UNTIL RETRIBUTION BURNS

BEAUTY IN LIES BOOK THREE

ADELAIDE FORREST

Copyright © 2021 by Adelaide Forrest

All rights reserved.

No part of this book may be reproduced in any form or by any electronic or mechanical means, including information storage and retrieval systems, without written permission from the author, except for the use of brief quotations in a book review.

Cover Design by Adelaide Forrest

Proofreading by Light Hand Editing

❀ Created with Vellum

ABOUT THE AUTHOR

Adelaide lives in her tiny house with her husband and two rambunctious kids. When she's not chasing all three of them and her dog around the house, she spends all her free time writing and adding to the hoard of plots stored on her bookshelf and hard-drive.

She always wanted to write, and did from the time she was ten and wrote her first full-length fantasy novel. The subject matter has changed over the years, but that passion for writing never went away.

She has a background in Psychology and working with horses, but Adelaide began her publishing journey in February 2020 and never looked back.

For more information, please visit Adelaide's website or subscribe to her newsletter.

CONTENT & TRIGGER WARNINGS

Beauty in Lies is a DARK mafia romance series dealing with topics that some readers may find offensive or triggering. Readers of Adelaide Forrest's Bellandi Crime Syndicate series should note that this series is much darker.

Please keep in mind the following list WILL contain specifics about the ENTIRE series and may spoil certain plot elements. Please avoid the next page if you don't wish to know specifics.

The following scenarios are all present in the Beauty in Lies series. This list may be added to over time.

- Situations involving dubious, questionable, or nonconsent
  - 13 Year Age gap, with both characters being of legal age at the time a physical relationship forms.
  - Forced Pregnancy
  - Branding
  - Forced Marriage under threat of death & violence
  - VERY graphic violence, torture, and murder
  - Drug use, attempted date rape, and dubious situations while under the influence
  - Kidnapping/Captive Scenarios
  - Knife Play/Violence
  - Somnophilia

1

ISA

A firm hand clenched the back of my shirt, gripping me tightly by the material and lifting so suddenly that the sound of fabric tearing filled the air.

Dark and impossibly cruel eyes met mine as he lifted me off my feet.

As if I was the kitten he'd tempted me with, he kept me at arm's length. Like I was a dirty and diseased thing he couldn't bear to taint himself with.

I screamed as my body was tossed backwards. Cold water filled my lungs suddenly when I broke through the surface, sinking fast and rapidly caught in the current. I kicked my legs, lost in the darkness of the river as it roared around me. Phantom shadows came from the depths, surrounding me as my body was swept away.

A sharp bite of pain caught my leg, ripping through skin —

"Isa!" Rafael snapped, drawing me back to the present as he grasped my shoulders and shook me roughly. I stumbled backward, slapping away his touch and desperate to get free from him. My back hit the opposite wall in the hallway, the impact making me feel solid compared to the liquid feeling that had taken over my body when I remembered what it was like to drown.

How it felt to be filled with the same water that surrounded me, as if I could dissolve into nothingness and cease to exist.

The man who had ruined me, who'd had changed everything in my life and taken my sister away...was my father-in-law. Dead or not, we'd somehow become bound by the bonds of marriage.

I wished I'd been there to watch him burn for what he'd done to me and my family, but fate, and my husband, had stripped me of that right.

"*Mi reina*," Rafael said, stepping toward me cautiously. My feet moved faster than my body could keep up, sliding further along the wall to keep that distance between us. "Stop and think about this. I need you to be very, *very* certain it was him."

"Stay away from me," I gasped, backing down the hall toward the kitchen where I'd left Martina. He reached out for me again, his face a complex mix of concern and rage as I threw myself back to avoid his touch. "Why?" I asked. Tears streamed down my face steadily as I tried to understand and tried to wrap my head around all the moving pieces in the game I hadn't even known we were playing.

Hadn't his father done enough?

I turned, running down the rest of the hallway and bursting into the open-concept living room. Rafael followed at my heels, the sound of him vaulting into motion behind me erupting in the more enclosed space.

I turned to look back, watching his face harden for a brief moment before I collided with a wall of muscle. I screamed as Sebastian wrapped his arms around me, holding me still despite my struggles and the foot I stomped on top of his.

"What's going on?" Andrés asked, stepping up beside me as Sebastian spun me in his arms. Facing Rafael, I watched his gaze settle on his cousin's hands wrapped around my stomach and my chest to hold me still.

"Unhand. My. Wife," Rafael growled, his voice dropping to a tone that bordered on animalistic.

"He will, as soon as you tell me why you're chasing her through my home, and she looks like she's seen a ghost. I *know* what your father taught you was acceptable behavior, Boy. I will not tolerate that in my house," Andrés argued, forcing Rafael's eyes to turn to him. Whatever he saw in Andrés' expression calmed the beast in him somewhat, and he stepped forward slowly to touch gentle fingers to my face as I flinched back.

"I promise you, I didn't know," he murmured, touching his forehead to mine as if he could make me feel the truth to the words.

"You expect me to believe that?" I said through gritted teeth. My throat clenched around the words, a sob that I wouldn't give into threatening to break free. Of all the people in the world, there couldn't be any way that Rafael obsessed over the same girl his father had tried to kill, and it was all just a coincidence.

It wasn't possible.

"I've been searching for answers. I have men looking into the accident in Chicago to find out what happened to you and who did it. I wouldn't have done that if I already knew the answer, *mi reina*," he reassured me.

I eyed him warily. Though his words felt like the truth,

I'd come to learn that coincidences didn't exist when it came to Rafael. In the place of happenstance there was only cool calculation and manipulation — a master hand on the chess pieces of life, guiding those around him to do exactly as he pleased.

My bottom lip trembled as I remembered how desperate he'd been for the answers to what happened in the river that he'd thought to coerce me into revealing them under the threat of branding. He'd stood nothing to gain in that moment aside from the information he lacked that had plagued him.

He must have thought he saw acceptance in my eyes, because he tore Sebastian's hands from my body, moving to draw me into his embrace. Dropping to the floor, I scurried out beneath his arms and rounded his cousin's legs, letting him unknowingly serve as a temporary obstacle as I scrambled to my feet and raced for the back doors.

My arms pumped with the desperation consuming me. A glance over my shoulder as I threw open the French door showed Rafael brutally shoving his cousin to the side to get past him. The breath froze in my lungs as I moved, my chest unnaturally tight as I ran.

The view of the shed up ahead in the distance served as a cruel reminder of all the ways Rafe had ruined me.

He'd taken an innocent girl who'd survived his father's wrath and done what he'd failed to do. He killed her—turned her into a phantom of his own making.

A murderer.

Even wanting nothing to do with that shed and the recent memory that threatened to slow me down, I turned my back on the docks and sprinted in its direction up the driveway. Closer to civilization and escape, even knowing in my heart that the flight was pointless.

I stumbled, my heel tilting to the side as I traversed the slight incline with ragged breaths. The roll of my ankle shot pain up my leg, a whimper escaping my throat as I looked behind me. Rafael was quickly closing the distance between us, his face twisted into a murderous expression as he ate up the head start his cousin's interference had provided me.

"Isa, stop," he ordered, his low and impossible quiet voice traveling through the air. The sound shouldn't have reached me, but something in that command felt like I would hear it anywhere. No matter where in the world I was, no matter where he was, the instinctive desire to submit to his will overwhelmed me.

Only the panic coursing through my veins drove me to keep moving, to stumble along the path with the limp from my sprained ankle. Even knowing it was futile and that Rafael would *always* catch me and drag me back to the pits of Hell with him, I kept going.

That feeling settled down my spine, the slow caress of a nightmare whispering along my skin when he came close enough to almost grab me.

One more step, and I could already feel the heat of his arms reaching to wrap around me in the next moment. The harshness of his grip as it would lift me off my feet.

I ducked, dropping to the ground and crab walking backwards on my hands as the devil himself loomed over me. Even in the moment with his expression calm and placating, cautious, as if I were a wounded animal he only wanted to help, that darkness lurked in his stunning gaze. The animalistic tilt of his head as he studied the prey he'd well and truly caught once again left little doubt as to just what kind of punishment he would deliver as soon as he pulled me into his evil embrace.

A shadow emerged from the other side of the driveway, a

figure moving between us as if he didn't fear death itself. Joaquin stepped over my body, positioning himself so that one foot was to either side of my thighs. "Get up, *mi reina*," he said softly, glancing over his shoulder at where I panted on the ground beneath him.

I drew my legs out from between his, leaving him standing in front of me as I pushed to my feet and winced at the pain in my ankle when I righted myself.

"Move," Rafael ordered, and the bass of his voice coated my skin. That panic and terror settled over me once again, a distinct reminder of the time when I'd genuinely feared for my life while he tormented me.

I knew Rafael wouldn't kill me, but I also knew there were things far worse than death. The pain of knowing that I'd fallen for him twice, and that everything had been a lie both times, *that* threatened to crush something that went deeper than flesh and bones.

"That's enough, Rafael," Joaquin reprimanded, holding his position despite the way Rafael's fury coated the air.

I watched in horror as Rafael pulled his gun, pressing the barrel against Joaquin's forehead. My guard didn't flinch, staring back at *El Diablo* with defiance in his face. "Give me *mi reina*," Rafael growled, the monster not bothering to hide beneath the surface. It didn't matter that he'd known Joaquin far longer than he'd known me. I didn't doubt his vindictiveness or the reality that he would shoot him if Joaquin did not obey.

Nothing and no one would get in his way when it came to the woman he claimed as his property.

"Then treat her like *mi reina* deserves. Not like an animal that you hunt down in the night," Joaquin returned, his voice a threatening growl despite the gun pressed to his head.

"Rafe, don't," I whispered, my voice pleading as I looked around Joaquin's shoulder. Neither man spared me a glance, too lost in their mostly silent war as they studied each other.

"She shouldn't have run," Rafael said finally, the gun drawing away from Joaquin slightly. He didn't put it away, not completely, when the other man remained between us.

"You shouldn't have chased her," Joaquin said, quirking a mocking eyebrow. "Even those who have done nothing wrong will run when they're chased by the devil in the moonlight."

Rafael clenched his jaw, rage consuming his features as his eyes settled on mine briefly before turning back to Joaquin. "You will move, or have you forgotten all that you owe me?"

Joaquin stilled, every muscle in his body locking tight as his eyes darted to glance at me over his shoulder. He sighed, his chest loosening with the loss of air. "If you hurt her, I will owe you *nothing*."

I watched him in a panic as he stepped to the side slowly, my body turning as if in slow motion to escape the inevitable.

Rafael's arms wrapped around me from behind as I screamed, turning my body until I faced him, then he tossed me over his shoulder. The ground threatened to swallow me whole as Rafael walked, moving toward the docks by the water and the boat that waited for us with the privacy he undoubtedly wanted for dealing with his wayward wife.

My panic slowed as my eyes met Joaquin's, watching the hard set to his jaw and the remorse in his eyes fade away.

Something inside me hollowed, the sway of Rafael's rapid stride lulling me into the familiar embrace of floating in that place where pain didn't exist.

My head buzzed as blood rushed to it, a reminder of

everything I'd felt in those moments when I'd been underwater. Instead of fighting it, I sank into that familiar feeling.

And I welcomed the void like a dark embrace.

2

ISA

I was only vaguely aware of Rafael boarding the yacht, of his deep command for his men to vacate and leave us in privacy. My back collided with something soft as he shifted me off his shoulder and dropped me, the bounce threatening to jar me out of the peaceful void I'd retreated to.

It had been so long since I'd gone there, so long since I tried to embrace the respite it offered. Rafe made me feel too much. He made me want things I had no right to desire, and the safe retreat in my mind had become nothing but a memory.

Until the realization that nothing I believed had been true once again. Until the need for retribution burned within me, impossible and unattainable in the face of the power that was Rafael Ibarra.

Men who claimed to care for me stepped aside when all was said and done, because no one could come between us.

No one except me.

I turned my head to the side, staring up at the house in the distance. The moonlight shimmered off the water in the pool, the blue and bronze of the tiles striking as the water rippled around the small waterfall at the edge. My head continued to buzz with the remnants of my blood rush, helping me drown out the sounds of whatever Rafael did while I worked to ignore him.

He spoke, the ripples of his voice coating my skin as if from a distant memory. The distance it gave me offered clarity of my mind, a separation from the sensations Rafael would undoubtedly pull from my body whether I wanted them or not. He wouldn't care if I fought or if I cooperated, because he would take what he thought he owned regardless.

My body was his. He owned it, and there was no questioning that fact, even when I struggled to grasp the latest revelation in our marriage.

The vague sensation of hands trailed over my stomach, pulling the fabric of my dress up until my skin was bared to the moonlight shining down on us. The gentle press of his mouth against my skin should have been jarring; it should have been a reminder of everything that would come in a matter of months whether I was ready or not.

My eyes drifted closed, shutting away the image of stars twinkling in the sky. Stars that Rafael had counted as a boy with the mother his father had taken from him.

Was I a repaid favor? A way to wrong the father he'd hated so deeply?

I shook off the thoughts, clenching my eyes shut and burrowing myself deeper into the hollow inside me. That place where nothing hurt, where the lack of pain would welcome me hovered just out of reach.

There, but not. Just as I remembered it, but just beyond my reach.

Rafael's mouth dipped lower, the treacherous touch of his flesh against my skin.

I drew in a fortifying breath. Sinking farther into that hollow, I felt my body grow heavy with exhaustion. A breath in and then one out, I focused on the feeling of my lungs stretching and the way each breath drew in through my nose.

I found peace in the way my stomach expanded, feeling it expel as I blew out through my mouth slowly. Rafael's hands could do what he wanted, his mouth could touch whatever part of my body he pleased.

But I'd take away everything that made me, *me*.

If he wanted an obedient pet who wouldn't run when he betrayed her, it wouldn't matter much to him. "Do you truly believe I knew about my father?" he asked, his voice deceptively soft. Even sounding as if it came from the other side of the yacht, the darkness in that tone couldn't be missed.

He wanted *mi reina*. He wanted the queen he claimed to value so much only to betray with secrets and lies that had plagued our relationship from the very beginning.

I'd been foolish enough to take him at his word when he'd told his uncle he had no secrets from me. I guessed that only went for business that didn't matter.

I quieted my mind, shutting out the racing thoughts that kept me from going truly unaware. Rafael's fingers dug into the skin of my hip, his short nails dragging over my flesh. The pain nagged at my senses, trying to pull me back to the world of light.

Darkness surrounded me. The very same darkness I'd called home long before the devil entered my life, letting it cocoon me in warmth when I needed comfort.

When I needed to feel accepted for the temptations and dark sins running through my mind.

Cold touched my hip, the bite of a shallow cut stinging as the lace of my panties snapped in two. The sting of metal against the other side followed, until Rafael's harsh hands yanked the scrap of fabric away from my body. Touching his hands to the insides of my thighs, he pushed them open until he stared down at the center of me.

Knowing he watched me when I couldn't see it, knowing his eyes were heavy on that part of me he claimed as his own, I scrambled to grasp the edges of the darkness to pull around myself like a protective barrier. I didn't want to feel what would come next.

I didn't want to hate him more than I already did.

Moments of time passed while he drew his hands away, and only the sounds of his movements filtered through the foggy haze that I pulled around myself and clung to. Curiosity tugged at the edges, but I refused to open my eyes to see what he might be doing.

I clenched my jaw as he dragged the flat of the knife over the inside of my thigh, the tip giving a kiss of pain when it curled toward the top. It was already wet, the surface of it covered with something thick and viscous.

"Come out and play with me, *mi reina*," he murmured, touching the fingers of his free hand to the top of my pussy. He used them to spread me wide, leaning forward and licking me from entrance to clit in a slow glide that set my nerve endings on fire. I shoved it away, forcing my breathing to stay slow.

Something hard touched my clit, pressing gently and circling it slowly. Maddeningly. I swallowed back the feeling, refusing to let the warmth rising in my belly touch me in my mind.

Reminding myself that my body wasn't me, I didn't

attempt to stop the sensation from building. Only working to separate myself from it.

It was just sex, not a melding of my soul with the man that I loved, because the man I loved was a nightmare—a phantom come to torment me in my waking hours.

The rounded edge of the object rubbed over me, sliding to the ridges along the edge of what I knew had to be the hilt of his knife. He slid it lower, moving through my sensitive and overheated flesh until he pressed that rounded end against my entrance. It was hard and unforgiving as he worked it inside me, stretching me open slowly.

I swallowed back my nerves, the knowledge of the knife so close to my body making it harder and harder to escape into the prison of my mind. To the only place I'd found freedom in a life that had seemed ever more confining.

Until him.

He moved it in and out of me, slowly and carefully tormenting me with the knife. Finally leaving it as deep as it could go, he leaned forward and wrapped his lips around my clit. One of his hands came down on the inside of my thigh, sliding along my flesh with that same thick fluid that had covered the knife.

Finally, unable to suppress the need coursing through me, I opened my eyes and peeked down at the red staining my bare thigh. At the blood as he rubbed it into my skin, as if it could mark me in ways he hadn't already achieved.

His eyes met mine, triumph shining in them as he smirked into my clit and gave it a final swipe of his tongue before he leaned back on his knees. My gaze dropped from his face to angry, bleeding wounds on his chest.

To my name carved into his heart all over again, covering the fading marks from the first time. These went deeper, the wounds jagged slashes that made my throat clench tight. The others had been temporary.

These would scar in a way that never faded.

Raw. Jagged. *Angry.*

They were the perfect summary of our relationship, of the tumultuous emotions and the harsh circumstances that brought us together. They showed the toxic obsession that we felt with one another, even knowing it would lead us straight into the flames of hell and be our destruction by the time it was all over.

The blood on my thigh seemed to warm, a tingling spreading through me with the confirmation that it was his and his alone. Not the consequence of the murder we'd committed only hours before.

He leaned over me, the blood on his chest touching the front of my dress. The contact with his wounds must have been agonizing, but he didn't seem to care as he pulled the knife free from my body and raised it.

A scream caught in my throat, the sound erupting into the night air as that blade came down to my shoulder suddenly. All my thoughts and assurances that Rafael wouldn't kill me fled my head in the face of that weapon coming for me, of the brutal determination etched into the lines of his face.

He severed the straps on my dress, being careful to only nick my skin with the tip of the blade as he cut them away. Pulling his body away long enough to tug the dress down and free my breasts, he touched his bare skin to mine.

That blade moved to my neck, touching the side of it hesitantly. As if even Rafael questioned the depths of what he would do next. Fear made my bottom lip tremble, the haze of my mind forgotten in the face of the nightmare staring down at me. Covered in his own blood with madness dancing in his eyes, he reminded me of a monster who'd been locked in a cage for years then had suddenly been freed from his confines.

"You think you can run from me?" he growled, pressing the blade deeper. The warmth of my blood surrounded the puncture, mixing with his as I felt the slow trickle along my skin. With that knife touching my throat, he reached his free hand down between our bodies and guided himself inside me with a harsh thrust.

Pinned by the knife at my throat and his cock invading my body, I couldn't move to fight his domination of me. I couldn't retreat into the void with the threat of death so overwhelming.

"Rafe," I whimpered, suddenly so filled with him that I couldn't breathe. One wrong move and it would all be over. My body accepted him inside me, even as I screamed inside my head.

He took me slowly, and if it hadn't been for the knife at my throat I might have thought he made love to me. With his dangerous eyes intent on mine, he grabbed a fistful of my hair and turned my head to the side. I lost the contact of his gaze, feeling his knife drag a shallow cut over the side of my throat until it touched the sensitive nook between my neck and shoulder.

"It is unfortunate for you," he said, punctuating the words with a sharp thrust of his hips as he twisted the knife in his hand. The tip pressed into my skin, the flesh parting around the blade as pain burned through me. "That my name is much longer than yours."

"Stop," I said, his grip on my hair holding me still. He ignored the plea, focusing on my neck where he moved the knife and carved through my skin. I cried out, thrashing my legs around his hips as he continued.

"You will never be free of me." The blade left my skin as he finished the R, sinking in next to it as he continued on with his name. He didn't worry about my legs kicking, not with the way he held me pinned down with his body weight.

I'd been so content to give him my body and hide in the fortress of my mind, I'd let myself forget that my husband was a monster.

That he would stop at nothing to consume all of me.

"Rafael!" I screamed, not daring to move my arms to fight him off. Even with the pain pulling me apart, I knew that it would be nothing compared to what could come if he slipped. If he lost control of me and cut deeper than he wanted.

"You think you can hide from me?" he asked, continuing to cut through my flesh as he carved his name into my skin where *everyone* would see. There'd be no hiding it, no disguising it as anything other than a primal marking from a man who would slaughter anyone who touched me. I wouldn't be able to explain it away as an artistic representation of our love if I ever saw my family again.

I whimpered, the glide of his cock between my legs turning painful as my body tried to shove him out. Even my body couldn't accept *this*. "Stop," I begged, tears staining my cheeks and dripping down onto the cushion of the yacht. This was not the kind of pain that added to pleasure, but white-hot agony threatening to tear my soul free from my body.

"You're mine, Isa. Your body. Your heart. Your very fucking *soul*. If you keep forgetting that, I'll run out of places to mark your flesh," he said, tossing the knife to the side as he finished with the etching in my skin.

I blinked past the pain, staring at the cushion where my

head rested as I raised a hand to touch the mess at my shoulder. It came away slick with blood.

I had the odd thought that it was fortunate the cushion was already red, my gaze narrowing on the trembling fingertips of my other hand as it dragged over the cushion. I felt nothing in my fingertips, the odd sense of shock claiming me as Rafael grasped my chin in his hands and turned my eyes to his. My shoulder screamed with the motion, a ragged gasp pulling free from my lips. There was sympathy in his eyes as he studied me, his brow furrowing as he touched his forehead to mine and sighed.

His hand went between my thighs, touching my clit and stimulating it with slow and gentle presses that dragged me closer to that spot where pain and pleasure combined. My neck and shoulder throbbed, aching as he leaned forward and dragged his tongue over the wounds.

I moaned before I could tamp it down, wincing when he finally released my hair and those crazed eyes met mine. His lips crashed down on my own, consuming me with a frenzied kiss that tasted metallic.

Taking one of my hands in his, he guided it to the mess of blood on his chest. My fingers trailed through it as I touched his wounds, and then he turned my hand around and touched them to my lips to smear my mouth with it.

Heat built in my core as he drove harder and deeper, consuming me with rough thrusts that I felt everywhere. I wanted to kill him. I wanted to fuck him.

I wanted to bleed him.

I reached out a hand to touch his wounds, digging my nails into his chest as he groaned and leaned forward until his chest touched mine once again. I wrapped my arms around him, sinking nails into the flesh of his shoulders as his thrusts turned punishing and lost their rhythm. All I could do in the moments where he consumed me with his body was hold on and take it, take all of him.

"I fucking love you," he murmured, a growl in his throat as he said the words as if he could imprint them on my soul the way he'd etched his name into my skin. "And I will accept *nothing* less than all of you, *mi reina*." Those traitorous fingers of his stroked me higher and higher, until I came around his cock with a quiet cry and sank my teeth into his shoulder.

He pounded into me harder, using me to find his own release until he flooded me with heat. I spoke after I caught my breath. "I hate you," I whispered, clinging to him despite the harshness of my words. "You're just another cage."

"I wouldn't have to be if you stopped fighting your nature. You aren't meant to be my prisoner, Isa. You're meant to be my queen. *Pero me lo darás todo,* or I'll simply take it for myself."

3

RAFAEL

I swept the hair off Isa's neck, staring at the name I'd carved into her skin. She tilted her head to the side, soft and compliant as I ran the washcloth over the wounds and cleaned away the blood. The taste of her on my tongue, of the blood that coursed through her veins, tormented me.

I briefly wondered if my obsession with her would ever settle. If there would ever come a moment where I was just content with having her in my arms and didn't feel the need to possess her every waking thought and every dream.

If I didn't need to consume her nightmares and make them part of me.

"I didn't know," I murmured, watching her reflection as her body twitched in my grip. The reminder of what she saw as a great betrayal immediately tensed the body that had been relaxed after the adrenaline surge that consumed her. The aftercare of having me clean her wound had settled her down, until she'd practically purred in my grip in spite of what I knew had to be painful. "I swear to you on my mother's grave, *mi reina*. I didn't know that my father threw you in that river."

She turned those stunning eyes up to me, the brightness of them in the wake of her tears startling as they met mine. Never in my life had I sworn *anything* on my mother's grave. Nothing had been important enough for those words and the sacrifice they embodied. I ran my nose up the uninjured side of her neck, breathing in her unique scent to settle myself.

Everything in me felt taut, agonizing in the wake of her revelation. With me overcome with the need to hunt my father and slaughter him all over again for what he'd done, Isa's choice to run had been the very worst thing she could have done.

She called to the predator, to the nightmare who needed to hunt. Fuck. *Kill.*

She nodded back at me, her gaze still wary as if she couldn't quite believe me. Logically, I knew I'd given her no reason to trust me and take me at my word. In time she'd come to understand I very rarely lied.

Only when I thought it would protect her from the realities she could not change and the facts of life that would only hurt her. My father's involvement in her drowning was not one of those instances.

I hoped she never learned the truth of the rest.

I dressed her in a pair of sleep shorts and one of my comfortable shirts that covered the fresh wounds on her shoulder. The last thing she needed to deal with was the pity from my aunt and the condemnation I would face from my family.

Marking her skin in the way I did should be a crime. I would punish anyone else who did it to a woman, but something about it just made sense for Isa and me. As if the toxicity of our love and the history we didn't understand demanded that we bleed for one another.

I pulled her into my arms, cradling her gently as I carried her off the yacht and back up to the house. She rested her head against my chest, settling in with a complacency that bothered me. I wanted her to fight me, to rage against the injustices done to her.

Not run and retreat into herself.

I strolled into the open back doors, my family studying Isa as I set her on the sofa and took a seat next to her. Keeping her cuddled tightly into my side, I drew in a deep breath and prepared to explain the very same thing that I myself didn't understand.

"What the fuck was that about?" my uncle asked, meeting my eyes over Isa's head. With anyone else, I may have hesitated to answer him. The reality of my father's involvement meant there may be very few people I could trust. Only the knowledge that he might know the information to fill in the gaps of my knowledge led me to answer him.

"I keep all reminders of my father's existence isolated to the spare office," I said. "Isa has never seen him until that photo in your hallway."

My uncle had known my father before the loss of his humanity turned him into a beast who acted on impulse without fear of repercussions. He'd clung to the hope that the brother he remembered still remained locked inside him, trapped beneath the madness that plagued him. That one day he would see the error of his ways and agree to do whatever it took to bring him back from the place where he danced at the edges of reality.

The knowledge of just how far his brother had fallen into his madness wouldn't come as a shock, but it brought back the painful memories I knew Andrés would rather forget. I almost wished I could spare him the pain of knowing that his own brother would drown an innocent child for no reason, but the answers I needed were far more important than his precious feelings.

"When Isa was five, a stranger tossed her into the river and attempted to drown her. She never knew his name, and he was never brought to justice because of his connections in high places," I said, watching as my uncle's eyes widened. "She never saw him again."

"What would your father stand to gain from harming a girl in such a way?" Martina asked, her hand raising to touch her mouth as she stared at Isa in horror. "The man was completely unhinged, but everything he did benefitted him. His selfishness wouldn't allow for anything else."

"He married Regina as a final fuck you to my mother, because burning her alive wasn't enough. If he truly only acted in ways that benefited him, he would have chosen someone younger and more likely to give him the sons he so desperately wanted," I reminded. My father had been a monster, and he would do something monstrous just to prove it.

I'd been forced to sit through many of his conversations with Pavel about his latest property acquisitions. Even from a young age, I'd known exactly what they meant.

People.

"Why did my father throw her in the river, Andrés?" I asked, glaring at the man as he fiddled with his hands nervously.

"I don't know," he admitted. "Your mother was a special circumstance. She always brought out the worst of his madness. What he did to spite her wouldn't necessarily translate to other people—"

"She was drowned on the anniversary of my mother's death," I said, wondering how I hadn't thought to make the connection previously. I'd thought it only a coincidence, a twist of fate, that the worst days of our lives were so irrevocably entwined. My uncle fell silent, his gaze dropping to Isa in sympathy as he accepted the truth.

My father had tried to drown my wife. The only question was *why*?

"What was he doing in Chicago?" I asked, watching as my uncle shook his head.

"He spent a great deal of time there or in Russia during the summers when you were with us. I'm sure you can imagine what he and Kuznetsov and Bellandi did with their time," he sighed, turning his eyes to look out the window. The lights on the back patio shone in the darkness, illuminating the path all the way down to the docks where the yacht waited to take Isa and me home. "The three men were inseparable, with Origen Regas clinging to them like the sycophant he was and just hoping to get in on the action. Much like the way Calix clung to you after he and his father came to stay on *El Infierno*."

"Calix is anything but a sycophant," I scoffed, not giving the time to defend him. Calix had found his place in life, and it had nothing to do with who his father was.

Exactly the way he would have wanted it.

"Is there anyone who is alive who would know why?" I asked, shifting Isa off my lap so I could stand up and pace. I knew of one man who could give me the answers I needed.

Unfortunately, I doubted my killing two of his sons had put him in a talkative mood.

My uncle stood, grabbing his cell phone off the island in the kitchen and stepping back toward me. "Aside from Pavel?" He laughed bitterly. "There's Samuel Suarez. He's your best hope," he said, waiting for my confirmation as he brought up the old man's contact information.

I nodded. The information wouldn't come cheap if he knew, because Suarez was nothing but a rat looking for favors instead of crumbs. He'd use my need for answers to his advantage, negotiating a deal I wasn't prepared to give.

For anything else, I wouldn't have done it.

But I'd do anything for *mi reina*. Even sell my soul.

Isa remained quiet on the sofa, holding perfectly still as she studied me and the tension in my body hesitantly. My uncle pressed the button on his phone to make the call, making his way toward his office at the back of the house. Torn between not wanting her to have any part in the conversation that I knew would follow and knowing that I couldn't leave her unattended with my cousins, I did the only thing I could and put my trust in the last person I wanted in that moment.

"Get me Joaquin," I barked at Thiago. My youngest cousin glared at me, but stepped outside to grab Isa's personal security from his spot where he hovered outside the family home. He stepped in, his dark eyes disinterested as he studied me and waited for instructions. "Keep an eye on her. She doesn't leave that couch," I ordered. He furrowed his brow, glancing down to where Isa had drawn her knees up on the couch. I watched his gaze travel over her body, checking for signs of injury and undoubtedly growing curious at the sight of her in my shirt given her usual attire of dresses.

He said nothing, sitting on the opposite side of the sofa from *mi reina* and watching as she flinched away despite the space between them. With a heavy sigh, I turned on my heel and left her with the man I knew would do as I demanded and keep Sebastian's wandering hands off my wife in the process unless he wanted a bullet in his brain.

"I understand that, Samuel, but I hardly think my brother cares if you keep his secrets anymore," my uncle barked as I made my way down the hallway. Stepping into the open office door and closing it behind me, I crossed my arms over my chest and waited for him to signal me into the conversation. "What can be such a big deal about a child he hurt?" He hit the screen, enabling the speaker phone so Samuel's accented voice filled the silence.

"I'm certain it isn't a big deal actually, but you seem to want the information. That makes it valuable to me," Samuel said, a smile in his voice as it carried through the room. "What do you want to know about some brat anyway?"

My uncle looked up to me as he considered what he could answer. Anything but the truth would have been more likely to get Samuel to cooperate, but there was also nothing we could say that would explain the sudden interest in a drowning incident my father had never been officially involved in. "She is an Ibarra now," he said finally with a sigh.

Samuel laughed, the boisterous sound echoing through the room. "Which one of your sons went slumming with American pussy and was too stupid to wrap it up?"

"She is the wife of *El Diablo*," my uncle returned as I clenched my teeth in an effort to contain my fury. The inability to beat the answers out of Samuel threatened to push my rage over the edge once again.

There was nothing I could do with him safely tucked behind the walls of his fortress in Colombia, and I was not a patient enough man to wait for him to come out of hiding. The old bastard would die before that ever happened.

He coughed, the sound of his palm slapping against his desk echoing through the space as his coughing dissolved into laughter. "Oh that's rich. They were *made* for each other."

"What exactly does that mean, Suarez?" I asked, uncrossing my arms and stepping forward to lean my hands on the edge of my uncle's desk. Glaring down at the phone as if he could feel my glare through the other side.

"Rafael!" the old man said jovially. "I hear congratulations are in order."

"How quickly a worm like you goes from referring to my wife as slumming to a congratulatory statement," I said carefully, working to conceal the wrath threatening to boil my blood.

"Careful, Rafael. I have the information you're looking for," he warned, his voice tinted with the arrogance I had associated with all of my father's friends as a boy.

"And what do you expect for this information?" I asked, curling my fingers around the edge of the desk and squeezing.

"I'm not certain," he said, his voice trailing off as he considered his options and what he could want from an Ibarra. I expected a request for some of the weaponry at my disposal thanks to my connection with the world's most notorious arms dealer, but he surprised me instead. "I don't come across many men I like, but your father was another story. I greatly enjoyed my time with him as my friend."

My uncle froze in his chair, giving me a tense look as we waited for the other shoe to drop.

"I'm sure you did," I said, filling the silence.

"I do not wish to insult his memory by giving his murderer what he seeks. A great many people believe in karma, Rafael. I have never been one of them. Until today," he growled, disconnecting the call as silence replaced his voice. My uncle's brown eyes met mine, a hesitant plea in them as I hardened to the harsh reality. I had never in my life regretted killing my father, and now his loss was what stood between me and the answers I needed.

"Fuck!" I yelled, sweeping the papers and things off Andrés' desk in my rage. There wasn't another person alive who could tell me what I needed to know.

Why the fuck had my father bothered with a five-year-old girl in the first place?

4

ISA

The walls were closing in around me. Martina sat beside me, her hand rubbing over the back of mine as we waited for Rafael and Andrés to emerge from the office with the answers we sought. Without being able to explain it, I already knew that those questions would go unanswered.

Nothing about my life had been simple. The mystery shrouding Rafael's father throwing me in the river couldn't be any different. Perhaps foolishly, I believed Rafe when he told me he'd had no knowledge of his father's involvement after swearing it on his mother's grave, but that belief could only stem so far without understanding what had really happened.

The connection was far-fetched. It was complicated and messy.

I'd let Rafael turn me into a nightmare, pulling the demon from inside me until I no longer recognized the person staring back at me in the mirror. I'd done it because, in spite of everything he'd done, I loved him more than I wanted to breathe.

I couldn't deny that he'd somehow seen that darkness in my soul and known it would complement his. He'd known that I had never been meant to stay in the light. Most girls who were attracted to bad boys wanted to offer them a path to the light, to show them the beauty in the sunshine. I'd let Rafael drag me into the night with him, dancing with the devil in the moonlight and seeing the beauty in the shadows.

The worst part was that I didn't regret any of it in the end. Because I felt more understood in the moments when the devil moved inside me than I had sitting in a room with my family. I felt more alive with my hands on the knife protruding from a man's heart, watching the life fade out of his eyes as his blood soaked my fingers.

"It will be alright," Martina soothed, her voice soft and reflective as she spoke to me. I turned my blank stare her way, my brow furrowed as I tried to understand how that could be possible.

"My father-in-law tried to kill me," I whispered. Speaking the words out loud somehow made them feel more real, as if the fact that they'd passed through my head time and time again since realizing the truth hadn't been enough affirmation. A hysterical laugh bubbled up in my throat, coming out in a choked sob as Martina shifted to wrap her arm around my shoulders.

"What is it?" Sebastian asked, narrowing his eyes on me. Since discovering the truth of what his uncle had done, I hadn't been able to look at him. I couldn't believe I hadn't seen it the moment I met him. He was the picture of Miguel, only younger and without the same harshness to his face.

Andrés wasn't quite the same, but close enough that I could see the resemblance now that I knew the truth.

Extra time would have been a gift he didn't deserve, but

my hand clenched as if a knife was still within my grip and I could drive it into his heart. If I'd enjoyed killing Maxim, I couldn't imagine the vindictive pleasure that would consume me if I'd been able to kill Rafael's father.

"Is he rolling in his grave to know his son has married the child he tried to murder? Or is he pleased since he probably hated his son in his final moments at the very least, considering Rafael burned him alive?"

Sebastian leaned back in his chair, his fingers gripping the arms as he watched me. Observing me and looking for signs of weakness, as I kept my face a blank mask even though I wanted to be overwhelmed by all I'd done and all I'd learned.

Rafael might have trusted his uncle and cousins, but I trusted no one.

Not even my husband himself.

"I would imagine he hated his son as the fire melted the flesh from his skin," Sebastian admitted. Martina's breath left her in a startled gasp as the weight of her arm left my shoulder. She disappeared from my side, retreating from the room as the conversation shifted to the more detailed aspects of the violence her husband and children lived in a daily life.

There'd been a time only days ago when I thought I would need to remain separate from Rafael's violence to function, so that I could live with the reality that I'd fallen in love with a murderer. Instead, I'd come face to face with the nightmare living inside his skin.

I'd looked the devil in the eye, and let him make me *his* demon.

Sebastian nodded when I didn't so much as flinch at the violent words, a twisted smirk transforming his face that reminded me so much of his cousin. That same darkness that resided in Rafael lived in him too, a monster waiting to reveal its true form when the timing was appropriate. "I hope he hates the knowledge that his bloodline will be tainted by me. I hope it haunts him in the afterlife," I growled, the words coming from somewhere deep within me.

From that well of darkness that I'd spent my life keeping suppressed.

"I believe I might have underestimated you, *mi reina*," he said. His voice was quiet as he glanced toward the hallway, as if he thought Rafael might disapprove of the name when it came from his mouth, but others had called me that name without consequence.

I suspected Rafael may not appreciate it coming from his cousin's mouth.

"You are truly not bothered by the knowledge that Rafael ordered his father tied to the pyre? That he set it aflame and stood close enough to feel the heat as his father screamed? What sort of man is capable of such a thing?" Even as Sebastian spoke the words, there was no condemnation in them. I knew without a doubt that he would have done the same thing if he thought he had an enemy, particularly one who would have harmed his mother.

"But Rafael is not a man at all, is he?" I asked, tilting my head to the side as a smile claimed my face. It felt strange, unhuman in the same way that Rafael's was when he was consumed by his darkness. "He's *El Diablo*. My only regret is that Miguel did not have to experience barbed wire tearing his flesh apart while water filled his lungs before he burned. That he wasn't raped as he did to Regina. He should have suffered for every crime he's committed against innocent people."

"So violent," he purred, standing from his seat with a

seductive grin. He moved to the liquor cabinet at the side of the room, pouring whiskey into a tumbler and bringing it to me. "Welcome to the family, Isa. I think you'll do just fine."

I nodded, accepting the drink and taking a deep swig of it despite the burn as it trailed down my throat.

"Fuck!" Rafael's roar came from the office, and Sebastian spun to the hallway as I dropped the tumbler on a side table and vaulted to my feet.

"Stay here," Sebastian ordered as he pointed at the sofa. The muffled sounds of a crash came from the office, the pure rage continuing to accompany the shattering of glass. He exchanged a brief glance with Joaquin, my bodyguard moving to grasp my arm in his grip.

"Fuck you," I snapped back, racing away from Joaquin before he could grab me. With the knowledge that whatever he owed Rafael had been enough for him to step aside and hand me over, I'd be damned if I did a thing he told me to.

Sebastian reached out an arm as I passed, catching me around the waist and trying to contain me as I dropped my weight to the floor so suddenly that he shifted off balance and tipped forward. "What the fuck?" he asked. As he struggled to regain his footing, his grip loosened so that I could get free and race ahead of him. I might not know how to fight, but I knew how to get away thanks to Joaquin's lesson.

"Isa!" Joaquin shouted, chasing after me as I threw the office door open and barged in on the chaos of the room. Andrés sat on the sofa, his head in his hands as Rafael destroyed everything in sight.

I'd never seen him so unhinged. His fury had always been carefully controlled and felt more like ice on my skin than what I knew must be blazing inside him. Watching him in that moment, I saw the devil who could stand among the flames and not be burned.

"Get her out of here," Andrés ordered as Joaquin emerged behind me. His arm wrapped around my waist, moving to drag me from the room as Rafael's blazing multi-colored gaze settled on us.

His body stilled, a jarring pause in his destruction as his fury fixated on that offending limb and every inch of me that Joaquin touched. In the space behind me, the sounds of Sebastian making his appearance felt like it came from the other side of a fog.

My world narrowed down to the feeling of Rafael's stare on me, on the animalistic way he watched every move I made. Somehow I knew that one wrong twitch from me would shatter the stillness in the room.

"Easy, Rafael," Andrés murmured. I was left with the distinct impression that while I may not know the Rafael who could lose control like this, there had been a time when he wasn't so restrained. My heart panged with the picture of a young boy raging against the injustice of his mother's murder and his father's abuse, so consumed by the violence inside him that he didn't know what to do to release it.

My need to calm him overcame the nerves pooling from the distinct impression that the center of this version of Rafe's attention was a very dangerous place to be. "I think you may want to take your arm off me. Slowly," I said, reaching out a hand to touch Joaquin's. He allowed me to pry it from my body, my gaze holding Rafael's as I moved slowly. His head tilted in that way of his, the movement much more predatory than normal. Like the devil was too close to the surface, a beast all but unleashed. I took a step forward, watching him draw in a steady breath as his eyes narrowed in on my hand. I raised it, the tattoo and brand that marked me as his stark against my skin.

Another breath.

No part of him moved except his chest as his lungs released the air trapped within them. Then he inhaled again, his nostrils flaring as if he truly was an animal and he could smell me. What would he scent if he could? Would he smell himself on my skin?

"Talk to me, Rafe," I murmured as I took another step. Andrés moved on the sofa, looking like he might intervene as I moved close enough that my fingers brushed against Rafael's shirt. His muscle jumped beneath my touch, his eyes gliding down to study the contact of my hand on his chest.

He raised a hand to mine, wrapping his fingers around my palm and squeezing tightly. I swallowed back my nerves, choosing to believe that, in this moment, in this way, Rafael would never hurt me.

He would claim me and mark me and take me, but my nightmare wouldn't damage me.

Those feverish eyes returned to mine, recognition finally settling in that piercing stare as I said, "I need to know what's going on."

He exhaled as he lifted my hand to touch his cheek. The stubble on his cheek scraped my palm as he pressed it in firmly, breathing deeply when I stepped into his chest and touched my torso to his. He wrapped his other arm around me, holding me tight as the office remained silent.

"He almost took you from me before I even found you. I'd have gone through my life without you, never knowing that you'd been taken from me," he murmured, seeming not to care if his cousin and uncle overheard the admission. It felt too close to revealing his love for me in front of others, and while I didn't have an issue with his family knowing how he felt about me, it felt like maybe Rafael would.

It hadn't been long ago that Regina had worried the

knowledge of his feelings for me would put me in more danger. To be loved by the devil was to be very useful to his enemies.

"He tried, but he failed. Did your phone call provide anything useful?" I asked, studying the tight lines of his face.

"He won't help us," Rafe said, shaking his head as anger seeped back into his face. It chased away the lingering sadness that had accompanied his concern of almost losing me. "We'll have to find the answers for ourselves."

I nodded, because if I believed in anything, it was Rafael's ability to do whatever it took to get what he wanted.

He'd find his answers. I just hoped we were ready for whatever they might reveal.

Martina's arms wrapped around me, while the male members of Rafael's family kept their distance. I couldn't blame them, not with the shadows that continued to lurk in Rafael's gaze and the memory of his reaction to Joaquin's attempt to restrain me. If any of the men so much as made a move too close to me, they might find himself lacking limbs.

Or a head.

Either was possible in Rafael's mood. While I thought I should hate the territorial bullshit of it, something about it soothed the frayed edges inside me after the last twenty-four hours.

I'd murdered a man in cold blood, and while he might not have been a good man, neither could I claim it was self-defense. Not when he'd been helpless by the time I stabbed him in the heart. I'd discovered that my connection to Rafael went farther than even he knew.

Even in the moments of knowing I couldn't and shouldn't trust my husband, his quiet ownership of me was a comfort.

"No one has ever pulled him back from one of his rages," Martina said quietly, drawing back with her hands on my shoulders to stare down at me. "After his mother's death, he was inconsolable. His father didn't want to deal with him, so he sent him here for us to attempt to bring him back from his devastation. That was the first summer he spent with us, and in the years following, the rages came with the season like clockwork." She paused, glancing over to where Rafael nodded at something his uncle said. The older man's eyes were gentle on his nephew, trying to convey something to him that I couldn't hear but understood was a private moment between the two of them.

"The anniversary of his mother's death was always the worst. We had to lock him in that shed on that day for years," she whispered, her eyes clenching closed as the reality of what they'd done overtook her. "He was unreachable and would hurt anyone who came near him. She might not have been perfect, but his mother loved him deeply. Losing her killed the last of what was human inside Rafael. Until you," she said. "Thank you for bringing him back to us." She leaned forward, touching her lips to my cheek before moving away to stand next to her sons.

"Hopefully we will see you soon, Isa," Thiago said from his mother's other side. "Family should not go so long between visits."

My heart clenched, thinking of my own family, and wondering if I would ever see them again. Rafael hadn't forbidden it, but my life with them seemed a world away. I seemed a world away from the girl they knew.

"Allow Thiago to come with you. Perhaps there is something he can do to help you find the answers you need," Andrés said, clapping Rafael on the shoulder.

"There's no need. For now, we're going home to sort through what remains of my father's belongings. Perhaps the answer has been right under my nose all this time, and I just needed the last piece of information to snap into place before I knew where to look," Rafe said, but his face was solemn. I didn't need him to speak to know he wasn't hopeful that it would be so easy.

"You can't honestly think it will be so simple?" Sebastian asked with a smirk.

"Nothing worth having ever is," Rafe answered, his voice dropping low. My toes curled in my sandals against my best intentions. His deep timbre was so similar to the tone he used when inside me, and the same as when he'd spoken to Maxim in the middle of torture.

There was something wrong with me.

Stepping away from his uncle finally, Rafe held out a hand for me. Giving me the semblance of a choice, and I smiled as I took it, knowing without a doubt there had never been a choice for either of us. Something deep had pulled us together from the moment he first saw me. Something rooted in our past and the history we had very little chance of ever coming to understand, coiling around one another like the vines of a climbing rose, thorny and dangerous even in its beauty.

"Take me home," I murmured, letting him guide me toward the back doors of the house.

5

RAFAEL

The night sky greeted us as we stepped outside and wrapped us in a familiar embrace. Joaquin emerged from the patio, a silent sentry at Isa's side as he walked us toward the yacht at the berth. Isa's movements were slow at my side, unsteady as if her exhaustion was finally catching up with her.

I reached over to scoop her into my arms, sighing as she tucked her head into my neck and breathed deep. It was impossible to believe we'd arrived in Barcelona earlier that day, and that everything had changed so drastically in a matter of hours.

By the time we reached the end of the dock, my men shuffled behind us and allowed me to make my way onboard. I nodded to Joaquin briefly, silently telling him he was off duty for the rest of the night and carrying Isa to the bedroom cabin. The sleek white lines greeted me as I stepped inside, and Isa lifted her head slightly to look around the space as if she hadn't been aware enough to do it the first time.

She'd been far too distracted by the murder she'd

committed to worry herself over the luxury of her new life with me.

I placed Isa in the center of the bed as gently as I could, taking a seat beside her at the edge and leaning forward to place my elbows on my knees. She shifted behind me, the warmth of her palm touching my spine through the thin cotton of my shirt as I studied the floor.

"Has anyone told you about my mother's death?" I asked, turning to meet the shock of her green eyes as she opened them suddenly. Her body was languid, as if sleep was the only thing on her mind.

A kinder man might have left her to rest, but the overwhelming need to talk came so rarely it would have felt like a foolish opportunity to waste. Her eyes widened as she moved to a new position, her face going alert as she seemed to realize the seriousness of my mood.

She nodded, pursing her lips as she waited for me to continue. Uncertainty swam in her gaze, an underlying hesitance that perhaps she shouldn't have known the truth about my mother's demise.

I sighed, returning her nod. I'd fully expected that answer, and the details of her murder were far from a secret. "I'm not surprised," I murmured, turning my body so that I could pick up a stray strand of her hair where it sprawled against the pillow. "Her heterochromia was more like yours, but her eyes were blue with a green piece at the top of her right eye." My hand drifted up to my face, unintentionally touching the skin under my blue eye. Suddenly craving the contact with one of the pieces of my mother I carried within me, I let the comfort of it wash over me as I prepared to open old wounds that were better left untouched.

My father's eyes had been dark, so deep a brown that

they bordered on the black of night. There was no trace of my father in me.

"She used to tell stories of how my father loved that they made her unique. That of all the women he could have been contracted to marry, his was special. He believed God had sent her to him, but still he did not love her. Miguel Ibarra was incapable of love, but from what I remember of my early memories and what Regina and others have confirmed, there was a time when he was good to her. When he was kind, particularly compared to the monster he became." I sighed, shifting my hand to cup her cheek.

"You don't have to tell me this," Isa murmured. She was always so in tune to my moods. Curiosity must have threatened to consume her, the gaps in her knowledge of my life so vast in comparison to the few details I didn't have of hers.

And yet she still gave me an out. A way to walk away from the difficult subject.

I would never deserve her, but she was mine regardless.

"I'm not certain which came first. My memories from the time when my mother was alive are hazy at best, but he became obsessed with religion around the same time he started murdering his men without reason. His paranoia knew no bounds, and his friend Franco Bellandi was going through something similar. They fed into one another's ridiculous notion that no one was trustworthy. Not even their wives and sons. Franco dealt with his problems by documenting everything and hoarding information. My father murdered and buried himself in his newfound Catholicism. He found a priest who encouraged his radical views, bringing him here to drag his people into the abomination he made of God inside the very Church where we were married." I stood from the bed and moved to the vanity at the side of the room. My eyes caught on the reflection in the mirror briefly before I turned away, unable to face the reminder of my mother so plainly. I stripped off my shirt, draping it over the back of the chair. "The Priest convinced my father that the disfiguration in our eyes was the mark of the devil. That my mother was a witch who had been sent to turn my father's soul against God. He believed I wasn't really his son, but the child of my mother's affair with the devil himself."

I paused, watching as the gears turned in Isa's head and she worked to connect the dots to the origin of my name. "*El Diablo?*" she murmured, furrowing her brow as she studied me.

"The name given to me by my father after my mother's death," I confirmed. "What I doubt anyone has told you, is that I was meant to die that day alongside my mother. He intended to strap me to the pyre across from her, so she could watch her spawn burn along with her. My mother pleaded with him, and she promised that she would go to the pyre willingly if he would just allow me to live. She sacrificed herself, walking toward a slow and painful death so that her six-year-old son could live," I scoffed, shaking my head as I spun away from her. "My father and the priest believed my mother would live and they would have their answer. Witches can survive the flames, of course. At least that's how it worked during the witch hunts. She was proven innocent in my father's eyes when she died, and me along with her though he made sure to brand me for crying as she burned."

"He wasn't stable, Rafael," she said, shifting toward me and drawing my attention back to her. "You can't blame yourself for the choice your mother made. *Any* real mother would beg for her son's life, no matter what the cost was. I would do it in a heartbeat," she confessed. Her voice trailed off as she realized the weight of her confession, and once again considered the reality that she would be a mother sooner than later.

I smiled at her, the motion feeling heavier than it should as the injustice of my mother's death threatened to make me combust. "My uncle would have you believe that my father was sick, that medication or treatment could have helped him. But the sickness that plagued him wasn't an illness that could be changed. He was a sociopath and a sadist. He got off on hurting people, and he thought himself a God. I'm no different, and I think that would be what makes my mother turn in her grave. That after everything I survived at my father's hands and everything she sacrificed, I'm no better than him in the end."

She swallowed, fidgeting slowly. "From what Regina said, your father was a rapist."

"How is that different from what I did with you? I may not have forced myself on you, *mi reina*, but I didn't give you a choice either. I took away your ability to consent by hiding the truth from you. If you'd known all I'd done, you never would have let me touch you," I said, my voice dropping lower with the next words and the dark truth that lingered in them. "And I think we both know that I would have stopped at nothing to have you."

"Why are you telling me this?" she asked. I reached further into the bed, grabbing the waistband of her shorts and tugging them down her legs. She didn't resist as I stripped her clothes off, watching me with wary eyes. "Why are you trying to make me believe you're a monster when I've finally come to terms with what you are and who I am?" she asked, raising her arms so I could lift the shirt over her head.

She winced as her shoulder and neck pained her, the

fresh wounds stretching until she returned her arm to her side. I shoved the pants down my legs and kicked off my shoes, climbing into the bed beside her.

Turning to her side, she stared at me and waited for the answer.

"Have you? Come to terms with who you are and who the man you've married is?" I asked, raising a brow as I cupped her cheek in my palm. She leaned into the touch, soft and sleepy.

It hinted at all the sweetness she'd had before I took her. Before I corrupted her.

I hoped one day she could be both *mi princesa* and *mi reina*. A combination of the queen who would defy me when I crossed the line and the princess who could take my dominance and return it with the sweet submission only she could make me crave.

"You ran from me," I murmured, leaning forward to tease her mouth with mine. "That does not feel like acceptance."

"I had good reason," she said, her hackles rising to the challenge. Her mouth tensed against mine, denying me the entry she thought I wanted. I just wanted to breathe her air, to draw her into my lungs and hold her there for as long as possible.

"There is never a reason to run from me. I *am* a monster, Isa. I always will be, but I'm *your* monster." I paused, letting the truth of those words calm the harshness of Isa's mouth before I dragged my lips against hers lightly again. "What I can tell you is that I lived most of my life in a way that my mother's death felt pointless. What exactly did she die to protect? Another murderer? But one way or another, she led me to you."

She shook her head, denying the pretty words, but I

needed to hold on to them. To grasp some kind of meaning to my mother's death. It made her murder easier, took away some of the lingering pain that came with her memory. "As sweet as the thought may be, that isn't possible."

"My father tried to drown you on the anniversary of my mother's death," I laughed lightly. "I think we are far beyond the notions of impossibility. She knew you needed me, and that I needed you. She brought us together."

"Careful, you might sound like a religious zealot if you keep discussing notions like that," she teased, letting me draw her into my arms. Her head touched my chest, resting against the brands that marked my skin from the way of life so ingrained in me that I didn't think I would ever be able to separate. Her touch brushed against the edges of the wounds that marked my skin as hers, her claim on my flesh undeniable and total.

"I don't need God when I have you, *mi reina*. You're my religion," I murmured softly, kissing the top of her head. She didn't respond, only the slight hitch in her breath confirming that she'd heard me. I held her as she drifted off to sleep, resisting the urge to run my fingers over the painful name scrawled into her flesh long after she'd fallen into slumber.

The answers we needed would come at a cost. I wouldn't let her be the one to pay it.

6

ISA

El Infierno rose out of the water like a mystical island, with nothing else in sight. It existed on its own, completely separate from the rest of the world in a way that shouldn't have been appealing. It was hard to imagine that such a beautiful place had been home to evil like Rafael's father. That the very house that I'd started to accept as my haven had once been home to the man who ruined my life.

I wanted answers. Enough that I was willing to dig through the hazards of Rafael's and my tenuous relationship to find them.

Rafael guided me to the lower level of the yacht and the McLaren on board. I sat in the passenger seat as he opened the door, watching one of his men open the hatch so that he could drive off the boat and onto the dock. As we went, I turned to stare back at the yacht, considering if the steps were similar to the ones Rafael had taken when I was unconscious when he'd first brought me to his home.

It seemed like a lifetime ago, but somehow wasn't even close.

Rafael was lost in his thoughts as he drove up the hill to the main house, eventually pulling into the driveway. The mid-morning sun shone down on us, making me want nothing more than to soak up the warmth of it and chase away the chill that seeing the photo of Rafe's father had left me with.

I didn't wait for him to open my door for me before I climbed out, staring into Regina's smiling face as she stepped out the front doors to greet us. She held out her arms, waiting for me to step into her embrace.

Those kind brown eyes stared down at me, sending a pang through me that I needed to call my family again. With everything spiraling around me, it was easy to forget that they weren't living the same whirlwind that I was. They sat at home, dealing with the return of one daughter while coping with the absence of the other.

One of the men grabbed our bags out of the tiny trunk as Rafe stepped around the car. "We're leaving for Chicago tomorrow. We need the bags packed with new clothing. Enough for a few days, and then I'll arrange for whatever we need to be purchased to remain at the house there."

"But you just got home," Regina said, pursing her lips and staring at him with the knowledge that she was missing some vital piece of information. I felt like I was too, because the news of going home to Chicago was a shock to me as well. I leveled him with a glare, considering stabbing him when he smirked back at me like I was amusing.

"Can you fill Regina in for me, *mi reina*?" he asked. "I have some business to attend to since we'll be off the island for the foreseeable future."

"When were you planning to inform me of our travel plans?" I asked, planting a hand on my hip and staring him down.

He twisted his lips into a smile, shaking his head as if I were ridiculous. "I just did." He kissed me briefly as he passed, leaving me floundering after him.

It wasn't until he'd disappeared into the building that I realized he'd left me to inform Regina that her dead, abusive husband had tried to kill me.

What a dick.

Regina moved through the bedroom and to the master closet, hauling a duffel bag and larger suitcase out from behind where my dresses hung. Her movements were urgent, despite the fact that we didn't need to leave until the next morning, as if she could feel Rafael's urgency as much as I could.

Given how young he'd been when his mother was murdered, I imagined she'd spent a great deal of time exposed to his moods and anticipating them. "If he manages to complete whatever tasks he deems necessary, the two of you will leave early. Patience has never been his strong suit, and whatever happened in Barcelona has him strung tighter than I've seen in years."

I sat on the edge of the bed slowly, staring at her as she perused my clothing and sorted outfits for me. I remembered how desperate I'd been to ensure I had everything I'd need for my trip to Ibiza. The sheer number of times I'd studied my packing list had left the paper worn and the edges torn.

The difference between that uncertain, unprepared girl and the version of me who didn't even care to give input into my wardrobe was staggering. There was no need or desire to obsess over what I would bring on my trip home or even what I wore daily. Rafael took care of those decisions for me, and at some point it had become a comfort to not have to make them myself.

My life had spiraled out of my control, my choices left to a man who wouldn't allow me to make decisions he didn't agree with. Yet somehow, even forfeiting those decisions, I felt more in control of my life and the world around me than I ever had back home in Chicago.

"So, tell me what happened, since your coward of a husband left that to you," Regina teased, crossing her arms over her chest as she studied me sitting on the edge of the bed with my head in my hands.

"I'm worried that speaking of it will bring back terrible memories for you," I admitted, furrowing my brow. I couldn't imagine being married to a monster like Miguel Ibarra. Having to navigate the depths of the mood swings and paranoia that consumed him must have been impossible. Finally free from him, she deserved to never have to hear his name again.

As impractical as that may have been.

She squared her shoulders, drawing back a deep breath to confirm that she knew exactly what I meant. "Tell me," she said, her eyes shining with her need to persevere through the flash of pain that crossed her face.

"When I was a girl, a man threw my sister and me into the Chicago River. We both nearly died," I said, uncertain how much she might have known. She nodded as she sat down behind me, her brow furrowed in confusion. "In Barcelona, I saw a photo of Rafael's father for the first time."

She swallowed as her hand flew to her mouth, undoubtedly following the only path I could be leading her down. "No." She shook her head, her brown eyes wide with disbelief.

I nodded, twisting my lips. "It was him."

"But *why*?" she asked. "Miguel was unhinged. There is no doubt about that, but he didn't go out of his way to hurt people when it didn't benefit him. If he'd tried to sell you to traffickers, *that* I could have believed, but to...." she trailed off as her hand shot up to grasp my chin suddenly.

I flinched back, startled by the frantic energy in the motion. She stared at my face as her breath wheezed out of her lungs. "My God," she whispered suddenly. She pushed to her feet, racing for the bedroom door and into the hallway. It took me a moment to react, standing and following after her as she set a brisk pace through the halls. She went further into the maze, turning at the end of the house to the last room at the end.

Something ominous slithered up my spine as she paused at the door to draw in a deep breath. Her brown eyes met mine, shadows moving behind them as she turned the knob and pushed the door in. The hinges creaked as if it hadn't been opened for years, then Regina stepped into the darkness and disappeared from view.

A moment passed as I stood there, rooted to the spot and unable to shake the feeling that, once I went into that room, nothing would ever be the same. My life as I'd known it would be forever changed, and I would realize just how deeply entrenched my soul had been in Rafael's world before I'd ever even laid eyes on him.

A light clicked on inside, and it was enough to draw my feet slowly toward the door. I pushed my way more fully into the dusty space that felt as if it had served as a tomb. Regina tore a sheet off the top of the desk, dust scattering in the air as she coughed and ran a trembling hand over the chestnut surface.

She moved away from it, tearing sheets off the boxes and

filing cabinets that filled the room. "What is this place?" I asked, stepping inside and swatting the dusty air away from my face. She settled when all the files were revealed, turning a stunned stare my way briefly before she set to tearing the lid off the first box. Sorting through the files, she shoved it to the side and moved onto the next, her anxious face making my own panic rise higher with every moment that passed.

"Miguel had many friends who were fond of young girls," she said. "That's why I said it would make more sense that he would sell you rather than kill you. I can't imagine you weren't a beautiful child. He would have benefited from selling you."

"I don't understand what that has to do with anything. No matter the reasoning, he *didn't* sell me, Regina," I said, moving toward her as another box was shoved out of her way. She stilled as she opened another, her hands hovering over the contents of the box as she stared down and all the air left her lungs. "Regina?" I asked, stepping closer.

When I stood directly in front of her, she finally turned her wide eyes up to look at me. The horror I saw in them was what finally forced my gaze down to the contents of the box.

And found my own face staring back at me.

7

RAFAEL

"Perez was happy with the shipment?" I asked, staring at Braxton Knight where he sat in the chair on the other side of the desk. The arms dealer was as ruthless as they came, often working as the middleman and walking into tense negotiations without fear. To harm him would put us all at a disadvantage. There was a reason the man was my sole contact when I needed weaponry.

"Yes. He was satisfied, as I'm sure you can see." He smirked, nodding to the briefcase filled with cash that rested on my desk.

"Good. My wife and I will be going to Chicago shortly, but while we're gone I need you to coordinate with Alejandro. I want all the ammunition stocked, make sure every last gun is working properly, and stock up on your extra toys. Show me what you've done when I get back, and you know I'll make sure you're paid well," I said, standing from the desk. I handed the briefcase off to Alejandro where he hovered at the edge of the room. With a nod, he took it and left to go make arrangements for the cash to be distributed among my accounts.

"Ohh, *wife*," Braxton teased. "That sounds positively domestic."

"Don't start with me," I warned, but my lips twitched in amusement. There weren't many men who could draw a laugh from me, but Braxton somehow made me chuckle when we invaded the homes of my enemies and were covered in their blood.

The man had a gift.

The door pushed open without warning, and both Braxton and I bolted to our feet with our hands on our guns. Regina stood there, her face strained as her lungs heaved with exertion. "What the fuck?" I asked, moving toward her.

"*Mi hijo*," she said, leaning forward with a hand pressed to her heart. "You must come. *Now*."

"Coordinate with Alejandro," I barked out the order to Braxton before I followed Regina out of my office. My heart was in my throat as we made our way down the short hall and through the kitchen. "What's wrong?" I asked, following as she hurried through the maze of hallways. She passed the bedroom I shared with Isa, making her way to the only room that could have elicited such a response from Regina.

But where was Isa?

If she'd wandered inside the tomb I'd created of my father's belongings after his death, there was no telling what she might have seen. His crimes against humanity were extensive, and all the hope fled that she might have been able to see beyond his involvement in her drowning one day. If she knew how much worse he was capable of, how could she ever stand to look at me again?

Isa stood behind the desk in the center of the room, staring down into a box that rested on top of it. When I entered the room, the breath left me in a rush.

The woman standing before me held no traces of *mi*

princesa, the innocence gone from every line of her face as she turned blazing green eyes up to me. "*Mi reina?*" I asked.

She grasped the edges of the box in her hands, lifting it and turning it until the contents spilled over the desk. Photo after photo fluttered to the surface, Isa's face staring up from each and every one of them.

I stepped forward, running calloused fingers over them as I looked at the sheer number of them in shock.

Isa's face as a child was as familiar to me as the woman who stared back at me now with her jaw clenched tight in fury.

"I can't believe I didn't see it. Her eyes should have been a dead giveaway, but there were so many children with heterochromia...." Regina trailed off.

"These were taken after the river," Isa murmured, her eyes darting from one photo to the other.

"How can you be certain?" Regina asked.

"I just am. Look at this one," she said, picking up one of the photos. "This is me, and that's Odina glaring at me in the corner. Before the accident, she would have been right by my side, but never after." She set the photo down, picking up another. "My grandmother bought me this dress for my eighth birthday," she said. I watched on with mounting dread as Isa ruffled through the photos on the desk.

The sheer number of them...she was different from the others.

"Are there any that might have been taken before that day?" I asked, stepping around the desk to wrap an arm around her shoulders as she studied them. I didn't know why, but it felt like that was important. Like it marked a significant change.

"I don't think so," she whispered. "These all feel like they were taken after. I don't know how to explain it. Why would he stalk me *after* he tried to kill me? Doesn't the reverse usually happen?" she asked, turning her eyes up to mine. Uncertainty crept in past her fury, her cheeks turning pink as her panic settled in. All her life, she'd been watched.

First by my father and then by me. I really was no different from the man who raised me.

"What age did the photos stop?" Regina asked her. "Miguel didn't die until five years ago."

"I think they stopped before then. If that's the case I would have been thirteen when he died," Isa said. "But I don't think I see photos of me after I turned ten if I'm honest. It's hard to say, but that's my feeling." She reached forward, brushing her hand through the pile of photos and giving them one last look over.

Calculating the math in my head, I knew it couldn't be a coincidence. Miguel may not have died when Isa was younger, but someone had. "My father wasn't the one taking these of you, though I don't doubt it was done at his request."

"Who?" Isa asked.

"Franco Bellandi died when you were nine. He was one of my father's closest friends, and he happened to run Chicago," I answered.

"That can't be a coincidence," Isa said, stepping away from my embrace to peer down into another one of the boxes that she or Regina had torn the lids off. "What about these other girls?" She reached into one of the boxes, pulling out a photo in each hand. A different girl stared up at her from each of them, a red x crossed over their faces. "What does the red marker mean?" she asked.

Regina looked at me with sadness in her eyes one more time before she fled the room, leaving the heartache behind in the tomb where I'd tried to trap it.

I hadn't been the one to pack up my father's records and belongings to place in the office, leaving that to one of the housekeepers as I'd been too busy dealing with the transfer of leadership at the time. I'd intended to go through everything once the transition was solidified, but never gotten around to it. "It means they were sold, *mi reina*," I murmured, stepping up behind her to peer down into the boxes sprawled at her feet and swallowing back the shame I felt knowing all the innocent people my father had hurt.

Isa swallowed loudly as her eyes closed and she turned to press her face into my chest, her fingers gripping my shirt tightly. "There are so many."

"There are," I agreed. "And most of them looked like you," I said, burying a hand in her hair and clutching her tighter to my chest. In each of the photos in the box, there was a child with multicolored eyes. Most were girls, but some boys were mixed in with the sheer number of lives my father had been involved in selling.

I could only hope that the victims were long since dead, because I didn't like to think of the life they'd lived if they hadn't been granted that death.

"This doesn't explain anything," Isa murmured. "If these photos were taken after he drowned me, it doesn't give even the barest hint as to why he did that. Regina said he had more to gain from selling me, and I'm inclined to agree after seeing just how many children he did that to." I knelt at her feet, picking a photo from one of the boxes. The red x was stark across the boy's face. Turning it in my hands, I studied the name and date on the back.

It too had been dated after Isa's drowning. "Are there any dates before the river?" I asked. Isa dug her hands into the photos, taking them out one at a time and sorting through them. Only the ones marked with red had dates though some without them had names, leaving little doubt as to the purpose.

My father kept track of who he sold the children to and when, and he crossed them off like a checkmark on a list when the sale was complete.

With the photos laid face down in front of us, Isa studied the dates. "They're all after the accident," she said, and there was a pause for reflection. As if she knew, with everything staring her in the face, that she needed to stop referring to her attempted murder as an accident. Why she ever had, I didn't know.

Maybe it helped her to not have to think about the fact that someone hated her enough to want to kill her, and she'd never known why.

"You were the first," I said, staring at her with sudden clarity. Whatever had moved my father to throw her into that river, *something* had shifted for him on that day. Enough that he'd suddenly developed an interest in trafficking children. "But why?" None of the photos revealed a name, but her eyes lit with knowledge regardless.

"You said that your father believed your mother was innocent *because* she died. I lived, Rafael," Isa said, her expression gleaming as she tried to follow the hints of clues in front of her. "What if all of this was because I didn't die? In the Salem Witch Trials, Trial by Water wasn't unheard of. I don't know what drove him to throw me in that river, but if he thought it should kill me and it didn't?"

"You're saying maybe your survival proved to my father that girls with eyes like yours were witches?"

"I'm not sure," she said. "I didn't know him, but you did. Would he do all of this,"– she gestured around the room – "if he thought we were the literal spawn of Satan because our eyes were different colors? It sounds ridiculous," she scoffed, shaking her head as she swept the photos of herself back into the box. "And we're no closer to knowing what made him throw me in the water in the first place, especially on the anniversary of your mother's death. It feels too convenient to be a coincidence, but there's nothing here that touches on what caused this."

"If the answers to those questions exist anywhere, it's in Chicago," I said, pulling my cell from my pocket and texting the pilot that I wanted to leave sooner than planned. There was too much at stake, and I couldn't shake the feeling that I was missing a very important aspect and my lack of knowledge would have dire consequences for us.

If she ever learned the truth, she may never forgive me.

My only saving grace was that Isa was more concerned with why my father had chosen to try to kill her in the first place. I knew him well enough to know the cruel bastard didn't need a reason.

Because if Miguel Ibarra had truly wanted Isa dead, she wouldn't be standing in front of me.

8

ISA

The sunshine shone in through the windows of Rafe's private jet, nearly blinding in intensity. I'd only ever been on a plane when traveling to Ibiza in the first place, and the difference between first class and the sleek luxury around me was shocking. I couldn't imagine what the differences would have been from coach to this.

"You'll let me see my family while we're there, right?" I asked, making Rafe look up from his phone finally. He had the innate ability to constantly be busy, but never make me feel ignored either. All it took was a word from me, and he'd shift his undivided attention my way.

Having that probing stare and his intense fixation settled on me was just as disarming as it had been my first night in Ibiza. I took a sip from my bottled water to distract myself as he quirked a brow at me. "Of course we will see your family while we're in Chicago. I have no interest in keeping you from them unnecessarily."

I spluttered, even though it shouldn't have come as a shock. Not with the way that Rafael was determined to infiltrate every facet of my life, but the thought of him sitting in my parent's living room was...laughable. He'd kidnapped their daughter, and he would waltz right into their home without shame. "We?"

"Yes, we, *mi reina*. Am I not your husband? That makes them my family by extension. Don't you think it is time that I met them?"

I paused, considering my words carefully. A conversation with Rafael was treacherous under the best circumstances, anything involving the word *husband* was even more so.

My head shouted alarms as I forced my lips into an appeasing smile. "I just thought it might be better to ease them into it. Let me go see them alone first, and I can inform them that I'm married before I shove my husband in their face when they aren't even expecting me to come visit. If we want them to like you, then there's a certain nuance to how we should handle the introduction," I explained.

Without taking his eyes off mine, he set his phone down on the table between us, standing in a slow unfolding of limbs that caught the breath in my lungs. He prowled around the table and toward me, stretching past my torso to touch the intercom button on the side of the plane.

"Yes, Señor Ibarra?" the female attendant asked over the speaker.

"The back cabin is off limits until further notice," Rafael barked. Removing his finger from the button, he released the locking mechanism on my seat and spun it to face the center aisle of the plane where he stood. Locking it into place once more with his foot, he cupped my face in his hand and dragged his thumb over my lip. "You're incorrect to assume that I care if they like me, *mi reina*," he murmured.

"Why wouldn't you care? If they're your family now like you say?" I asked, tilting my head. His thumb stroked my cheek under my eye, his fixated stare on the brown part marring the green, taking on an entirely new meaning now that I knew the truth of his father's obsession with children who had heterochromia.

His intense stare shifted to my face as a whole as he shook off whatever moment he'd been lost to. "All that matters to me is the fact that you're mine. They can love me. They can hate me. It matters little to me, because at the end of the day it will be my bed you fall asleep in. My arms that you seek in your sleep when your nightmares come for you. Though I do hope they tolerate me for your sake."

"My sister will tolerate you alright," I snarked, rolling my eyes to the ceiling as I thought about the various reactions my family might have to him. My grandmother would give him a glare so intense any normal man would quiver in fear. My parents would hate that he corrupted their innocent baby, and my sister would be so busy trying to manipulate him into her bed that there would be very little chance of me not ripping her hair out.

Rafael smirked, those wicked lips tipping up in the face of my jealousy. He'd always loved it when I acted territorial over him, though he hadn't given me much reason to have any real concern.

Odina was another story, and I wouldn't tolerate even the slightest encouragement of her advances. "I hope you know that if you touch her, I will cut off your favorite appendage while you're sleeping," I warned.

"My favorite appendage? Or yours?" Rafe grinned.

I tipped my head to the side, biting my bottom lip as I fought back the slight smile that tried to escape. It was so rare that the playful Rafe I'd known in Ibiza showed himself after I'd learned the truth. I had to admit that I probably had something to do with that, as the push and pull of our relationship as we learned to love each other as we were had been stifling at times.

I'd wanted to stab him just as often as I wanted to fuck him.

"Both," I admitted, watching as his eyes gleamed with dark heat and satisfaction.

"Maybe you need to remind me why you're my favorite twin," he teased, and only the wry smile that twisted his lips eased what should have been a sting. The statement should have played on my old insecurities, but somehow with Rafe it didn't.

If he'd wanted Odina, he would have had her. It really was that simple for him.

I slapped his thigh, watching as his cock twitched in his slacks in response to the sting from my palm. "Should I hide the forks?" he asked, reaching down to unbutton his pants.

I glared at him. There were no forks on the table sadly. It might have come in handy. "What are you doing?" I laughed, leaning back in my chair.

His free hand went to the head of my seat, supporting his weight as he leaned in and freed his cock. Pumping it with his massive hand, he stroked it from root to tip. Precum gathered at the tip, as if he was truly ready and waiting for me at any moment.

"What does it look like I'm doing? I'm waiting for my wife to wrap her pretty fucking mouth around my cock," he said, releasing his length to glide his hand beneath the curtain of my hair. He tugged me forward, all traces of amusement fading from his face.

I shoved back with my hands on his thighs, fighting the grip around my nape. "I am not going to prove to you that I'm your favorite twin," I said, narrowing my eyes on him in a glare. Even if the words hadn't stung in the way they would have from someone else, I still wouldn't reward that kind of statement with sucking him off.

"You're right. You never need to prove that to me," he said, his features softening for a moment as he willed me to understand that the statement had been meant in jest. I knew it as well as if he'd told me, but still couldn't willingly bring myself to part my lips for him. "But it seems I do need to remind you of something, *mi reina.*"

"And what's that?" I asked, wincing when his hand at my neck gathered my hair in his grip and tugged until pain exploded across my scalp.

"When I tell you to open your fucking mouth, you do it, *wife,*" he growled, all traces of everything soft and gentle gone from his face as he twisted my hair harshly enough to make me gasp. Using the opportunity to pull me toward his cock, his head slid over the tip of my tongue. I turned my eyes up to his to find him staring down at me as if daring me to do something as foolish as bite him.

I opened wider, letting him surge inside with a snap of his hips until he filled my mouth completely and nudged my throat. Drawing back and repeating the motion, he held my gaze as he used my mouth ruthlessly. Each relentless press of him brought tears to my eyes, and I knew from the heat blazing in his gaze that he loved seeing them.

He'd broken me, turning me into his nightmare. I hollowed my cheeks, sucking as he pulled back until only his head remained inside my mouth. "Fucking hell," he groaned, shoving deep and staying planted at my throat. The tears built as he increased the pressure, giving me no choice but to swallow around him and accept him even deeper. His strokes inside me were short, the angle of his shaft tipping up, making it more difficult for him to glide further down my throat.

He groaned his frustration, tearing free from my mouth suddenly as he lifted me out of the chair, turned me, and planted me onto my knees on the cushion. Flipping my dress up over my ass, he shoved my panties down my legs and drove inside me without warning.

There had been a time when I would've been horrified to admit how wet I was from the feeling of his cock in my mouth and nothing else, but all I could do as he drove deep was cry out. "Rafael!" I shouted, wincing when his hand came down on my ass.

The skin stung, a reminder of the time he'd done worse with a riding crop as he continued to fuck me. That memory would always be a bitter mix of sex and pain, knowing that what came next had seared my flesh and left me marked with his name in a permanent and irreversible way that he seemed determined to repeat as often as possible.

Just as the imprint of his ownership on my soul was everlasting.

He reached out one of his hands to press against the side of my head, pinning me on the cushion as he took what he wanted from my body. It didn't matter if it hurt, or if it left me feeling wrung out and used, because we'd both enjoy every second of it.

I slid a hand over my belly, touching the bundle of nerves at the apex of my thighs and working the flesh to add pleasure to the violence of his drives inside me. My body shook with the sudden orgasm that consumed me, convulsing as he continued to fuck me as if he hated me.

I knew better, knew it was a physical release for the stress of the last few days. And as much as I hated that I had to bear the consequences of another's actions, I couldn't deny that I needed the pain.

It grounded me. It reminded me that no matter what

had happened, Rafael's father hadn't torn us apart before we could ever come to be.

Heat flooded me as Rafael came inside me, pressing his hand against my lower back to hold me still as his length throbbed against the end of me.

When he pulled out of me and tucked himself back into his pants, he shifted me so that I stood and claimed my seat for himself. I was still half-disoriented as he tugged my panties back up to my waist and smoothed my dress down to cover me. Pulling me into his lap, he let me curl my head into his shoulder and held me.

The intercom sounded as he called the attendant, the sound feeling like it happened in another part of the world. My body thrummed with the aftermath of pleasure as my brain tried to wrap around my surroundings.

It wasn't until the attendant emerged into the main cabin that I fully understood what he'd done, inviting another person into the very room where he'd only just finished fucking me.

His cum was still inside me as he spoke to the attendant, requesting a glass of white zinfandel. I flushed beet red, burying my face further into his neck. The cabin smelled like sex, and if that hadn't been obvious enough, my disheveled appearance would have been. The attendant left us to go fetch the drinks he'd requested, and I groaned into his chest as he laughed at my discomfort.

"How could you bring her in here?" I scolded. "She *knows* we just had sex."

"I fail to see the problem with that," he grunted, his hand running through my hair in a gentle soothing motion that was such a sharp contrast to the fact that I wanted to fucking stab him again.

Where was that fork?

"Maybe I don't want everyone to know things like that," I hissed, pulling back from his chest to stare down at him. His leg was firm beneath my ass, the muscles in his thigh so hard they should have been uncomfortable.

"You're my wife." He grinned. "I think it is safe to say that everyone knows we have sex."

I groaned, burying my hand in my face as the woman returned with my wine and handed it to me quickly before scurrying off. "You made her uncomfortable."

"No, you being uncomfortable made her uncomfortable. You have no reason to be ashamed of the fact that I cannot keep my hands off you," he murmured, leaning forward to run his nose up the side of mine. He ran his thumb over the bandage covering his name, the light touch making the wound throb. "How does it feel?"

"How do you think it feels?" I asked with a roll of my eyes. Only Rafe could literally carve his name into me and then ask how I felt.

"I think it feels like you're mine." He shrugged, removing his hand from the wound as if the pain it might have caused me was inconsequential. Even with the dull ache that accompanied the wounds and the memory of the blinding white hot pain slicing through me, I knew he'd gone far easier on me than he had himself. His wounds were deeper than mine would ever be, cut through his flesh as deeply as he could manage without causing permanent damage to the muscle.

Shifting me to the side slowly so I could balance my wine, he grabbed his phone off the table in front of us as if the subject was settled in his mind.

When he typed in a password that was different than his, I stared at the home screen with a photo of a fork for the background in shock. Rafael's phone was filled with apps, but this one looked new out of the box. It was identical to the sleek and expensive one I'd seen him using otherwise in every way. He handed it to me, letting me take it from his grip as I shifted the wine to my other hand. "There will undoubtedly be times when we are separated in Chicago. I'm sure you will spend time with your family while I'm looking for answers in places that you cannot come," he said, and it sank in that he was really, truly trusting me with a phone of my own.

I hadn't had one since he'd knocked mine off the balcony in Ibiza, and I swallowed back the meaning of the moment as emotion clogged my throat. Had we reached the point in our relationship where he trusted me not to leave?

How had we gotten here so quickly?

"This is mine?" I asked, even though the answer was obvious. I needed the words and the reassurance they would give me, that maybe, just maybe, we could find a way to some kind of normalcy.

"You'll *always* have Joaquin with you at the very least," he said, nodding his head toward where the majority of Rafael's men had chosen to stay in the larger cabin at the front of the plane. The one in the back was more private, separated from what Rafe informed me was a small bedroom at the back by only a door. "But I still want a way to reach you. It is always to be charged, and you're to answer the phone any time I call you." My mouth dropped open in outrage, prepared to argue the point, but his face tensed in that way that I knew I would achieve nothing by making demands of my own.

Even if his were unreasonable.

"I can't *always* answer the phone," I said, softening my tone from the angry rage I wanted to throw in his face. "It isn't like you will."

"*Mi reina,* I would never ignore your call unless it were life and death. I do not plan on being involved in any of those scenarios while we are in Chicago, so it should be a moot point. I promise I will be as available to you as you must be to me," he said, raising a brow at me as if he dared me to try to contradict him.

"Fine," I groaned, setting the phone on the table. As much as I wanted to play with it and set it up to my exact specifications, I'd never even seen the brand Rafael used until him.

I wanted to experiment with it in private and not with his amused stare looking over my shoulder and judging how slow I was to learn the new device.

Dropping my forehead to his, I smiled down at him even as I wrinkled my nose. "Thank you for trusting me with it."

"Mi reina, I trust you with my life," he said. "What is a phone compared to that?"

9

RAFAEL

The streets of Chicago passed by in the window of the car, Isa's gaze intense on the city that had once been her home. Not even long ago, this place had been all she knew.

I watched from the corner of my eye as *mi reina* faded before my eyes, her spark lost to the familiar prison that had kept her confined within the expectations of others. If I thought that her family would ruin what we'd built together, that they might tarnish her journey to accepting herself, I would remove them from her life like the weeds they were.

She may never forgive me for such a thing, but I would always do what was best for our life together. Her family would never accept the woman she'd become, not if they ever discovered the truth, and my Isa wasn't someone who could keep a secret like that without it weighing on her heavily.

"My parents' house isn't in this direction," Isa said, finally turning her gaze away from the window as we skirted around the center of the city and headed for my home in the outskirts.

"No," I agreed. "It is not. We'll get settled at the house tonight and then go see your family tomorrow." The sun was already starting to set, and exhaustion was written into the lines of Isa's face.

"I want to see my family. They're worried about me," she protested, glaring at me intently. She was too oblivious to the tiredness that plagued her, far too used to it for my comfort.

I'd push her. I'd break her and destroy her.

But I'd also worship her and make sure she was taken care of, even when she fought me. "Tomorrow," I repeated.

"Rafe..." she started, trailing off as she tried to find the words to argue with me. Given that she was always so quick to respond, it proved my point that she was far too tired to deal with her family at that moment. If she thought they would just accept her new husband and his place in her life, considering all that had needed to happen in order for me to infiltrate her life, she would have a very rude awakening coming.

The battle she'd had with me would seem like a walk in the park compared to trying to convince her family we were the average happy couple and that I was worthy of her. Whereas Isa might have seen the appeal in lying to her family long-term to appease them, I wouldn't tolerate such a thing beyond the initial conversation before Isa could come home.

I would never be worthy of her, and I would drag her down to the pits of depravity to rule at my side. I already had.

I raised a brow at her, waiting for her to continue with a smirk on my face. I loved nothing more than when Isa challenged me, even if I was already on edge, given my father's bullshit and the prediction that *mi reina* would wither under her parents' pressure to be the perfect daughter they'd raised in a cage of expectations.

When she didn't continue, disappointment flooded me. Already she'd started to retreat into the more complacent girl who had existed before me. I'd snap her back to my rebellious wife if it was the last thing I did.

"Joaquin is to stay with you at all times while we're off *El Infierno*," I explained, studying her face for a reaction.

Her mouth twitched with the need to give me a scathing retort, ignoring the man in question's chuckle from the front passenger seat. "And that's different from when we're on the island in what way exactly?" she asked finally, crossing her arms over her chest.

I ignored it, even though pride surged in my chest that she still dared to defy me even after learning the truth of who and what I was. She'd watched me beat a man, pound barbed wire into his body until it threatened to tear open his gut, and she still looked at me as if I was the love of her life.

If that didn't make her fucking perfect for me, then I didn't know what would.

"You always answer your cell phone," I said.

"So you said," she agreed, her nostrils flaring at the repeated order that she hated.

"You go nowhere without my approval. That includes spending time with your family. If I don't like what they have to say to you, then you will no longer see them. If your sister starts shit, then I will remove her from the equation," I said, watching as her mouth dropped open in surprise. "I will not tolerate anyone making you feel like you're less because you dare to live the life you were born for rather than the one they chose for you."

"Because I was clearly born to be your murdering little demon," she snarked.

Joaquin chuckled in the front seat, finally turning back to look at Isa pointedly. "You didn't exactly hesitate, *mi reina*. I believe you are far more prone to murder than you would like to think about yourself."

"Oh do shut up," she said, flipping him off as he spun back to the front. "Any other rules, your highness?" she spat to me, glancing out the window as we rounded the corner at the end of the road and pulled up to the gate.

The couple who took care of the house in my absence had likely made sure everything was set up earlier in the day, and the security I kept on the property at all times was well in place. One of the men nodded from the booth by the gate, pressing the button to let us through when Santiago pulled the SUV up.

As he continued up the driveway, I turned to watch Isa's expression as one of my secondary homes came into view. Much larger than Isa and I would need to accommodate all of my men and security that had to come along with us, the stone building was vastly different from the open and airy feel of the main house on *El Infierno*. The Tudor-style house wasn't my personal taste, but given how quickly I'd needed to purchase something that suited my needs and expectations when we'd first come to Chicago for Bellandi's war, I couldn't complain.

The line of SUVs parked in the rounded driveway behind us as Isa gaped at the size of the house in shock. Shoving her door open and stepping down from the vehicle, she ambled up the front steps before I moved to follow.

She looked so tiny next to the vastness of the house, I couldn't help but wrap my arms around her back and touch my lips to her cheek. "Do you like it?" If she didn't, I'd sell it and buy a new one to her specifications.

"It's stunning, but isn't it a bit much?"

"All the men have to stay here as well since they aren't much good to me off property," I answered, taking her hand and guiding her inside for a tour of the house and emergency bunker that would culminate in a much-needed shower and meal.

10

ISA

In all my life, there had never been a day when I was more aware of my family's financial mess than that moment when we pulled up in front of my parents' house the next day. Given that most of my time was spent in beaten-down homes where I tutored and a run-down school that hadn't been cared for in decades, it shouldn't have come as a surprise that my outlook had been skewed.

It was harder to see poverty when it was all you knew. The peeling paint of our home just seemed normal. The grass had at one point been alive and thriving due to my grandmother's attention and the love she gave to the land. When she'd gotten sick, she hadn't been able to take care of it anymore.

When she'd gotten sick, I'd started helping to pay her medical bills. In the time since the surgery things should have gotten easier, but with college on the horizon they hadn't. My entire life stared me in the face, all the hard work I'd done to get a scholarship feeling like a total and complete waste with the man sitting in the back seat beside me as we stared at my parents' home across the street.

"Has it always been like this?" I asked him. He didn't hesitate before he answered, his deep voice filling the silence that had consumed the vehicle since we parked.

"Yes," he agreed.

We were far from the poorest house on the block. We weren't even in the worst neighborhood, where abandoned houses were more common than occupied ones, but the signs of our struggle could be felt in every crooked floorboard on the porch. They could be felt in the screen door where the metal at the bottom was dislodged. Jagged and dangerous, it popped out from the framing. In the old and weathered front door that had long since faded from the sunny yellow I'd chosen as a girl, when I'd had the brilliant idea that a fresh coat of paint on the door could make our house more welcoming for my friends.

"I can't leave them to this, not knowing how we live," I told him, spinning to stare at him intently. "Don't ask me to do that."

"I won't, *mi reina*. I'll take care of them, if they let me. I believe your parents will come around to my assistance eventually, but I'm not certain about your grandmother."

I frowned, trying to think about my grandmother's reaction to this man coming in and stealing me away in the night. Even if she had no clue how true the sentiment was, she would feel that way regardless. She would see it as him buying me, paying my family for the theft of their future and her legacy. I groaned, suspecting my grandmother would be the greatest battle in the fight for peace between Rafael and my family.

Rafael grew tired of waiting for me to make my move to step out of the vehicle, shoving open his door to make that choice for me. I'd spent the entire morning nagging him, pushing to get to my family's house, but now that we were there all that bravado was gone.

I wanted to go back to bed.

"It will not be easy, Isa. Nothing worth fighting for ever is," Rafael reminded me as he opened my door. "I know you're afraid, and you have good reason to be. But what does fear do?"

"It makes us feel alive," I said, accepting the hand he held out for me. Allowing him to pull me from the vehicle, I watched out of the corner of my eye as Santiago and Joaquin stepped out of the front seats. In the time since Rafael had first introduced me to the advantages of confronting my fears, I'd come to understand one simple truth.

It didn't only make me feel alive in those moments when he dangled me over the edge of a cliff or pushed me into the water of a natural pool. It made me appreciate the moments of quiet, and see the value in the things I'd once feared. It made me understand that the tinge of fear and anticipation I always had with Rafael didn't have to be a bad thing.

He excited me. He made it so I never knew what he would do or how he would react to any given situation.

He guided me across the street with my hand firmly encased in his, tension bleeding into the lines of his body as his shoe touched the sidewalk in front of my parent's home. No matter what words of encouragement he offered me, he cared what they thought. If only because he cared about my happiness.

He knew as well as I did that this first meeting with them couldn't possibly end well.

"Stay here," he barked to Santiago and Joaquin as we started up the crumbling walkway. The stones were uneven, jagged where winter's frozen ground and the thaw in the spring had shifted the earth beneath them. I moved carefully, stepping over the raised sides to avoid twisting my ankle and wondering how I'd ever sprinted up to the house.

Everything was unfamiliar, even the place that had been my home and my sanctuary for eighteen years.

The door burst open suddenly, my mother's frame filling the front porch. With a hand covering her mouth, tears stung her eyes as I paused on the walkway. Rafe's hand clenched mine tightly, grounding me against the surge of emotions that came from seeing her. Dark circles stained the skin beneath her eyes, her cheeks more hollow than I could ever remember seeing.

"Isa?" she asked in a quiet voice as she finally drew her hand away from her mouth.

"Hi, Mom," I said, the quiet words seeming to crack through the air as she sprang into action. She hurried down the steps too quickly, racing over the uneven walkway until her arms surrounded me and she pulled me into her embrace. Rafe had no choice but to release my hand, and even then I could feel his displeasure in the act.

With my hands around my mother's thin frame, I patted her back awkwardly. Even in the moments when I could be nothing but grateful to be back with her, the sinking feeling that nothing would ever be the same in our relationship hovered on the horizon.

How could she ever love me, when I was no longer the daughter she'd raised?

"Waban!" she yelled when she finally pulled back. The neighbors next door poked their heads out the window, and I winced as I felt their gaze slide up over me in my expensive clothes with a man at my side. I knew what many thought of girls from our neighborhood when they found themselves a wealthy boyfriend, and it had never felt more pungent than the moment when all that bitterness was turned on me.

They knew nothing of my marriage, just like they knew nothing of the other girls who'd found a way out of the endless cycle of poverty that trapped so many. But that wouldn't stop them from whispering.

"Don't cry," I said, reaching up to touch her cheek with my hand. I brushed away the tears streaming down her face, guilt stabbing me in the chest as I thought of how worried she must have been. While my relationship with Rafael and time on *El Infierno* had felt like a whirlwind to me and flown by, I imagined it must have felt like a lifetime to a mother worried for her daughter.

"You're alright? Truly?" she asked, pressing her lips to my forehead.

"Yes," I said, and even if the words glazed over everything I'd been through with Rafael up to this point, they weren't a lie. When I thought of how things could have played out as a consequence for my foolishness in going to Ibiza in the first place and being naive enough to fall into a temporary relationship with a man I didn't know, I'd been incredibly lucky.

My father's footsteps thudded down the porch steps, his shocked brown eyes meeting mine briefly before he tugged me away from my mother and crushed me to his chest. "Isa," he muttered, swaying side to side as his fingers ran through my hair. His voice murmured gently, a soft thank you on repeat that I didn't think was for me, but to the ancestors for returning me home. To God, for bringing me home safe.

To any being he might have ever believed in, even vaguely and in a distant sort of way.

"You're never leaving the country again," he said, a sob catching in his throat as he tried to huff a laugh.

My heart stalled, reminded of the truth that I knew we would need to confront. They wanted me to be home for good, but this place wasn't my home any longer. "We should move inside, *mi reina,*" Rafe said softly, drawing me away from my father with the words.

I turned, nodding to him and drawing away from my father to take Rafe's hand in mine. The tense lines of his jaw relaxed, reassured by me actively seeking him out despite the presence of my family.

"Yes, let's go inside," my mother said, nodding her head though she looked at Rafael in confusion. It occurred to me that neither of my parents had made any indication that they even saw him, and I'd been so consumed by the reunion that I hadn't even realized how odd that felt. "Thank you for bringing her home. I can't thank you enough."

My mother turned, heading for the steps with that confusion still etched on her face when Rafael followed at my side. I realized with a start that she thought he'd just delivered me home.

She didn't realize that the strikingly beautiful man beside me was the very same man Chloe had warned them about. The murderer who had stolen me away. As we approached the stairs, my grandmother emerged in the doorway, her aging face tight with suspicion.

"*Nōhsehsaeh*, what have you brought home?" she asked, her eyes not on me, but settled on Rafael's face. Her lips stayed pressed together tightly, her words hovering in the air as she stepped back into the house and made her way to the living room where she dropped into her favorite chair.

My parents stood together in front of the old fireplace that they never used, staring at me expectantly. I looked up to Rafael, finding him staring down at me. The fact that he waited for my cue and allowed me to begin the introductions warmed the space in my chest that had filled with guilt at seeing the physical symptoms of my parents' worry. I turned to my husband. "Rafe, these are my parents, Waban and Leonora, and my grandmother Alawa." Ignoring the tension in the room at my brief mention of his name, I soldiered forward even though I knew that what would come would be far worse than the slight hint. "This is Rafael," I said, squeezing his hand. I knew they would recognize the name, that it would fill in the gaps of their knowledge.

The room went still as they processed my words, the joy melting off their faces as they turned to look at the murderer in their living room. "Her husband," Rafe added, turning that tense stillness to pure silence.

Nobody breathed. Not even me as I turned and leveled him with a glare.

What a dick.

11

RAFAEL

Isa glared at me, no doubt hating the fact that I'd chosen to let the cat out of the bag so quickly. I resisted the urge to smirk at the fury on her beautiful face, filling those stunning eyes with the fire she'd discovered within herself on *El Infierno*.

Somehow, smiling in the face of her family's shock seemed insensitive.

"Husband?" her mother asked, raising a shocked eyebrow to her daughter. Isa fidgeted, trying to draw her hand away from mine, but I kept my grip tight and did my best to not let her go, even going so far as to not make it obvious that I would restrain her with my touch. The last thing I needed to do was give her family any reason to believe the story Chloe had spun about the abuse she suspected Isa suffered at my hands.

I'd listened with my own ears over the audio feed I'd never removed when Isa came to Ibiza as Chloe told Isa's family everything, explaining that their daughter hadn't returned home because she'd been taken by a monster.

"Yes," Isa confirmed finally. "Rafe is my husband."

Her father practically vibrated with the need to avenge the daughter he suspected had been taken from him, but he wisely kept still. Still enough that I could recognize the restrained aggression for exactly what it was. "You barely know each other," he said finally, his gaze intent on his daughter for a brief moment before he turned his eyes to me. "My Isa is young, and I'm certain you've swept her off her feet with your lies. You should be ashamed of yourself for taking advantage of her like this."

"How have I taken advantage of her exactly? If that was my intent, it would have been far more logical for me to leave this relationship as a temporary arrangement and send her on her merry way when I was through with her," I explained, my voice cool and detached as I described what most men would have done with the virgin who had unknowingly wandered into a pit of vipers just waiting to snatch her up and devour her.

Nothing would have remained but bones when they were through with her.

"I don't know, but it is not acceptable that my sweet daughter went to Ibiza and she came home married to a man who her friend says is a criminal. The Isa I know and raised would not tolerate that," he said, lifting his chin with pride. There was no doubt that he loved Isa with all his heart and that he believed he'd done right by her.

I couldn't even regret the way she'd been raised in the end, not when it kept her from getting into too much trouble until she had me there to protect her.

"The sweet daughter you believe you raised never existed in the first place. She came to Ibiza practically screaming for adventure without even knowing it, because her life in Chicago had been smothered in her responsibilities," I said. Isa moved at my side as if she might protest, spinning to face me as I drew her tighter into me. "She would never tell you that, but even she knows it's true. You protected her. You raised her, and you even love her. But you never showed her how to *live*."

"Rafe," Isa murmured, her voice gentle as her hand touched my arm. There was a tremor to the sound, the only thing that alerted me to the fact that I might have moved too quickly for her parents to understand. Wrapping their head around the fact that their daughter was married was one thing, dismantling everything they thought they knew about her was foolish.

Isa herself would show them with time, and as much as it killed me to wait, that part of her evolution had to come from her.

"I'm sorry for worrying you," Isa said as silence descended once again. "As you can see, I'm safe. I married Rafael because I love him, and I hope you can accept that."

"You haven't left us much choice," Isa's grandmother said from her chair. Her gaze leveled on me for the first time. "When I told you to have fun and live a little in Ibiza, this was not what I had in mind."

"This wasn't exactly the kind of relationship I could have ever planned to find," Isa said, her tone hesitant as a laugh bubbled up in her throat. There was no chance to have planned on discovering she'd been stalked and had no choice in our relationship, was what she meant but couldn't say. A wry smile twisted my lips.

"And what of his criminal activities?" her mother asked, pursing her lips as she shoved down her distaste. From what I knew of her, she was an advocate of waiting until marriage. Perhaps she would be grateful that I'd made an honest woman out of her daughter in the end, even if my order of operations was slightly reversed. "You're okay with those?"

"Mother," Isa sighed. "Did Chloe have any proof of these crimes? I know her. She means the best she possibly could, but we both know she's dramatic. She heard a rumor and rushed to tell me of it. Rafe is very well-known in Ibiza and owns a number of respectable businesses. Tabloids and such will always print nonsense, and people whispering about criminal activities doesn't make it true." Admiration welled within me as I thought over her words. Isa had never answered her mother's question, nor had she confirmed or denied that I *was* a criminal.

She'd danced around the subject flawlessly, making her mother's face twist with concern as she thought over her daughter's statement. "I love Chloe. You know that, but nobody can deny that she's got a penchant for drama."

Her grandmother chuckled as she shook her head. "I've never known you to lie, *Nōhsehsaeh.* Has he truly corrupted you so much that you would feed your family his words and call them yours?"

"I told no lies," Isa said, jutting her chin up as she stared back at the matriarch I knew she admired more than anyone. "And I speak for myself, more now than I ever have before. Make no mistake, I am exactly where I want to be."

Her grandmother pursed her lips, a hard stare settling on me that I felt down to my bones. "What have you done to my granddaughter?"

"Loved her," I said simply. "For exactly who she is and not what I want her to be. That is more than I can say for you and the legacy you cling to."

Isa stilled at my side, a deep sigh shuddering from her lungs. She moved to speak, to try to salvage the situation that was quickly falling into chaos around her. "I don't want to fight."

"Then perhaps you should have left your *husband* in

Spain where he belongs," her grandmother said harshly. I stood, ready to guide my wife from her parents' home rather than deal with the scorned matriarch who had lost her only chance at continuing the heritage she worked her entire life to preserve.

The front door opened behind us, closing quickly as a voice so similar to Isa's filled the silence of the house.

"Mom?" Odina asked, rounding the corner from the hallway and stepping into the living room. She froze as her gaze landed on Isa where she stood in the center of it.

On the sister she'd hoped I would ruin.

Her eyes that were so close to Isa's trailed down over Isa's baby blue dress with long sleeves, to cover my name and the brand for the time being, and the heels on her feet. Her nostrils flared as she studied the flawless sheen to Isa's hair as it fell over her shoulders in cascades of waves. When her eyes finally landed on her sister's hand wrapped within mine, she raised her glare up and over my body until it landed on my face. Her gaze narrowed further, seeming to condemn me for the fact that Isa didn't wear the marks of my abuse.

"The prodigal daughter returns," Odina sniped, wiping the pissed off rage off her face. Whereas Isa's anger filled me with the need to help her flourish, Odina's washed over my skin like a disease.

Toxic, and full of so much hatred that I wondered how Isa wasn't already dead. The thought made me itch to wrap my hands around Odina's neck until the life faded from her eyes that were too like Isa's—a cold mockery of her beauty and warmth.

"I'm glad you're home," Isa said, smiling at her sister more kindly than she deserved. She made no move to approach Odina, and the sisters faced off while the rest of the family remained quiet as if they were waiting for a bomb to drop.

It might have been less tense.

"I moved your stuff to the corner of the room when it didn't seem like you would be coming home. I suppose I can move it back," Odina said. The words probably seemed giving to her family, an olive branch that they were praying for.

A truce, but I knew better than that. The curiosity in Odina's gaze made me more than confident that she only wished to fish for information regarding my place in Isa's life.

"That's not necessary," Isa said. "I won't be moving back in."

"Oh," Odina said, dropping her eyes to our hands held together once more. She stilled when her gaze landed on the rings I'd placed on Isa's finger the day we married, her mouth parting in shock as her face twisted with something cruel.

"Rafe, I'm sure it is obvious," Isa scoffed. "But this is my sister. Odina, this is my husband, Rafael Ibarra." Isa leaned further into my side, absorbing the heat from my body as she twisted so that her breasts pressed into my side. I released her hand finally to wrap an arm over the back of her shoulder and drape it along her waist.

The physical nature of her claim on me didn't go unnoticed or unappreciated, even with the awkward silence from the rest of her family. It pleased me to know my wife was territorial, and that she would mark me as her property whenever she had the opportunity.

Her father cleared his throat, breaking the silent competition between sisters so he could get back to the topic that mattered to him in that moment. "We did research after

Chloe came home," Isa's father said. "There is no lack of articles about you and speculating about your business practices."

"Yes," Odina chimed in. "It was very concerning. Our precious Isa would never be involved with an animal like that, so what exactly are you doing here?"

"Odina," her mother scolded.

"What? Let's face it. Dating a murderer is much more a me thing to do than an Isa. Though I suppose they were made for each other," Odina said, making her mother go still. The family turned wide eyes to me, the dirty laundry aired before a stranger not sitting well. Odina smirked at Isa, no doubt expecting her sister to cower in the face of the deepest shame she hid from the world.

"I have no secrets from my husband," Isa said instead, meeting Odina's eyes with a proud smile. "He is very aware of the mistake I made all those years ago, so if you intend to drive a wedge into our marriage, you will have to try much harder than that, *sister.*" Her smile turned mocking as Odina's mouth turned down in a frown of disappointment.

"None?" she asked. "So he's aware of the fact that you nearly murdered your twin and finds that acceptable for the woman he chose to marry? What does that say about him exactly?"

"That he's more forgiving than you?" Isa asked, tilting her head to the side. "I've felt guilty for that day for far too many years. I won't allow it to own me any longer. I was a child, and I did something foolish. *You* have done far worse in the years since then, and you do not have the excuse of being a kid anymore. Move the fuck on, Odina. I sure as hell have."

Begrudging respect bloomed on her grandmother's face as Isa spoke the words. "Language, *Nōhsehsaeh,*" she scolded, but a tiny smile threatened to reveal itself. She quickly suppressed it.

"You're such a fucking cunt, Isa. Did you finally get tired of being so perfect all the time?"

Isa shrugged, her face impassive as she studied her sister's rage. "No. I just got tired of being your whipping girl."

I tightened my hand at her spine, pulling her tighter into my side as pride welled within me. I hadn't thought she would stand up for herself so thoroughly. My one regret was that she didn't seem able to turn the same ferocity on the rest of her family and the questions that felt like they would be endless.

"Would the two of you stop it?" her mother asked, hanging her head and rubbing her fingers over her brow. "Isa has been home a matter of minutes and you're already at each other's throat. We need to discuss what we are going to do about this..." she trailed off, pausing to look down at Isa's rings in distaste. "*Marriage.* That's what is the most important right now."

"Of course it is. Everything about Isa is what's important," Odina said with a roll of her eyes. She ducked out of the room, making for the stairs at the back of the house and stomping her entire way up them.

Her mother sighed, dropping her fingers from her face to stare at Isa with a shake of her head. "I can't believe you didn't invite us to the wedding at the very least."

"It wasn't exactly planned," Isa said evasively. "He surprised me with a very romantic ceremony overlooking the water. I couldn't say no." Her voice went dreamy on the last words, the romantic notion she slid into her statement nearly making me snort.

I had the distinct impression that her mother would

have a very different opinion of me putting a gun to her daughter's head.

"I'm sure," her mother said, her glare settling on me. "How convenient for him that we weren't present to talk you out of such a foolish thing."

Isa's eyes widened as she studied her mother, moving to put her body in front of mine. "I know you think I'm still a child and incapable of making my own choices. But I promise you, I knew exactly what I agreed to when I married Rafe. The only game he plays with me is chess, and, unlike most men, I know exactly where he stands."

"Oh, Isa," she sighed. "What do you know of men?"

Isa pursed her lips as she considered her response and pulled away from me to take her mother's hands in hers as she tried to compel her to understand, and her voice softened. "I only need to know one man, and I know him far better than you ever could. Please do not question my judgement in this. It won't end well for anyone."

"What will he do? Take you away from us again?" Isa's mother asked, as she turned her glare my way. "We've been there—"

"My home is in Spain now," Isa said. "But we're here visiting for the near future. We should make the best of that, not spend it fighting over the choices I have made that are *done,* Mom."

"You're going back to Spain," Leonora breathed in shock.

"Of course. Rafael's business is in Spain. Our life is there."

"What about your life here?" her mother asked, ripping her hands out of her daughter's grip. "What about your family and your responsibilities to the center? What about college?!"

"I am Isa's family now," I said, stepping in finally as I

reached the end of my patience. The constant questioning was unnecessary, but even more than that it was the tone with which her mother spoke that sent me over the edge. The dismissal of Isa's choices may not have been spoken explicitly, but it was there nonetheless. "I would like for you to have a relationship with her for her sake, but it isn't entirely necessary."

Her mother paled at the threat. "What?" she asked.

"If you truly believe the rumors Chloe told you about me, then you are either incredibly brave or exceedingly foolish to think that your questions will have any sway whatsoever in the choices Isa and I make. Trust me when I say that Isa is *mine* now. Her priority is no longer to be your daughter, but to be my wife. As her husband, I will do whatever it takes to protect her. Even if that means keeping her from the family who wants to put her in a box and tell her who she is supposed to be. I think it's time we leave for today."

"How is that any different than what you're doing, if you just steal her away at the first sign of trouble? She hasn't expressed any interest in leaving," her father argued.

"Because with me, Isa can be anyone she wants to be as long as she's mine," I argued, holding out a hand for Isa. Her eyes fell to it, darting back to her mother's incredulous face. She didn't miss the shift of power in the room. Isa wouldn't leave the house unless it was her choice, even at my guidance.

She could choose to stay, or she could choose to put her trust in me yet again and place her hand in mine. She ground her teeth, glaring at me sharply but eventually she did exactly what I'd known she would.

She chose me.

12

ISA

What the fuck just happened?

I moved over the hazardous steps of the walkway in a daze. My mother's and grandmother's eyes bored into my spine as we made our way toward the SUV. The questions in their heads felt almost tangible when I turned back to glance at them and found them staring at Santiago and Joaquin in confusion.

I forced a slight smile to my face, wanting to reassure them that I would see them again. I didn't doubt Rafael's words that he would separate me from my family, but he wouldn't do it after the first meeting. He couldn't expect miracles in one hour spent together. Even he wasn't that unreasonable.

I hoped.

"Are you fucking kidding me?" I hissed as soon as the car doors closed. I turned to snarl at Rafael, ready to throttle him for his insufferable bullshit. "'Your daughter is mine now'?!"

He laughed, a deep chuckle that vibrated up his chest as he folded me into his side despite the fact that I felt like a hellcat ready to claw his damn eyes out. That had been the most infuriating conversation I'd ever had, between his aggravating attempts to defend my decisions and my mother's determination to question every choice I'd ever made.

"You told them you couldn't say no," he said, the sound of his laughter hissing through his teeth as he tried to restrain it. I snorted, placing a palm against my forehead as I realized that I *had* said that.

"Oh my God, why did I say that?" I asked. I'd all but told them the truth several times, and if anyone ever told them the full story of what had happened, then they would remember the little subtleties that had wormed their way into my words. "You all but told them you'd kidnapped me and that you would do it again!"

"It's the truth," Rafael said with a shrug. Joaquin groaned in the front seat, seeming to find us as insufferable as I found his boss.

"You need to have more tact in handling my family. Introducing yourself as my husband was ridiculous. We should have had the foresight to take our rings off—"

"No," Rafe growled, his eyes turning serious as he narrowed them on my face. "Those rings never leave your finger, *mi reina,* or so help me I will find a way to permanently attach them to you."

Sadly, I didn't doubt he meant it.

"This is never going to work out if we can't make them believe that I chose this. Which is going to get harder every time you make a comment about cutting them from my life. They'll never buy into me being okay with that," I said. "Because I wouldn't be. You cannot keep me from my family, Rafe," I argued.

"Watch me," he said, his lips twisting with a scowl. "I won't let them try to turn you back into the girl who did everything she was told. You stood up for yourself in there." He nodded his head toward the house as Santiago pulled away from the driveway. "Aren't you pleased with that?"

"Of course I am," I sighed, pinching my nose between my fingers. "You act like they mistreated me. They didn't."

"No, they just allowed Odina to do that without ever making a move to stop it," he accused, and the truth stung as those words hit me straight in the chest. "I won't tolerate any of her bullshit where you're concerned."

"Neither will I," I admitted. I wasn't sure when I'd stopped feeling so guilty for the danger I'd unknowingly put Odina in. Maybe it was just the time away from her that allowed me to see how toxic she was and how she kept me buried in those emotions. Perhaps it was knowing that Rafael's father had been the one to throw me in the river.

What chance did a five-year-old girl have against Miguel Ibarra?

"I don't think you understand," he said, turning and leveling me with a fierce look that left little doubt as to how serious his next words would be. "She will disappear, and it will be a much less pleasant disappearance than you had, *mi reina*. She has already endangered you once."

I sat in silence, staring into his intense eyes as he willed me to understand the words he wasn't speaking. Not wanting to make things worse, I neglected to mention all the times Odina had knowingly put me in danger before the drugging. "If she does it again," he drawled. "I'll fucking kill her."

Rolling my neck as I sat up in bed early the next morning, I stretched as quietly as I could. Rafael slept peacefully behind me, his massive body sprawled out and taking up most of the bed. He was so breathtaking to look down at when his face was relaxed in sleep, it didn't seem possible for a man capable of such evil to be so handsome.

I knew he'd probably disarmed my family with his appearance the day before, until they couldn't believe that the man who stood before them was the same man Chloe had accused of murder. I contemplated what that meant of their research as I moved through my morning routine in the bathroom as quietly as I could.

Tugging the robe hanging on the back of the bathroom door tight around myself to cover the slip I'd worn to bed, I stepped back into the bedroom and crept through the space to the door.

I padded my way downstairs on bare feet, wandering into the kitchen. Joaquin and Santiago sat at the island, staring at their phones and drinking coffee. Crossing my arms over my chest, I stepped behind the island. "Have you eaten?" I asked, quirking a brow at them.

"Can't cook," Santiago grunted. Joaquin shook his head as his eyes trailed down to the peek of skin at the top of my robe.

"Are you naked under that?" he asked, grimacing as if the thought pained him.

"Nope," I said, not bothering to mention that what I had on wasn't much better. "Eggs okay?" Santiago and Joaquin hummed their agreement, watching me as I moved about the fully stocked kitchen. Grabbing sausage out of the fridge along with the eggs, I set to hunting down the cutting board and other things I would need.

Adjusting to a new kitchen was always miserable, but there was something relaxing about cooking for the first time since my trip to Ibiza. At least, without the watchful eye of Regina teaching me how to roll *Ensaimada*. I grabbed a few potatoes out of the pantry, peeling them quickly while Joaquin watched me.

"Where's Rafael?" he asked finally.

"Sleeping in today it seems. I get the impression he doesn't adjust to time changes very well," I said.

"Never been a problem before," Santiago said, shrugging his shoulders. "Were you up late?"

Joaquin elbowed him in the side as I snorted back a laugh, dicing and tossing things into a frying pan. "I'm going to refrain from answering that in favor of preserving your life."

"Smart choice," Joaquin agreed, chuckling as Rafael emerged down the stairs as if he'd been summoned.

"Speak of the devil, and he shall appear," I chuckled, turning wide eyes to him when he froze in the middle of the kitchen. He stared at the robe covering me, his eyes sliding down until they landed on my bare legs. I rolled my eyes, knowing damn well the dress I'd gone to visit my family in the day before was shorter.

"Get out," he grunted. Both men nodded, retreating from the kitchen with haste as Rafael moved to close the space between us. I raised a wooden spoon, pointing it in his face until he stepped into it without concern.

"Don't you start with me," I argued. "You don't have a shirt on."

"The house is not filled with women, *mi reina*," he

growled, taking the spoon out of my hand and dropping it to the counter next to the stove with a thud.

"You're in my way," I said, raising an eyebrow at him as he stepped into my space and guided me back toward the island until he was between me and the stove. Reaching behind him, he turned the dials on the stove to the off position, his fixated stare falling back on me the moment it was done. "I was making breakfast."

"Breakfast can wait," he said, placing his hands at my waist. He lifted me up onto the counter, depositing me against the cold stone that stung my ass where the robe and nightie slipped up with his grip. "I don't appreciate it when you get out of bed without waking me, especially not when you come down and flaunt your tight ass for my men to see. I like to start my day inside you."

"I was not flaunting my ass!" I laughed, slapping his chest as he placed a hand at each of my knees and shoved my legs apart. Staring down at the space between them, a growl vibrated in his chest when his gaze settled on my pussy.

"Where are your fucking panties?" he asked, sliding his hips between my legs and burying a hand in the hair at the back of my head. He gripped harshly, tugging my head to the side as his mouth touched the bruise on my opposite shoulder from his name where he so often bit me to mark me. It had faded slightly before seeing my parents, but I couldn't blame them for asking a multitude of questions.

"We both know why I can't wear underwear to bed," I said. Because he had a tendency to rip them off me in his urgency.

"That does not explain why you didn't put them on before coming downstairs," he murmured into my skin. That wicked tongue of his shot out, licking my flesh erotically as I tilted my head farther to the side to give him better access.

My hips inched closer to him, seeking more contact between our bodies as he built that need inside me.

My best days started with him inside me.

His other hand pulled the sash of my robe open, spreading the silk fabric to the sides so that he could stare down at the teal nightwear I'd slept in. He inched it higher on my stomach, baring me to his gaze entirely as that wandering hand trailed over my skin and between my legs.

Two fingers slid through my slick heat, and I arched my back as he guided them inside me and pumped slowly. His thumb circled my clit, working me over on the kitchen counter where his men had been thirty minutes from eating breakfast.

A sudden paranoia washed over me, and I turned my head to look toward the opening from the main room to the kitchen. Silence met me, not a single one of his men anywhere within sight. "They wouldn't dare," Rafael groaned, pulling his face out of my neck to touch his forehead to mine and watch the parting of my lips. Those skillful fingers of his worked me until I writhed on the counter, fucking his fingers to find my release.

It seemed like a lifetime before that I'd come down to make breakfast, and a world away from the reality that his men were in the other room and probably knew exactly what was happening. "How do you want to come, *mi reina*?" Rafael asked, his voice a groan as he dropped his lips to mine and swallowed my whimper. "Does my queen want me to drop to my knees and lick my pussy until she screams, or does she want my cock?"

"Cock," I gasped, my hips following him as he pulled his fingers out and tugged down his sweatpants to free himself. He drove inside me with a loud groan, my flesh clutching at him to keep him inside as he pulled his hips back and thrust forward rapidly until he sheathed himself fully in my pussy.

Placing his hand at my throat, he pushed me until I lay on my back. Something clattered off the other side of the island and thumped against the floor after my head brushed against it. That hand wrapped around the front of my throat, squeezing tightly until my vision blurred and all that remained were Rafael's intense eyes boring into mine. "You do not come downstairs dressed like this again," he ordered.

I nodded the little I could, resisting the urge to sputter indignantly as I struggled to breathe. My hands flew to tug at his hand, to pull him away from my throat as shadows hovered. He released me just in time for everything to rush back before unconsciousness claimed me, the world narrowing down to the space between my legs and the sensation of him driving inside me furiously. All the other nerve endings in my body felt like they disappeared, so all that remained was the place where he touched me.

He tugged me further toward the edge of the counter until my ass hung off it, only his grip at my throat and other hand at my hip keeping me stable and aloft as my body bent backward to accommodate him. "The only person who gets to talk about your cunt is me, and it is *mine*." Fury coated my skin as his drives turned ruthless, knocking into the deepest part of me as my legs hung limply in the air. I came around him with a scream, only the hand he used to cover my mouth preventing the shrill sound from reaching every corner of the house as my weight dropped further onto him without that hand at my throat to pin me in place.

"Fuck," he groaned, pistoning his length in and out of me until he roared his release and filled me with heat. When he pulled out and let me drop my feet to the floor, he helped support my weight until the boneless feeling faded from my limbs. Tucking me back inside my robe and covering my skin, he turned on the burners while I stared at him in confusion.

I glared at him, turning to go to the bathroom to clean up and change, but his hand on my arm stopped me. "Where are you going?" he asked.

"To change," I answered.

"You wanted to flaunt your ass in that before, now you can do it with my cum dripping down your legs," Rafael said, his cold voice accentuated with a cruel smirk. "Remember that the next time you decide to disobey me and wear something like that in front of my men, *mi reina,* because I will fuck you every single time just to prove who owns you."

"You're an asshole," I said, clenching my thighs together to stop the tickle that I felt between my thighs. "You don't *own* me. I am your fucking wife."

"The two aren't mutually exclusive," he laughed. "I didn't need to buy you to own you, not when you gave yourself to me so willingly." I moved to the stove, cracking eggs into a bowl furiously when it became clear that he meant every word and wouldn't allow me any reprieve to clean myself off. "We're going to see a friend after breakfast. I'm feeling gracious enough that I'll let you clean yourself off before then."

"Thank you, *El Diablo*. How fucking generous of you," I spat, tossing a grape tomato at him. The bastard caught it as if he was superhuman, popping it into his mouth and claiming his seat at the island with his phone.

I had a feeling he would very much enjoy the show of me trying to keep his cum inside me while I cooked.

The "friend" we went to visit turned out to be the infamous Matteo Bellandi. If I'd thought the security at Rafe's Chicago house was intense, it was nothing compared to the modern system of the Bellandi Estate. Knowing that the man's father had been friends with Miguel didn't fill me with any kind of warmth as we made our way up the long, winding drive.

"When can we see my family again?" I asked as Santiago pulled the car up in front of the house. An older man stepped out, greeting us with a kind smile even before we exited the vehicle.

"We'll give them a couple of days to consider everything we told them. I hope it proves to be enough time for them to come to their senses," Rafael said, shoving open his car door. Joaquin opened mine for me, and Rafe appeared just in time to hold out a hand for me to take. The white and pink floral fabric of my dress dropped almost to my knees, hanging off my shoulders as I stood and gave him a smile. The bandage covering my wound made me feel ridiculous in nice clothes, but I hadn't fought it when Rafe laid out the pretty dress.

"I hope you're right," I murmured, contemplating the blinding hatred I'd seen in my grandmother's eyes when she looked at Rafael. I had no doubt deceiving her about the kind of man Rafe was would prove pointless, but there was a small glimmer of hope that she might see the way he helped me find my desire to stand up for myself and find that endearing at the very least.

The man stepped up as we moved toward the front of the house. "Rafael," he greeted, a kind smile consuming his face.

"Don," Rafe said, and there was a trace of warmth in his voice that I wouldn't have expected.

"You must be Mrs. Ibarra," Don said, nodding politely but making no move to shake my hand or make any form of greeting behind the words.

"Isa is fine," I said with an uncomfortable laugh. Rafe's glare felt heavy on the side of my face, undoubtedly taking my hatred for the formality of the name as a denial of his claim on me. I was far too young to be Mrs. anything.

"Matteo is inside. He's eager to finally meet you," he said, turning and striding into the house. Rafe and I followed at his heels, Joaquin and Santiago trailing behind us and showing how comfortable they were inside the house. There was no doubt they'd all spent a considerable amount of time here before.

They veered off as we stepped into the kitchen, an immaculate space that was clearly well-loved and taken care of by someone. A beautiful brunette stood at the counter, her daughter seated on it in front of her and working to stir the contents of a bowl, with her pink tongue pinched between her teeth.

"Just a bit more, Little Moon," the woman murmured, turning her surprised gaze up to us as we entered the space. A shock of sea-green eyes met mine, startling for how vivid they were and framed by endearing freckles and plush lips that many women would have envied. "Rafael," she said gently, picking up a wet cloth from the counter and cleaning her daughter's fingers.

Lifting the little girl off the counter to place her on the floor, she stepped around the island and leaned in to touch her lips to Rafe's cheek affectionately. "Ivory," he greeted, smirking at what he had to know was jealousy surging in my veins.

It was ridiculous, given she was the wife of his friend, but knowing she was far closer to his age and probably his level of experience didn't help. Having been face-to-face with the more wordly version of me in my twin the day before certainly hadn't either.

I was a virgin who'd had no clue what sex looked like with any other man, and I couldn't even begin to fathom how irritating it was to have to teach his wife everything regarding sex.

The little girl raced around the island, her dark hair that flowed past her shoulders flying behind her as she flung herself into Rafael's arms when he knelt to scoop her up. "Rafey!" she shrieked, her lungs filling with air as he rested her on his hip.

"How's the moon girl?" he asked, grinning at her with a lightness I hadn't ever seen on his face before.

"We make cookies!" she said excitedly, pointing to the bowl where she'd been stirring for her mother.

"Did you know I love chocolate chip cookies?" he asked. "Isa does, too. She loves sweets."

"Mhm," the little girl hummed. "For you!"

"There's a reason you're one of my best girls," Rafe said, turning a broad smile to me, before he tugged me around his side. "Isa, this is Luna. She's Matteo and Ivory's," he said, turning his attention to the woman. "Where's your worse half?"

"Here, you dick," the man who must have been Matteo said, appearing at the mouth of the hallway on the other side of the kitchen, with a baby boy held in one arm.

"Bad word!" Luna yelled, shoving at Rafe's chest as she demanded he put her down. She ran for her father, allowing him to pick her up with his free hand and nestle her into his chest.

"Matteo, this is Isa," Rafe said with a laugh, curling me into his side possessively in the absence of the little girl who demanded attention.

"His wife," I inserted, giving him a mocking smile that he returned with a deep chuckle.

"Turnabout is fair play," he said, tucking a strand of hair behind my ear. Matteo strolled forward, shifting his son into Rafael's arms. Rafe abandoned his grip on me to cuddle the baby into his chest. Ivory's sea green eyes stared out of his round face, a light dusting of dark hair on top of his head as he babbled up at Rafe. "You must be little Brio. Lucky you look like your mom," Rafe murmured to the boy.

"Wife? It seems Rafael has withheld some information," Matteo said with a tentative smile. He held out his free hand for me, shifting Luna higher on his hip. I took his hand, shaking it as he drew me forward out of Rafe's grip to touch his lips to my cheek playfully. Just a brief touch of his lips against my skin, I couldn't stop the flush that spread to my cheeks instantly when he pulled back.

While there was no denying that Ivory was stunning, it was easy to see why she belonged at Matteo's side. Unease slithered up my spine, feeling out of place next to Rafe as he drew me back to him. "Asshole," Rafe muttered.

"But you said turnabout is fair play," Matteo said, his tone light and mocking as he studied us together.

"Ignore them," Ivory said, stepping forward and rolling her eyes as she took my hands in hers and looked at my rings. "You're so young! I don't even want to consider what that devil of a man did to get you to marry him so quickly."

"He put a gun to my head," I said. I kept my tone light, but Ivory's eyes narrowed on my face as if she knew Rafe was capable of just that.

She sighed, smiling through it as she shook her head. "Somehow I don't doubt it felt that way."

The air went still as she spoke, and I turned to find Matteo's gaze narrowed in on my arm and the tattoo that must have been brought closer to his scrutiny when Ivory grabbed for my rings. Ivory seemed to ignore the pulse of fury rolling off her husband, whether she was just used to it or not, I didn't know.

"Don, take the kids outside, would you?" Matteo yelled to the other room. The older man appeared almost instantly, folding the baby boy into his embrace as Matteo set Luna on the floor and they fled the room as Ivory finally turned my arm from side to side and studied the brand in horror.

"Rafael," she murmured, touching a hand to her mouth as she released my other hand. The light sweater I'd worn momentarily covered his name carved into my shoulder, and I briefly wondered if there would ever come a day when I felt like I could *not* hide it. Probably not.

"Did we or did we not have a deal that you were not to abuse her?" Matteo asked Rafael, his voice dropping low enough that I spun to face him where he glared at Rafael as if the two men might come to blows. He stepped forward, grasping my forearm tightly and running his thumb over the raised flesh of the *El Diablo* brand on my forearm. "So tell me, Rafael. *What the fuck is this?*"

13

RAFAEL

Everything in my body narrowed down to the sight of Isa's delicate arm encased in Matteo's harsh grip. His thumb stroked over the brand, glaring at me as if he had never been more disappointed in my actions.

Admittedly, there had been some pretty shitty ones.

"Take your fucking hand off my wife," I growled a warning. He couldn't understand that the brands united Isa and me, that they were another part of my claim on her body and her claim on my *soul*. I shrugged off my suit jacket, tossing it over one of the stools before I uncuffed my sleeve and rolled it up my forearm to reveal my coordinating tattoo.

Matteo's gaze narrowed in on the *mi reina* brand close to my wrist, some of the anger bleeding out of his gaze. Ivory backed away to the other side of the island, wisely leaving us to determine what agreements may or may not have been violated.

"The brands were part of our wedding. Some people exchange rings, we got brands. What we do in our marriage is none of your business," I said, raising an eyebrow at him.

"Excuse me?" Isa asked, tearing her arm out of Matteo's grip so suddenly that he actually released her. She spun to glare at me, placing a hand on her hip and cocking it to the side. "*We* did no such thing. I had no part in this, but I'll be damned if some man I don't know gets all indignant because of an *agreement*. What the hell does that even mean?" she asked, spinning and pinning Matteo with the fire of her glare.

He cocked a smirk, staring down at her with a furrowed brow despite his obvious amusement. "It means I gave him permission to take you so long as he treated you well."

"In other words, you gave him permission to kidnap me and then tried to ease your conscience with this bullshit notion that I'd be cared for. Don't bother with that, because the only person who benefits from it is you, with your own guilt," she said, smacking my arm as I hooked it around her waist and tugged her back into my arms.

Ivory laughed beneath her breath, trying to stifle the sound as her husband leveled her with a grin. "Fair enough," Matteo said, turning his eyes back to Isa and giving her a look that was full of all the confusion I was sure most people felt when they faced the spitfire of her personality, which came out more and more with every day that passed.

She was *mi reina* for a reason.

"I like her," Ivory said, drawing her husband's stare back to her. "It isn't often that someone puts your stubborn ass in your place."

"Of course you would," Matteo smiled, the easy gesture making something inside me settle. Isa moved her hand to my other cuff, unbuttoning it and rolling my sleeve up my arm as we waited in the awkward silence. She patted the skin, running caressing fingers over the area in a slow tease that made me want those fingers on other parts of my body despite the unfortunate audience.

Since I didn't have an interest in spooning out Matteo's eyeballs, I'd have to keep my dick in my pants for the time being.

"Well, now that I've made a terrible impression of being self-serving—" Matteo started.

"Which you are," Ivory input helpfully.

Matteo continued on as if his wife hadn't spoken, though his smile widened. "Why don't I make my exit? Rafael, the files are in the basement." He didn't ask about the bandage on her shoulder or what horror might be concealed beneath it, and, even knowing it would probably become a battle another day, I was glad for it.

I wasn't sure who might kill me first if I stripped off my shirt to show Isa's name carved into my chest: my wife or Ivory's husband.

I leaned forward, touching my lips to the side of her head affectionately. "You'll be okay with Ivory?" I asked.

Isa looked at the woman who smiled back at her, then shrugged as if she couldn't really say otherwise with her right there. "Why can't I go with you? I thought we were here to find out about the river."

"We are," I responded, turning her in my arms so I could look down at her and tuck her hair behind her ear. With her intense eyes on mine, I sighed. "But Franco Bellandi's files are no place for you. Make cookies, spend some time with Luna. I wish I could be with you instead."

"He's right. You don't want to see the kinds of things my father kept documentation of," Matteo agreed, crossing his arms over his chest as he returned to the back hallway. The entrance to the basement was located at the end, and I wondered if it would be as dark as I remembered it when we finally went downstairs.

I didn't fear the dark, instead welcoming it like I was returning home, but Isa would have been a different story altogether. Some kinds of darkness were complete, like a void that eclipsed all the light and nothing else existed.

She wasn't ready for that.

"No offense, but you don't know the first thing about what I've seen," Isa said, warning Matteo that she wasn't some delicate flower to be protected. I might have agreed with her, but there was a distinct difference between looking at photos and videos of innocent people suffering and feeling the blood of a murderer coating her hands.

Matteo nodded, though he didn't speak to tell her the thoughts that were so clearly running through his head. A dismissal of just how emotionless Isa thought she might be, and I imagined that if she was with me long enough she would become desensitized to certain things. It just wasn't that day.

"Stay here, little demon," I said, teasing her as I touched my lips to hers. "I'll tell you if we find anything." Pulling away from her arms and ignoring the fury that radiated off her at being dismissed so casually, I followed Matteo down the back hall toward his office. Walking past it and to the entrance to the basement, Matteo flicked on a light for the stairwell. "Good to see the lights have been fixed."

"It would be hard to sort through my father's records without them," Matteo laughed, making his way down the new stairs and into the basement itself. The main space was large enough, giving the illusion that it might be the only part of the massive basement. Where there would normally be a false wall at the back, the two halves of the false wall were thrown open to reveal a small group of Matteo's men sorting through the endless files of Franco Bellandi. "It's not as organized as it once was, but everything should still be here. We just have to find it."

"We're looking for why he would have thrown Isa in the river. How would your father have filed that?" I asked, pinning him with a look and then studying the sheer vastness of the amount of files. It would take years to comb through everything and even then there was no guarantee that we would find the answers within them. Who knew what a man like Franco deemed worthy of documenting?

At the back of the file room in the basement was a small passageway that led to the escape tunnels that had been carved beneath the suburbs of Chicago. The elaborate maze made me remorseful that I lived on an island, because if anyone ever managed to attack us there, we would be limited in terms of our escape options if we needed to.

"What did Isa mean when she said I had no clue what she's seen?" Matteo asked, watching his men comb through the documents.

"She killed Maxim Kuznetsov," I said. Matteo raised his eyes, nodding his approval as he no doubt pictured something similar to what Ivory had done. Murder in self-defense wasn't murder at all.

What Isa had done was different.

"Slid the knife right into his heart while he stared up at her like she was the angel of death," I murmured. "I know you'll disagree with me on involving her in that, but she needed it even if she doesn't know it yet."

Matteo shook his head, a smile tugging at his lips. The Bellandis protected their women, shielding them from the violence and consequences of the men's actions at all costs. I was sure my willingness to show Isa the darkest depths of my soul seemed unfathomable to him.

Their women were made of sunshine and everything light, keeping their husbands from falling to the darkness. Isa was a queen of nightmares, finding her home in the darkness with me.

"Ryker says you're dead set on killing all of Pavel's sons," Matteo observed. "Are you sure that's wise at this point in your endeavor? You don't want to make too many enemies too quickly."

"They have to die," I said evasively. I wouldn't explain my reasoning, not when there was little chance of making him truly understand without revealing information better left in the past. "Pavel will suffer watching all his children murdered by my hand, and then I'll finally allow him to die."

Matteo nodded as if he'd already known the answer, watching one of his men wince as he opened a folder and sorted through the undoubtedly gruesome photos that he'd discovered.

On one wall, Matteo had taped the pictures of Isa that I'd sent before we departed for Chicago. Several of her from various stages of her life lined the walls, making it easy for Matteo's men to identify her in case they came across a photo rather than her name. "Viktor Kuznetsov has a house in Brighton Beach," he said, and I turned my eyes to his sharply.

I'd thought I had documents of all the Kuznetsov properties around the world, monitoring them to know when any of the assholes left their fortress in Russia. "It will take some time to find out if he's there or when he might be. I'll put my contact on it. Would you have a jumping point for entrance?" he asked, raising a brow at me as we finally moved into the file room and each picked a box off the floor to sort through.

"Mariano and Luca Rossi are in New York. That should

be close enough to work," I answered. "If they aren't willing to help, then Calix will have to do."

"As long as he doesn't have any sign of you flying into the city, either should work." I nodded my head in agreement, turning my attention down to the box in front of me. File after file stared up at me, filled with every sort of horror a person could imagine.

The sales of people. Information for blackmailing the police or government officials. It was endless.

It was also nothing new.

***

I never wanted to touch another piece of paper or folder file by the time Matteo and I decided to make our way up the steps and rejoin the land of the living and light. The ghosts that lurked in those folders would haunt a better man, staining him with the taint of their gruesome and untimely deaths.

The things Franco Bellandi, my father, and Pavel Kuznetsov had done for the sake of their own greed and violent vices knew no limits. Depraved didn't even begin to cover it.

The kitchen was empty when we emerged into it, and Matteo didn't hesitate to make his way back to the main living space and out the side doors. In the garden beside the house, we finally found our women. Isa sat on a blanket on the stone pavers that wound between the garden beds, her legs curled underneath her as Luna hung off the back of her shoulders like a monkey.

"Auntie Isa!" the little girl squealed, rubbing her cheek against my wife's as she turned her stunning eyes back to look at her. "More!"

Isa giggled, lifting a cookie off the plate at the center of the blanket and feeding it to the monkey of a child. Brio sat facing her, a cookie happily clutched in his tiny hands and munching away as he smiled at my wife as if he adored her already.

"She'll make a great mother," Matteo said, chuckling at my side when he looked at my face. I'd always known I wanted Isa to be the mother of my children, an instinctive need to claim her fully and completely. "Here's hoping it makes up for having you for a father," he said, knocking into me with his side as he moved to go and claim his wife.

Isa continued to feed Luna cookies, pulling the little girl over her shoulder to sit on her lap so she could talk to both the kids. From my spot by the door, I couldn't hear exactly what she talked about, only see the motion of her lips and the sweet smile that consumed her when she stared back at their happy faces.

It was at that moment I realized the desire for Isa to be pregnant with my child so quickly was only partially because of my need to claim her. I also felt the overwhelming desire to be a father, to watch her snuggle and feed our own child that she looked at with all that love in her eyes. Before Isa, I'd thought I would go my entire life without providing an heir to my father's legacy, out of spite. There had never been a desire for children or a long-term relationship with any singular woman.

With a single glance, Isa had taken everything I thought I knew about myself and stripped it away, replacing it with the overwhelming urge to have it all. My Empire, my wife, and the children who would make our lives complete.

I moved as if in a trance, my feet carrying me to close the distance between us before I even consciously registered what I was doing. Isa turned a startled glance to me, the smile fading off her face at whatever she saw in my expression. Sitting on the blanket beside her, I snatched a cookie off the plate and popped it into my mouth to occupy it so I wouldn't say something to scare her off. I couldn't throw a wrench in the relationship that had only begun to bloom, instead choosing to appreciate the unguarded moment watching her with Luna and imagining it as our child one day soon.

It didn't matter that Isa was so young she'd only just become legal. All that mattered was the sight of a toddler on her lap with chocolate-stained lips, who smiled and blabbered on about the flowers, pointing out colors even as she butchered the pronunciation of the names and Isa corrected her in that quiet, encouraging way I thought all mothers should have.

"What's got you so quiet?" Isa asked finally when Luna stood from her perch on Isa's lap and made her way to her father. The fact that she hadn't abandoned Isa the moment he emerged spoke to just how enraptured Luna had been with her.

Nobody was more exciting than Matteo, in Luna's world.

She reached forward suddenly, a massive smile on her face as she grasped Brio beneath the armpits and lifted him into the air. Perching him on her lap, she bounced him playfully. "You're good with them," I said, choking back the threat of unusual emotion as warmth bloomed in my chest. Isa blushed, her hand trailing toward her stomach as she followed the line of my thoughts.

It was only a matter of time.

14

ISA

"Did you name *Moon* after Luna?" I asked as we emerged from the restaurant and went to walk along the river. My heart was in my throat as it always was, trapped in the memory of what had happened the last time I walked alongside the river so freely. I'd avoided it like the plague since the accident that wasn't an accident, staying as far away from the dark water as I possibly could.

Something about having Rafe by my side soothed me and made me want to face that irrational fear. His father was dead and gone, never again to throw me into the river and drown me for some unknown reason. Never to stalk me and obsess over a child who'd survived his attempt at murder. The presence of our shadows at our back probably added the notion of some level of protection as well. I didn't know Santiago well, but I knew Joaquin well enough to know he would keep me safe.

From everyone who wasn't Rafael, anyway.

"Yes," Rafe agreed, a warm smile on his face as he leaned over the railing for the water. I kept some distance, not willing to step quite that close. "I rebranded the hotel after I went home, and *Moon* just seemed appropriate. I didn't really consider that it was for her, but I suppose it was. Ivory was who set the events of the war in motion, and if that had never happened I wouldn't have needed to come to Chicago."

"I imagine lives would have been saved," I said, shaking my head to push back the hope in his voice. War could never be seen as a good thing.

"Some, but others would have been lost to the trafficking operation that we stopped. The men who died knew what they were fighting for. They were good men, good people, and I imagine it wasn't easy to say goodbye to some of them. But I think we honor their sacrifice by living, and by focusing on all that we accomplished through that fight," he said. "Besides, if I hadn't come to Chicago, I never would have met you. I can never regret that no matter how many people died for it."

"You didn't exactly meet me," I said, refuting the reality of that statement as he pushed off the railing and stalked closer to me. The breeze on my face felt like a relaxing balm on a warm summer night, cooling me despite the humidity to the air.

He grinned, that dark tinted smile that I'd fallen so head over heels in love with before I ever understood the place where it came from and the depths of his darkness. I never could have guessed that he'd drag me into the darkness with him.

He moved so suddenly that I almost didn't even see him, lunging for me and tackling me to the ground. The sidewalk stung my back as we landed and skidded across the concrete, tearing the skin from my flesh as the sound of a gunshot cracked through the air.

His body covered mine completely, his hands tucking my head into his chest the best he could and those broad arms shielding the sides of my face with his own body. "Rafe!" I yelled over the sound of repeated gunfire, hoping to dislodge the man using himself as a barrier between me and bullets.

"On the count of three, run for the car," he said, grunting as his body jerked to the side. Warmth seeped through his clothes immediately, filling me with dread as I registered what the sticky substance dripping onto my chest was.

There was only a grunt of pain to indicate he even felt it, a single sound that resounded through me as my terror mounted. "You're shot," I gasped, reaching up a hand to press against the wound in his shoulder. Even through the fabric, the warmth of his blood seeped free, staining his white shirt with bright red in the shadows.

"I need you in the car, *mi reina*," Rafe rasped, fury in his voice. He pulled a set of car keys from his pocket, pressing them into my hand urgently. "One. Two." He paused, lifting his head to glance around him. *"Go."* He vaulted up with shocking agility, despite his injury, and pulled the gun from his back pocket. I ducked low as I scrambled to my own feet, making for the stairs at the edge of the walkway that would take me up to the parking lot where we'd parked the SUV.

The sound of harsh breathing and heavy footfalls sounded behind me, making me spin backward in fear of who might be following. My eyes met Joaquin's, his shock of furious dark eyes roaming over me and checking for injury before he tucked me under his arm and hurried me to the foot of the steps. "Rafe," I said, wheezing past the catch of my breath in my lungs.

"He'll be fine," Joaquin argued. "He can take care of himself." We raced up the steps, leaving the gunfight next to the river and stepping into the more illuminated parking lot. Joaquin pushed me forward, turning to watch our backs and make sure no one followed us up the steps.

My feet took me closer and closer to the SUV, and I pressed the button on the fob to unlock the doors before I could reach it.

Heat suddenly knocked me back like two molten hands at my shoulders, shoving me away from the raging inferno in front of me. Time slowed as my feet left the ground with the force of the explosion, my body weightless for a few brief seconds before reality crashed back in.

My legs hit the ground first, crumpling beneath me and unable to absorb the force of the impact. My head cracked against the pavement, my sight lost to a blinding white light as the heat in front of me became unbearable and my skin felt molten.

There was no sound, only the void inside my head and the throbbing pain of every inch of my body. I shifted my legs on the pavement, the slickness of blood coating them as ringing filled my ears and I forced my eyes open. Joaquin stared down at me, panicked, his lips moving silently.

He exhaled a sigh of relief, his body drooping with the force of it. Reaching down, he prodded the back of my head gently. When he pulled it back, the red stain of blood covered his skin. He muttered something, his face twisting in fury as he turned back to look at the blazing inferno where the SUV had sat waiting for me.

I was struck with the terrible knowledge that, if I'd waited even seconds longer to unlock it, I'd be dead. Burned alive like Rafael's mother.

"Hurts," I groaned, my lips feeling cracked as I forced them to move and form the words.

Sound trickled in, the pain in my ears only amplifying the throbbing in my skull. "You've got to get up, *mi reina*," Joaquin said, his voice soft as if muffled by a pillow despite the urgency on his face. Sirens split the silence of the night, a ringing shriek in the distance as I turned to my stomach and forced myself up onto hands and knees. Gunshots peppered my hearing periodically, confirming that the fight was far from over.

And there was no vehicle to protect me.

Standing slowly, I unfolded my body to full height and winced as I looked down at myself. At the pink skin on my arms where the heat from the explosion had barely kissed my flesh.

Joaquin took my hand, guiding me to the shadows at the side of one of the buildings. He folded me into the wall, bracing his body over mine as he kept a watchful eye on the light at the corner. Tucked safely into the shadows, he heaved a sigh as he watched. "You're okay," he whispered, running a hand over the lump at the back of my head as my body swayed and nausea burned my throat.

The gunfire stopped, the air consumed by silence except for the approaching sirens.

I stilled as a figure appeared in the lights of the parking lot, coming to a sudden stop in front of the SUV and staring at in horror. The sound of the furious roar was distant, like it somehow came from another world and pierced the veil between the living and the dead. The wind caught my name, carrying it through the air as Joaquin took my hand and guided me away from the wall.

I didn't want to go, didn't want to be out in the open where bullets sliced through the air and explosions turned my world upside down. "It's okay," Joaquin said, tucking me into his side and guiding me out into the light, despite my mediocre struggles.

Rafael sensed the movement as I pulled away from Joaquin's side, determined to stand on my own two feet despite the sheer agony that claimed my body. I felt the moment Rafael's eyes landed on me, felt the simultaneous and overwhelming relief and fury in them as he took in the sight of me alive.

Even if it felt like I was only just.

I couldn't imagine what he saw staring back at him, but he darted forward suddenly. By the time I realized my legs were crumpling underneath me, he'd caught me in his arms and supported my weight. "*Jesus. Fuck,*" he groaned, touching the back of my head to clutch me to his chest. I whimpered in pain, feeling his hand still as he registered the wetness matted in my hair.

Santiago dragged a man up over the top of the steps with his hand at his throat, and Rafael's entire body tensed as he turned to level the man with his fiercest glare. Anyone with reasonable intelligence would have withered up and died at the ferocity in it. The pure, blinding rage as his arms trembled around me took my breath away.

Rafael shifted me into Joaquin's grip, stepping to meet Santiago and the man halfway. Cocking his fist back, he struck the man in the jaw with all the strength in his body as he curled his abs into the punch. The man crumpled to the ground at Santiago's feet, spitting out blood and a tooth as I watched. "She will burn," the man growled, his stare shifting beyond Rafael to meet my eyes. "And all of you along with her."

Rafael kicked him in the face, snapping his head back as he fell in an unconscious heap. "Is he dead?" I said, and while I'd thought I whispered the words Rafael and Santiago's attention snapped back to me.

"No," Rafael growled. "He only wishes he was." He came back to me, plucking me into his arms as headlights appeared in the parking lot. Three black vehicles and a beat up old van rolled in. The cars I recognized from the house as belonging to Rafe's men, but the van was unfamiliar. "Fucking take care of him. I want him *alive,* Ryker," Rafael growled to the muscular man who stepped out of the driver's seat.

"Got it, *Devil*," the man said, his face twisted in a grimace as he grabbed the unconscious man by the shirt and dragged his limp form over the pavement and tossed him into the back of the van. Closing the doors with a final slam and a lock, he turned back to us. His eyes landed on me, sympathy in them as he offered words I thought he meant to be encouraging. "He'll suffer for every pain," he said, hopping into the driver's seat as Rafe brought me to one of the cars.

"Who was that?" I asked, forcing the sound up my sore throat. "The man who said I would burn?"

Rafael tensed as he settled me across his lap in the backseat of the car, Joaquin climbing in beside us and Santiago taking the vacant front seat. "Timofey Kuznetsov," he growled. "Pavel's youngest."

I didn't dare to ask the other question plaguing me or give it a voice, not when I didn't think I was ready for the answer. Not then. Maybe not ever. Because he hadn't threatened Rafe's life.

He'd threatened mine.

"The shooters were aiming for me," I said, pressing tighter to his chest. He didn't answer, confirming my thoughts with his silence. I swallowed, shoving back the concern for the future and wondering what this meant for our safety and ability to stay in Chicago.

We needed answers, and nothing would get in my way of finding them. Especially not men who seemed to think they'd be better off with me dead.

15

RAFAEL

The doctor finished stitching the cut at the base of Isa's head, having had to shave just enough of her hair to keep it out of his way. She grimaced when she straightened as soon as he was finished, sitting up and resisting the urge to touch the injury. "Hearing better now?" he asked quietly. She nodded slowly, and I heaved a breath of relief that her hearing hadn't been impacted permanently.

Hearing Joaquin yell her name after the explosion, not being able to find her and only seeing the flames engulf the very same SUV where I'd tried to send her for safety, I'd feared the worst.

I'd thought she'd been stolen from me in the flames.

"I didn't feel any deformities," Matteo's favored doctor continued. "So I don't think we need to worry about a cracked skull or severe trauma to the brain itself. A concussion for certain, but nothing unmanageable. The rest of your wounds are relatively superficial. Scrapes and bruises. Even the deeper wound on the back of your knee has stopped bleeding and will heal without stitches. You were *very* lucky," he said, moving to the sink and rinsing his tools.

"I know," Isa murmured softly, accepting the bottle of water I handed to her. Her face was pinker than normal, the heat of the explosion having irritated her skin. It was a minor consequence when compared to the potential reality of her face being nothing more than a pile of ash.

The doctor moved to my side, the forceps already in his grip as I pulled my shirt over my head with a grimace. The burn of the bullet in my flesh drew another wince from me as I lowered my arm so that he could study the shoulder briefly. The skin around it was angry and red, and Isa's eyes narrowed in on it in frustration.

The stubborn thing had tried to convince me that I should be taken care of first, as if she hadn't survived a fucking car bomb. "You're lucky too. It doesn't appear to have hit anything vital," the doctor said as he poked his fingers against the area surrounding the hole. The metal of the forceps sank into the wound, wrapping around the bullet and gripping as he slowly pulled it free. I gritted my teeth against the pain, holding Isa's eyes and trying to will her to see that I'd be fine.

Her worry over me should have been touching, and it might have been any other day. Now all I could think about was getting her home to *El Infierno* immediately.

"What does she need to do for recovery?" I asked as the bullet popped free from my skin and a fresh surge of blood trickled out of the wound. He worked quickly to disinfect it, stitching the skin back together like someone who had treated far too many bullet wounds in his life. Working for the Bellandis, I didn't doubt it.

"Rest mostly. I'll leave her something for the pain, but mostly nothing too straining for the brain. No long periods of television or reading, nothing too social or upsetting. Just keep her home and make her get lots of rest," he said.

"Easier said than done. When is she okay to travel back to Spain?" I asked.

"At least a week."

"I'm not going to Spain," Isa argued, crossing her arms over her chest defiantly. She winced as all the little scratches and spots where the pavement had scraped off her skin stung, but didn't relent.

"You're going back to the island as soon as he deems you okay for travel," I said, watching as he finished the stitches and moved to pack his belongings like a smart man. He could probably sense the fight coming.

"No upsetting her," he said.

"Upset is better than dead," I growled, making the man nod his head and retreat from the room.

"You aren't sending me back! Not without you, and especially not after how we left things with my parents. I can't just disappear and make them think you kidnapped me or got rid of me or something," she said, turning to glare at Joaquin as he stepped out of the main room and followed the doctor out. There was no chance of any of the men wanting to be around for the coming argument. I stood from my chair, scooping her into my arms despite her protests about my own injury, and carried her upstairs.

"You were almost killed," I pointed out. "I think that's more important than whatever your family might think. You can call them and explain something came up so they know you're alive."

"I mean it, Rafael. Our answers are here, and like it or not Timofey seems to know something. I know you well enough to know you aren't leaving, and neither am I. I want answers, and I want to be here when you find them. If it's safer, then I won't leave the house. I'll stay here or go to the Bellandi estate during the days and spend time with Ivory and Luna. My family can visit us here. This place is a fortress. There's a reason this guy attacked us when we were wandering around in public."

I heaved a sigh, knowing she wouldn't relent. I could force her on the plane, but the only thing that would accomplish was making her hate me. I'd broken her to rebuild her into a stronger woman who could stand at my side and survive in my world.

I couldn't exactly fault her when she did everything I'd ever wanted her to do.

"Fine. But you do not leave this house," I warned, settling her into the bed gently so she could get some sleep.

"Where are you going?" she asked, realizing that I didn't make any move to get into bed with her.

"To get some answers, and no, you cannot come," I said, touching my lips to hers gently. "You need to rest."

She sighed her frustration. "Stay with me until I fall asleep at least?" With a breath of relief, I curled up in bed beside her, drawing her into my arms. Her heat enveloped me, her skin feeling too feverish to be comfortable following the explosion. I held her tight, trying not to touch any of the dozens of injuries on her back, legs, and arms.

Remembering the feel of her body curled beneath mine and hoping I would be enough to stop any bullets that hit us, I waited until her breathing evened out finally.

I went to get my fucking answers.

By the time I arrived at the warehouse, Ryker had started without me. The impatient fuck never took kindly to men who tried to hurt women, let alone kill one of ours.

Timofey's head hung forward, one of his eyes swollen shut as he turned to watch me with the one that was still functioning while I entered the freezer and closed the door behind me. "Your father never would have let another man do his dirty work for him." Timofey wheezed. "Then again you aren't half the man he was."

I ignored him, moving to the table with Ryker's favorite tools set out on display. Timofey was entirely naked, his hunched body an attempt to hide the pathetic cock and balls that had long since shriveled up and tried to crawl inside his ass. Ryker wasn't above castrating rapists, but that would come later.

I picked up one of Ryker's best knives, moving to lean forward in front of Timofey. Grabbing a fistful of his greasy dark hair, I yanked his head back until that swollen eye tried to blink at me. The unhurt one worked to glare, nearly closing shut with his attempt to be intimidating. Either Timofey already knew he would never again see the light of day, or he was too stupid for his own good.

Either way, he would be food for the fire when I'd learned everything I could from him.

"Matteo is on his way," Ryker said, crossing his arms over his chest and leaning against the table to watch. He'd never taken kindly to me playing with his toys, but no man in his right mind would get between me and the man who'd tried to hurt my wife.

"Good for him," I grunted, touching the tip of the knife to the tattoo on Timofey's chest. "Do you know how Leonid squealed when I cut this from his body? I'm amazed that all of Rome didn't come to his rescue." Digging the tip of the blade into his flesh, I drew an outline around the tattoo that marked him a Kuznetsov. That marked him as everything I hated and needed to rid the world of.

"My father doesn't give a shit about his sons. All you're managing to do by killing us is pissing off his children. We could be your allies — "

"I don't think so," I huffed with a laugh. "I don't work with people who get off on raping kids, and your father raised you to be *just like him*."

"So did yours," Timofey argued, his voice rising into a scream as I slid the knife into the skin I'd outlined, carving it off the muscle beneath. He wheezed, his breath coming in deep, soul-wracking pants. "If you can step out of his shadow, so can we."

"The problem is that I never stepped outside the shadows, Timofey. I still very much call them home," I told him, peeling back his skin as his one good eye met mine. "I just don't drag innocent people into them with me."

"Just your fucking wife," he said, spitting pink tinged saliva onto the floor.

The freezer door opened as Matteo arrived, his overwhelming presence adding to ours to fill the freezer with far too much pissed off fury. Matteo might not know Isa the way I did, but he'd met her. He liked her and had been ready to go to battle for me.

He glared at the man in the chair as if he might cut off his head himself. "I'm fairly certain his wife is none of your concern. Perhaps if you hadn't been so stupid as to threaten her, you may have been granted a swift death."

"Yeah, like my brothers? I saw the little gifts he sent home to my father. He would have tortured me either way."

Matteo raised a brow at me, making me shrug in response. I wouldn't apologize for making sure Pavel's sons knew pain before they left this earth. Not while knowing what kind of torture they put women through on a daily basis.

"He isn't entirely incorrect," I admitted. "Though an hour or two of suffering hardly compares to what I'll do to him now that he nearly killed my wife."

"Can't argue with that logic," Ryker said with a chuckle. "I'd keep you alive for weeks. Come and play with you every single day just so you remember what pain is. I have a friend who likes to fuck rapists, too. I'm sure he'd love you."

"There is one fault to your logic," Timofey wheezed, his lips twisting with a dangerous smile as he latched his one open eye onto my face. "Your precious Isabel has belonged to my brother Dima far longer than she's been yours."

I went still, the blood rushing to my head as his words washed over me like an ice bath. "What are you talking about?" Matteo asked, glaring at him and shaking his head from side to side.

I tore my eyes away from Timofey's face, moving to the barbed wire on Ryker's table as I worked to ignore the man digging his hole deeper with every word from his mouth. The barbs dug into my skin as I gripped it in my hand, moving back to where Timofey sat. I slid it beneath his thigh, chuckling at the hiss of breath that escaped his lungs as the weight of his leg sank back down and the points dug back into his skin.

"Dima wanted her something fierce. Then again, he always did like his bitches scarred," Timofey said, his voice trailing off into a shout as I wrapped the wire around his thigh and pulled it tight. The barbs shredded my skin, reopening the wounds from when I'd done similar to

Maxim and adding my blood to the wire that I would use to give Timofey a scar just like Isa's.

Fury flooded me when his shout trailed off, pleading filling his eyes. "I can tell you so much that you don't know."

I turned back for the tools. "How did Dima know Isa?" Matteo asked, suspicion burning in his eyes.

"Miguel Ibarra and Franco Bellandi sold her to him when she was a girl," Timofey wheezed, his breath fading into a laugh. Matteo and Ryker's bodies vibrated with fury, with the need to avenge the child that had been handed such a shitty future as a young girl.

Timofey huffed a disbelieving breath as he studied me, understanding dawning on his face. It was Matteo's incredulous stare that turned my head his way, staring his fury in the face.

"You already knew," Matteo breathed in shock.

Straightening my shoulders, I didn't bother to nod. The only affirmation I gave Matteo was to meet his gaze and not show a hint of remorse. I might not have been able to save Isa as a girl, but I'd do everything in my power to protect her now that she was mine.

She'd been mine since the moment I'd laid eyes on her photo when my father sold her.

I just hadn't known it yet.

16

RAFAEL

"It would be far easier for me to help you find information if you weren't withholding what you know," Matteo said, crossing his arms over his chest as we stepped out of the freezer and into the main part of the warehouse. There was no trace of kindness in his accusing eyes, only a hardness I'd seen far too often since returning to his city.

I wasn't one of his men who worshiped at his feet.

"If I'd thought it was relevant, I'd have mentioned it. I didn't exactly realize that it might all be connected until Isa identified my father in the photo. Even then, I still had no reason to believe Pavel recognized her." I sighed, pinching the bridge of my nose between two fingers. My shoulder twinged with pain as I forced it to move, ignoring the stitches that pulled at my skin.

"Explain to me how it could *not* be relevant that your father *sold* your wife to your enemy," Ryker said, raising a brow at me as he lurked in the shadows.

"She was one of hundreds," I stressed, gritting my teeth against the insistence that I needed to explain myself. "I didn't realize who she was until I looked through the photos Don and Alejandro gathered from her childhood. It was a vague memory of her face, and I wasn't certain until Alejandro found the contract and confirmed her name."

"One of hundreds?"

"My father had a thing for kids with strange eyes. He sold them to buyers all over the world," I explained, making Ryker heave a sigh.

"You thought she was just one of the lucky ones who wasn't taken before your father died," Ryker said, nodding his head to the side.

"Nothing else made sense. There was no reason to think it was any more complicated than that," I agreed.

"Until the photo of your father," Matteo groaned, touching a hand to the rough walls of the warehouse and staring toward the fridge. "Why did Kuznetsov want her?"

"I'm not sure. I remember her photo, but it was almost thirteen years ago. I can't remember the specifics of their conversation, and I tended not to listen to the gruesome details when they were talking about kids."

"Why wouldn't he take her right away? Why was she left with her family for so long? That's the part that doesn't make any sense to me," Matteo said, glancing to Ryker with the reminder of exactly what kind of family life his enforcer had lived before coming to the Bellandis.

"She was too young," Ryker said. "Dima prefers women to children. A five-year-old wouldn't interest him. He would have wanted to wait until she was a preteen at least."

"She was to be delivered on her thirteenth birthday," I agreed.

"Does she know?" Ryker asked, pursing his lips as he considered what that might mean.

"No," I grunted, shaking my head. "She doesn't have a

clue, and it is going to stay that way." I cast a warning glare to Matteo who twisted his lips in thought.

"This is unraveling faster than you can control. You don't want her to find out that you've known all this time and never bothered to tell her, Rafe. Take it from me. Secrets like this? They cause wounds that never really heal."

I grunted, confirming I'd heard his warning, but nobody would tell me what I could or could not keep secret from my wife. "Keep him alive. He knows more, and I'll be damned if he doesn't suffer for what he did to Isa for as long as it takes us to find out what that is." Turning and making my way out of the warehouse, I was met by Santiago and three other men at the car.

After the attack, we wouldn't be taking any chances where safety was concerned. "Where to?" Santiago asked as he climbed into the driver's seat of one of the SUVs from the house. The fact that it was the exact same make and model as the one that had blown up and nearly taken Isa with it made me dig my fists into the seat beside me.

"Back to the house," I ordered, desperately needing to feel Isa in my arms. Picking my phone out of my pocket, I hit Alejandro's number on speed dial.

"How is she?" he asked, undoubtedly having received a report from Joaquin through his brothers.

"She'll live. I don't think he expected that to be the outcome of the night," I said, sighing as I thought over the options. "It seems the Kuznetsovs want her dead."

"Are you sending her home?" Alejandro asked. "I'll have the plane ready whenever it's safe for her to travel."

"No. She insists on staying here, and, given how the meeting with her family went, I can't exactly blame her. I want you to send at least ten more men, including Gabriel and Hugo. She's not permitted to leave the house, so she'll need people she's familiar with to keep her from going stir crazy."

"I'll put them on the next flight," he agreed as I ended the call abruptly. Fortunately, the house was fully stocked with every weapon I could possibly need after the war we'd fought the last time we'd been in Chicago. I just needed the men to wield them.

As Santiago drove through the streets of Chicago to bring us back to *mi reina*, I considered Matteo's words. I never wanted her to know that she'd been sold as a child.

Especially when I'd been there and done nothing to stop it.

The space in my chest that I'd thought to be a void before Isa came into my life throbbed with pain at the look of betrayal I could picture on her face. I'd let my father sell my wife, never thinking anything of it beyond the horror that came with each and every life he'd ruined. If I hadn't burned him alive, Isa would have been dead long before I could spot her in Chicago and fall into her trap.

She could never know the truth.

17

ISA

Ringing filled my ears, the sight of the fire in the backyard where Rafael's men and the Cortes brothers who were off-duty sat around the pool and socialized drawing me in and holding me captive. I curled my arms around myself, feeling the scabbed over scrapes on the back of my arms as pain flared from the wounds.

The flames drifted to smoke, the wisps of it lost in the air as it rose to the night sky overhead. Three nights in a row I'd been left in the house while Rafael went to torment the man who'd tried to kill me. He left shortly after breakfast every day, going to Matteo's house to oversee the investigation in the basement. Only coming home briefly at night to tend to my wounds and see how I was feeling, he'd quickly tuck me back into bed to get more rest before leaving to deal with the man who'd tried to harm me.

As if just the sight of my lingering wounds was enough to drive him back to the point of rage where he needed to take it out on Timofey's flesh.

The words he'd said with such cold, calculating malice as Santiago dragged him up the steps echoed in my head, muffled by the ringing that filled my ears with the memory of heat licking my skin. Gabriel stood from the fire, leaving his brothers to catch up with the men who must have been his friends. They'd arrived the night after the accident along with the additional security Rafe summoned.

Even if I'd wanted to leave the house, the knowledge of just how many people would need to accompany me would have made it impossible. I didn't know why it bothered me so much that people I'd never met might want me dead, but I couldn't shake the feeling that there was something deeper to it.

Something that went far beyond me being a way to hurt Rafael.

Of all the choices for a way to threaten me, a way to kill me, he'd chosen to *burn* me.

"You okay?" Gabriel said, appearing behind me and making me spin away from the window to face him. Sound crashed into my head following his words, the voices of the men from outside and the cheeriness to their entertainment too loud with the sudden intrusion. My head throbbed, almost missing the vibrations of my thoughts and the familiar embrace of a painful memory.

"Yeah," I said, looking away as my cheeks warmed. It wasn't the first time the quietest of the Cortes brothers had approached me in the days since the explosion, his eyes too knowing and his voice too gentle. Of the three of them, he was the one who'd kept his distance the most while Hugo deceived me. And yet when Hugo and Joaquin seemed content to give me distance, he was the one who pushed through to draw me out of that haunting place.

The place where the lines between the living and the dead blurred, shadows dancing in my vision as bright white light was licked by flames.

"Liar," he said with a chuckle, smiling as he stepped up next to me. He stared out at the fire, grunting at whatever antic the men around it engaged in. I watched them, but I didn't see them.

I couldn't see anything but the flames.

"Where do you go?" he asked, turning his body so that he stared down at me. "When you get quiet?"

"I don't know what you're talking about," I said, forcing myself away from the window and making my way toward the kitchen for some water. I couldn't look at fire without remembering the painful cracking in my lips, the dryness of my throat as all the moisture in the air evaporated in the heat. I tugged the refrigerator open, grabbing a bottled water off the door before I turned back to face him.

"You've always done it," he said, following me and leaning his elbows on the counter. "Before Rafael, it was in your room at night. You were so *silent*. It was like you didn't exist. Did you go back to that river?"

"That's none of your business," I snapped, slamming the bottle of water onto the counter without even taking a drink.

"What about now? Is it the river or the explosion that makes you stare out the window like you can't even see us?" he pushed, following me toward the stairs as I went to retreat. He hurried around me, stepping into the path I would need to take and blocking off my only exit from the inquiries I didn't want to answer.

"Stop it," I said, the pleading note in my voice taking me by surprise. I'd thought myself beyond the trauma of the river, thought I'd worked through the worst of it, but my inability to talk about it with Gabriel hinted at the lingering effects that I suspected would never really go away.

"If you think I'm being pushy, just you wait until Rafe realizes what's going on with you," Gabriel snorted a laugh.

"He's distracted with Timofey Kuznetsov and not here to see you like this. I have to admit you put on a good show for his sake, but he won't be this absent forever."

"I don't think he's well-versed in understanding the effects of trauma. He was shot and didn't even bat an eye. I bumped my head and can't sleep," I scoffed, bumping his shoulder with mine as I pushed past him to get to the stairs.

"Probably more than you think. He might not show it, but I promise you he was just as affected by the explosion as you. Except it isn't fear for his own life that drives him to that warehouse every night to get answers. It's fear for *yours*. He would die one thousand times over before he willingly allowed any harm to come to you. Just talk to him, Isa."

"What good will it do? I'll still be stuck inside watching the fire burn from a safe distance. I'll still be terrified of being burned alive." I sighed, shaking my head. "Even if he knows I'm scared, he can't do anything to change it. It will only make him feel worse than he already does. I'd like my husband to stop hunting the phantom threats to my life and come home at some point."

"He'll come home, *mi reina*. You need him to be home with you. Ryker is perfectly capable of getting answers from Timofey, and Rafael knows it. He's there because he feels like he needs to be and trusts that you would tell him if you weren't okay," Gabriel murmured, turning his back on me as he made his way back for the backyard. "Get some sleep."

I turned on my heel, making my way up the steps and passing one of Rafael's men where he lurked outside our bedroom. He nodded as I went in, wordless but polite until I finally closed myself into the private space.

I grabbed a nightgown, stepping into the bathroom and depositing it on the counter while I started the shower. Cold water sprayed from the shower head, casting a chill to the room as I stripped off my clothes and stepped beneath the icy rainfall.

The cold surrounded me, raising goosebumps on my skin as I tipped my head back and sank into the shivers of my body. Letting them consume me, letting them remind me that the fire outside wasn't the one that had nearly covered my skin, I heaved a sigh as I worked shampoo through my hair. My fingers brushed over the bald spot at the back of my head where stitches tied my skin together, the sting of shampoo against them grounding me against the chill.

Curling my hair over my shoulder, I combed the conditioner through my hair slowly, my lips trembling as I chased back the dark eyes in my memory. One trauma bled into another, the haunting image of Rafael's mother's face as I'd seen in the photo hovering at the edge of my vision.

Her screams echoed in my head, the sound of a raging fire filling my ears as the cold water of Chicago poured over my skin and brought me back to the river where everything had begun.

"Isa!" a male voice yelled urgently, making me lose my footing on the slick shower floor as I spun to stare into Rafe's unique eyes. Concern knotted his brow, turning his lips into a frown as he reached into the shower. Fully clothed, he didn't seem to mind the water drenching his suit as he turned it to warm. "You're freezing."

He stepped into the shower with me, working the conditioner from my hair. The shivers wracking my limbs somehow felt more pronounced with his body pressed into mine. He didn't bother to wash my body, shutting off the water as soon as my hair was rinsed and pulling me out of the shower to wrap me in one of the massive, plush towels hanging on the rack.

"What were you thinking?" he asked, scrubbing the towel over my skin until I was dry and staring into my eyes as he knelt at my feet to dry off my legs. I winced as the towel rubbed over my wounds, pinpricks of pain emerging from the icy void of nothing the shower gave me.

I didn't answer as he wrapped the towel around my body, stepping back far enough to strip off his drenched suit quickly. The fabric flopped to the floor in a heap, his arms reaching forward to snag me behind the knees and back as he lifted me into his arms.

The towel pinned my arms to my sides, leaving me trapped in his hold as he made his way out of the bathroom and for the massive bed in the center of the room we shared. "Your shoulder," I said, squeezing the words past the rattling of my teeth.

"Shut the fuck up, Isa," he growled, setting me on the edge of the bed. He carefully pulled the towel out from around me, glaring down at my naked body as if it offended him and guiding me to lie back in the bed. He slid in beside me, tugging me forward until my head rested on his chest, then covered us in the blankets. "What were you doing in the cold shower?"

"Am I allowed to speak now?" I asked, hating that the venom in my voice was diluted by the tremble to my teeth and the way I sank into his warmth. He winced as my feet pressed against his legs, seeking the comfort of his familiar embrace.

"Now is not the time to get smart with me," he warned, running a hand through the hair on the side of my head affectionately to contrast the harshness of his words.

"I just like the cold," I said, burying my face in his neck and wanting nothing more than to pretend the conversation didn't need to happen. I couldn't explain the shame I felt, knowing he'd been shot and went on with his day like it didn't affect him.

"Since when?" he asked, his body going still beneath me. "The explosion?"

I didn't answer, finding it impossible to grasp the words to explain when I didn't understand it myself.

"Isa," he said, his voice a stern warning.

"Yes," I mumbled. "I know it's stupid. You were *shot*, and yet you go out there every single day and don't worry about it happening again. I just—" I paused, the breath expelling from my lungs in a sudden rush as tears stung my eyes. "How am I supposed to get in a car ever again? How do *you* get in a car without being terrified?"

He sighed, clutching me tighter to his chest. "*Mi reina*, why didn't you say anything?"

"Because I can't do this," I said, my breath hitching with the sob that felt like it tore free from my soul. "I'm not strong enough—"

"Don't you dare. You're strong enough to survive me, and you're strong enough to survive these people who mean nothing," he said.

I stared into his face, realizing he didn't understand. Even with the threat to my life, it wasn't the fear of my own death that kept me up at night. "I'm not strong enough to lose *you*," I said, wincing when he flipped me to my back and hovered over me.

He stared down at me as he finally understood, his eyes warm in the dim lights of the bedroom. His forehead touched mine, a ragged sigh leaving his parted lips. "You won't ever lose me," he promised, but the words were hollow with the knowledge that he couldn't control death.

Even the devil didn't have that power.

"Every time you leave, I stare out the window with my

heart in my throat. I can't *breathe* in those moments until the car is out of sight, and then I sit here and I think about how the fire felt on my skin, and I wonder if that's how you'll die. If the skin will melt off your bones while I sit here waiting for you to come home. I don't want to be helpless anymore, so that I can go with you," I said.

"The condition of us staying in Chicago was that you stayed home. You're safest here," he said, his tone deepening as he prepared to argue.

"I know," I whispered back. "I'm not asking for you to let me go with you tomorrow. I'm asking you to help me not be such a liability. You took a fucking bullet for me, but if I'm going to die, then I want to do it with you."

"You're not going to die," he argued, his brow furrowing as he stared down at me. The tense lines of his lips made something in me settle, knowing that he would fight death itself to keep me by his side.

"If you're gone, I don't want to exist without you. I don't care if that makes me fucked up or stupid. I didn't survive everything you did to me and forgive you for it just to live my life without you."

"You just said you were afraid to get in a car, *mi reina*," he said, his voice going soft as he tried to reason with what I knew had to feel unreasonable. "I can't stay here, even if there wasn't work to be done, if we want answers."

"I'm not asking you to," I admitted. "I just want you to teach me not to be helpless. I don't want you to have to cover my body with yours the next time this happens, or send me to the car so I can be safe. I want to at least be able to function in the situations we might find ourselves in. I know you want me to stay home and protected all the time, but that isn't an option for me."

He groaned, pulling his weight off the top of mine and

sitting up. He stared down at me where I clutched the blanket to my chest. "It's not as easy as taking you into a field and teaching you how to throw a punch. If you want to fight in my world, there are guns involved. Knives. *Bombs.* Even amidst all of that, your own fear is your worst enemy. If you want to stand any chance of not freezing in the face of all that terror, you have to get used to being afraid for your life. Are you ready for that? For what that will do to you as a person and what it will mean to have fear be a constant companion until you no longer feel it?"

"Yes." I nodded, feeling like I'd signed the last piece of my soul away to the devil. He'd started calling me *mi reina,* recognizing the shift from *mi princesa* long before I was ready.

But as the nod he gave me in return settled into me, I knew I'd let go of the last pieces of the girl I'd once been. The only difference was the thought no longer filled me with dread.

I wouldn't miss her.

18

ISA

Rafael helped me smooth out my hair and get it to lay flat to cover the scar at the back of my head. With a maxi dress and light sweater to cover up what remained of the other scrapes and Rafe's name on my body, we'd chosen to conceal my injuries rather than admit the truth to my family.

Somehow, I didn't think they'd be too receptive to my marriage if they discovered I'd been in a shoot-out and nearly blown up by Rafael's enemies.

They were funny like that.

"They're going to freak out," I mumbled, watching him pour scotch into a tumbler. He surprised me when he closed the distance between us, lifting it to my lips. The cool glass brushed against my mouth, making me part for him on an exhale. He guided me back carefully with his hand cradling the back of my head, pouring a sip into my mouth.

It burned a path down my throat, and he paused to give me time to swallow before he gave me another sip. "You're running on fumes. The best thing you can do now is let them see how we are together," he said, taking the tumbler away from my mouth. He pivoted his hand, covering the stain my lip stick had left on the glass with his plush lips and drawing back a seductive swallow of scotch.

"So you're saying I should stab you?" I asked, quirking a brow at him.

He smirked, shaking his head lightly. "I have no doubt they would approve of that," he said, setting the glass on the end table beside the couch. "But if you want them to believe you choose to be with me, then you should probably refrain from trying to murder me for the evening."

"Shame," I muttered, picking up the glass where he'd set it. I tossed back the rest of the fiery liquid, letting it warm my belly against the dread that built there with every second that ticked by on the clock on the wall. "Does it make me a bad person if I hope she doesn't come?"

He didn't miss a beat, knowing exactly who I meant without question. "If it does, I'm probably worse since I would prefer she dropped dead," he said, a sardonic grin on his face. I couldn't quite tell if he meant it as a joke, or simply tried to play it off as one to ease the sting of wishing death on my sister.

"Rafe," I scolded, chuckling as I swatted at his arm. "You can't say things like that. Bad juju."

"*Mi reina*, if bad juju truly exists, don't you think I have bigger things to worry about?" he laughed, guiding me to the dining room where the table was already set up for dinner. I didn't dare to think of what my family would think when they drove up to the gate out front or got a good look at the house.

Or the armed guards patrolling outside. That would be interesting to explain.

Shit.

"This was a terrible idea," I said, glancing down at the

immaculate place settings that the caretaker of the house, a kind and gentle woman named Marisole, had set up for us before leaving for the evening. I'd been offended at the time, thinking Rafael thought I couldn't manage to set a table for myself.

But when I saw what she'd done, I had to agree with him.

The simple lines of the rustic setting she'd arranged were breathtaking against the wide planks of the table. She'd placed greenery artfully in a way I would have never been able to do. Most nights at home growing up, we'd been lucky if we were all home to eat together, let alone with a fully dressed table.

"They have to come face to face with your wealth at some point," Rafe laughed, nudging a fork to the side when he looked down and saw it was slightly crooked. "Now is as good a time as any."

"There is wealth and then there's the kind of wealth you have—"

"We," he said, not bothering to look at me as he made his way to the window.

"What?"

"You said the kind of wealth I have, but you should have said *we have*. You're my wife."

"And you're ridiculous. There is no chance of them ever looking at this kind of in-your-face money and thinking it's anything but yours," I argued, shaking my head as I looked out the window. I watched for a few moments in relative silence, twirling my wedding rings around my finger as Rafe stepped up behind me.

"How's your head?" he asked, pressing his lips to the back of it.

"Fine. It doesn't even hurt anymore," I said, leaning into

his touch. The doctor had come to remove my stitches earlier in the day, my week of rest finally over. I would have been lying if I'd said I wasn't disappointed that we'd chosen that night of all nights to have my family over.

The heat that flared in Rafael's eyes promised he wondered why we'd done that too. "It's not too late to cancel," he said, grinning down at me.

I chuckled, leaning up to invite him to kiss me. He gave me what I wanted, bending forward until his mouth touched mine and he coaxed me open for him. With nothing but his tongue on mine, he made me feel like I was desperate to go upstairs and remind myself that bed had far more fun uses than the ones where I laid in it alone and bored out of my mind.

I pulled back as movement appeared at the gate, the sight of my mother's old Ford rounding the corner. They paused, speaking to the guard in the exterior booth as I was sure my father asked for directions to find the address I'd given him. "I think it's safe to say it's too late," I said, leaning up to kiss him one last time.

He groaned into my mouth, driving me mad with the need that would keep me anxious through our dinner. It was only the sight of them pulling through the gate and making their way up the driveway that drew me away finally, knowing they'd be able to see us through the window.

Neither of my parents would want to see me wrapped up in Rafael in that way, married or not.

The car stopped in front of the house, and I watched in horror as my parents and grandmother stumbled out of the car, blinking back shock as they took in the enormous stone manor that Rafael owned as what was apparently one of many homes he—*we*—had around the world. "What were they thinking bringing her here?" he grunted, his annoyance matching mine as Odina stepped out of the backseat.

Where my parents' faces were filled with all the wonder I'd imagined I would see, Odina glared at the house with the loathing I'd come to recognize as being reserved for me. Her jaw clenched as she ground her teeth to clamp down on her aggravation, undoubtedly wondering why in the hell I'd managed to end up with the rich husband.

She'd always blamed me for everything I had and she didn't, no matter what I did. It had just taken me far too long to realize that I could never do right by her.

She wouldn't let me.

"They were probably thinking that she's my sister and she has just as much right to make me feel like I made a huge mistake as they do," I sighed. I couldn't even fault them for it, not given what Chloe had probably told them about Rafe, and not given the fact that I had disappeared for a period of time.

I'd have been ready to rip Rafe's throat out if he'd done it to my daughter too.

My father took my grandmother's arm, leading her up the steps to the front door. I moved away from the window, hurrying to pull it open for them before they had to deal with knocking and feeling awkward. I forced a broad grin to my face, fighting back the swirling nerves in my gut.

"Hey," I said, leaning forward to kiss my grandmother on the cheek. She pulled away from my dad, walking fluidly through the room as if she needed to remind the devil I'd married that she was anything but frail.

As if anyone needed the reminder that the matriarch of my family was alive and well. Until I'd met Rafael, she was the most intimidating person I'd ever met.

"Isa," my dad said, leaning in to give me a quick hug. He

backed off slowly as his eyes found Rafe lurking in the dining room, an appeasing smile on his face. I recognized it instantly as the one that he'd used when we'd been in Ibiza, the one designed to put me at ease so he could lure me into his trap.

By the time I'd realized what he was, I was already prey caught in his clutches. Seeing it directed at someone else and knowing exactly what it was disarmed me, making me falter in my step to hug my mom. She looked at my feet in heels, tutting gently with a hesitant smile on her face. "You never did like heels."

"Death traps for your feet," I agreed, stepping to the side so Odina could make her way inside without touching me. She waltzed past, making herself at home in the grand entryway as she tended to do and spinning to look at the mostly open concept main floor.

She whistled, looking over to the stairway that led upstairs and the hallway at the back of the main floor. "How big is this place?"

"Big enough," Rafael said evasively. "I travel with a large group for business and security purposes." He stepped into the entryway, taking my grandmother's hands in his and leaning forward to kiss her cheek. "It is my hope that with the initial unpleasantness out of the way, we can have a lovely evening and get to know one another better," he said, tossing my mother one of his breathtaking smiles.

Would it have been so much to ask for the charming Rafe to make an appearance the first time he met them?

I shook my head, chuckling at my mother's shocked expression as my grandmother took the arm he offered and allowed him to guide her to the table. "He has the manners I never could get you to acknowledge, Waban," she said, winking at my father as she took the seat to

Rafael's right. My father rolled his eyes, offering me a mocking arm and guiding me to the other side of the table.

Even though the food wouldn't arrive for some time, I settled into Rafael's left as he tucked in my grandmother's chair. Odina huffed in annoyance, walking herself over to the table and sitting next to my grandmother. My mother took the seat next to me, leaving my father to take the one on her other side.

"Wine?" Rafe asked, uncorking a bottle of red and pouring it into my glass expertly. He moved around the table, playing the dutiful host in the absence of staff since we'd thought it would make my family feel more comfortable if they weren't being served by the caterer and waiters.

I'd wanted to cook, but doctor's approval to come off my bed rest or not, apparently that was too much effort for me too quickly.

"Well, if he really is the devil that Chloe said he is, he sure is a pretty one," my grandmother muttered, taking a sip of the wine Rafael poured her. I snorted a laugh into my glass, chuckling as Rafe gave her a beaming, arrogant grin that showed he knew *just* how beautiful he was.

"Alawa!" my mother scolded, her face shocked as she stared at her mother-in-law. As if anyone could ever expect my grandmother to mind her tongue.

"Who knew the devil was such a gentleman, right?" I asked, smirking at her as she smiled at me.

"I can hardly take offense," Rafe said, smoothly bending into his seat at the head of the table and waving off my mother's outrage. Even dressed in jeans and a casual shirt to put my family more at ease, Rafe leaned back in his seat like a king on the throne.

It would have been impossible not to recognize that he

held all the power in that room, even if a stranger were to happen upon the scene.

"Is someone else joining us?" my mother asked, glancing at the empty seats at the end of the table where we'd placed a setting for the brothers.

"Hugo and his brothers Gabriel and Joaquin. They should be here any moment. They're just wrapping up some work in the back," Rafael said.

"You know Hugo?" my mother asked, her head perking up at the mention of the boy she adored like her own son. His invitation to a family dinner had been entirely strategic. Even though I'd only barely forgiven him for his deceit, I figured the least he could do to make it up to me was help pave the way with my family.

"It's a small world. It turns out that Hugo's family works for me. I believe in loyalty within my business, so the Cortes brothers were due to come intern with me when they returned to Ibiza," Rafe answered, grabbing my hand off my lap and holding it within his as he gave me a secret smile. He placed our joined hands on the table, my rings facing up and practically blinding as the lights reflected off of them.

My mother's shoulders sagged slightly, the breath wheezing out of her while Hugo appeared at the end of the hallway as if we'd summoned him. She stood from the table, moving to greet him with a kiss to the cheek and a broad grin. "We were just talking about you."

"Good things I hope," he chuckled, leaning in to kiss my grandmother's cheek before taking the chair at the end of the table. The seat surprised me until Gabriel emerged into the room. Gabriel smiled politely, greeting my family as he took his seat next to Odina.

All the Cortes brothers hated Odina for what she'd done to me, but Gabriel thought there was a special place in hell for people who purposely tried to harm their siblings. Watching him settle in beside her, I knew there had to be a strategy to the seating arrangement.

Gabriel had volunteered for Odina duty, trying to intimidate her into cooperating. "I'm sorry I'm late," he said with a smile. As my parents greeted the brothers, I turned my eyes to Rafe's and let the warmth of his effort wash over me.

I'd worried that our dinner would go the same as our first meeting and quickly devolve into disaster, but he'd worked to ease up on the over-the-top insistence that he was my life. Working to make my family comfortable went a long way where I was concerned.

"Is Joaquin joining us?" my father asked, latching onto the brother he'd always preferred. The quiet one who would protect me from doing anything foolish when my family wasn't around to keep an eye on me.

"He got caught up on the phone," Gabriel answered, making my father frown in disappointment. "I'm sure he'll come as soon as he's free."

"Well, I would be lying if I said I wasn't disappointed that you've chosen a life that will take you so far from your roots," my grandmother said, changing the subject with her sad eyes meeting mine as I looked away from Rafe finally. I reached across the table to take her hand in mine, ignoring my mother's protest that it was rude to do it.

"From what Chloe said, it doesn't seem like Isa had much choice in the matter," Odina said, sipping at her wine with a malicious grin. The words I'd been about to speak to my grandmother to reassure her that I would carry on our heritage, just in another part of the world, slipped from my mind.

Rafe leveled her with a glare, and the fact that the gruesome look on his face made heat bloom between my thighs should have probably served as a reminder that there was something seriously fucked in my head.

Murderous wasn't sexy, or at least it shouldn't have been to any normal person.

"Tell me, Dear Sister," I said, tilting my head to the side as I mocked her. Every moment spent in her presence showed me the truth more vividly. She hadn't been my sister for a long while; I'd just been too blinded by my hope that we could find a way past her anger. "Do I look like I have any interest in playing these games with you? Move on with your life, because I sure as fuck have."

"Language," my grandmother warned, sipping her wine and glancing at me over the top of the glass. She might have started out as the person I most feared disliking Rafael, but that quickly changed. She'd always been able to see what was right in front of her, and while there may be murky secrets, I had no doubt she could feel the love I felt for my husband and know it was genuine.

Even if it had been born in darkness.

"Oooh, Isa bites back now," Odina said, giggling as she feigned a shiver. "I wonder who taught you that." Her eyes slid to Rafe at my side, her gaze tracking down his body in a way that made me feel murderous. I curled my hand around my fork, wondering if the parting of flesh when I stabbed her would feel more or less gratifying than Rafael's had. "And if I can have a taste."

I leaned forward, my eyes intent on hers that were so like mine as I bared my teeth in a snarl that reminded me of the one Rafael gave when he went murderous. Instead of fearing what that meant for me, I embraced it. "Watch it. You have no idea what I'm capable of," I warned.

She leaned forward to match my pose, so that we were two identical copies facing off on either side of the beautiful dining room table. "I know *exactly* what you're capable of," she said, her lips tipping up into a cruel smile. "You've always been a bitch. It's nice that you're finally letting everyone see it."

"Careful, Odina. I'm not the one who keeps her sins a secret with her own family, am I? The last I checked, everyone in this room knew exactly what I did wrong all those years ago. I spent my life trying to make up for it. Have you ever owned up to what you did to me?"

She paled, leaning back in her seat as she pursed her lips. "Odina?" my mother asked, raising a brow at her in question. There was no secret that Odina had done everything she could to make my life miserable over the course of our lives. They just didn't know how severe her hatred had grown while they struggled to find a way to tame her bullshit behavior.

Knowing that Rafael had been there the day that she'd drugged me, even if my own memory of it was hazy, it had probably been foolish to bring it up. But even Odina had to know that claiming Rafe's presence over a year before I knew him would be difficult for anyone to believe. Especially when I had several witnesses who would insist otherwise.

"She's being dramatic. Nothing happened," Odina said, rolling her eyes as she crossed her arms over her chest.

"You keep telling yourself that," I argued, pushing my chair out from the table. I stood, holding my chin high as I stared at her. Rafe smirked into his wine, sipping delicately despite the tension in the room.

The man could have fed on sin and thrived on anger. Knowing him, watching me go toe to toe with my sister for what felt like the first time probably turned him on.

"A word?" I asked, nodding my head to the hall that led

to the bathroom and offices at the back of the house, entirely separate from the one that went to the majority of the bedrooms that Rafael's men claimed as theirs.

"Of course. I missed your lectures," Odina said, pushing her own chair out abruptly. She lacked all the finesse I'd come to expect of people after spending so much time with Rafael. Her anger made her movements sudden and uncoordinated.

"Girls," my mother heaved out a disappointed sigh, her voice trailing off as my father quieted her with a placating hand on hers.

"Let them work it out," he murmured, his voice fading as I made my way to the hallway and led my twin to the office where Rafael worked during his time in Chicago. Shoving open the French doors, I stepped into the space and spotted my book still open on the coffee table in the sitting area where I'd left it earlier that morning.

Odina glared at it, studying the chess strategy as if it was something distasteful. I closed the doors behind her as she moved into the room, cutting off our conversation from the prying ears in the dining room. There was only a matter of time before Rafe grew tired of letting me handle my own conflict.

He wouldn't take kindly to Odina's attempts to bully me out of my own family.

"Does your husband have a penchant for romance and fantasy books?" she asked, walking along the shelves at the side of the room and running her hands over the spines of hardcover books.

"No. He likes to make sure I have everything I might need. He had the house stocked before we arrived," I admitted, not liking the way her touch on the books that had been a thoughtful gift from my husband grated on my skin. It felt too intimate, having her touch something that was so clearly *mine.*

"How sweet," she spat, retracting her hand as if the books were suddenly written in poison that seeped into her skin.

"What do you want, Odina?" I asked, shrugging my shoulders as I stepped closer. "We're here visiting. We'll go back to Ibiza before you know it, and you won't have to see me. You didn't need to come here tonight."

"I'm sure you would have loved that. Having them all to yourself without me in your way," Odina said, spinning to face me with her legs shoulder width apart like she was ready to throw down. I'd never been one to physically fight my sister. But whereas before it had been because I didn't believe the answer to our problems laid in violence, it had become a question of whether I'd be able to stop before I killed her.

Nobody infuriated me like her. Not even the great *El Diablo.*

"That's not what I meant. I'm trying to tell you that I am not in your way unless you put me there. My relationship with Mom, Dad and Grandmother isn't ever going to be what it was now that I don't live here anymore. They may come to tolerate Rafe, and I certainly hope for that, but they'll never like him in the way I want. You don't need to act like we're in a competition,"

"I don't want to talk about them," she said, smirking cruelly as she tilted her head to the side and ran her eyes up my body. "See the funny thing is, you don't look hurt to me. I wanted him to *break you.*" She leaned in, snarling brutally and crossing her arms over her chest.

"Sorry to disappoint," I said, smiling sweetly in the face of her hatred.

"I remember him. You don't forget a man like that. He was there that night with Wayne."

"I'm not sure what you're talking about. I don't remember that night, because, as you might remember, I was drugged. It seems a little far-fetched to believe that he would have been at a high school party. To what aim exactly?" I asked, touching a hand to my jaw and looking at her with eyes that were filled with sympathy.

"Protecting perfect, precious Isa," she hissed through clenched teeth. "Hugo promised me Rafe would hurt you." I crossed my arms, pulling the sleeves up inadvertently and realizing my mistake too late. Rather than trying to correct the fact that she could see the tattoo and brand on my body if she looked, I chose to hope she didn't notice.

Explaining *that* was the last thing I needed to do.

"There are lots of different ways to break a person, Odina. You of all people should know that some of the deepest hurts happen under our skin. I may not look hurt to you, but I promise you know nothing of my life," I argued.

Her eyes fell to the tattoo on my arm, the brand feeling like it blazed to life all over again under her scrutiny. "You call yourself his wife, but he branded you like cattle. You're *property*, aren't you? Nothing but a whore for him to fuck when he's feeling some kind of way."

"This is one of those moments where you shouldn't talk about things you don't understand," I warned, stepping closer until her face was directly in mine. Odina was less than an inch taller than me, putting us nose to nose. Toe to toe, staring at each other with only inches separating us that somehow felt like an uncrossable chasm. "Yes, he branded me. Would you like me to tell you how much that hurt? Or would you like to hear how he wears my name branded on his skin too? Does that sound like I'm property to you, or is he mine?"

"Go back to whatever hole you crawled out of. I hope this time he kills you," she said, fury twisting her face as I ripped away the last pieces of vengeance she'd clung to. I'd suffered at Rafael's hands. The pain of my evolution was something that felt necessary in hindsight, but it didn't stop me from remembering what it was like to feel my heart crack in two when I learned of his deception.

I wouldn't have wished it on her, even if she deserved it, and *that* spoke to Odina's hatred far more than any words she ever spoke could have. She'd wanted me broken; she just didn't know I would emerge from the ashes stronger than ever. It didn't stop every word she spoke from feeling like a knife in my chest, but the final acceptance that there would never be anything I could do to make her forgive my mistake gave me a sense of peace all at the same time.

"I think that is quite enough," Rafael said, and I spun to face him. I hadn't heard the doors to the office open, but that wasn't what surprised me. He'd always moved silently, a predator in truth—capable of stalking his prey without them ever seeing him until it was too late. His hands were clenched at his sides, his face cold and impassive. Giving away nothing of the anger I could feel radiating off his body in waves, he stepped closer until he stood next to the two of us. "It is not just Isa that you have to fear any longer."

"Wonderful. Now my perfect sister has the perfect husband to use to lecture me on my life choices. How quaint," Odina said, rolling her eyes as her glare turned from Rafe and back to me. "Control your dog."

"I'm confused. Am I his whore or is he my pet? You can't have it both ways."

Rafael's head tilted to the side, a tiny fraction that most people wouldn't have even noticed. But I saw it for what it was: Odina coming to the end of the very short leash he'd allowed her. She might as well have wrapped it around her own throat.

"You and I both know I am far from perfect," Rafael said, his voice dropping low. Odina's eyes snapped to his, her lips parting as she finally recognized the predator in her presence for what he was. Rafe took one more step into her space, making her back up a step as she swallowed. "I am not a man you want as your enemy, Odina." Another step into her space, and she backed up more until her spine struck the bookshelf where she'd run her grimy hands all over my reading material. His hand came up to touch her throat, wrapping his fingers around it with a fierce intensity that he'd *never* used on me.

"Rafe," I protested, watching as she gasped for breath.

"There is no faster way to become my enemy than to insult *mi reina*. I have severed limbs for less," Rafael growled, keeping his face distant from Odina's. Despite the fury to his words, there was no trace of anger in his expression. Only a cool detachment that showed how little he cared if Odina lived or died.

The choice would be hers in the end.

Odina wheezed, trying to breathe around the tight grip on her throat. I stayed planted to my spot, watching with rapt attention as he showed me everything he could have been with me. Cold. Unfeeling. Indifferent.

Odina raised her hands to clutch at his forearms, her nails digging into the fabric of his shirt as her eyes came to me, filled with pleading and hope that I would interfere on her behalf. I said the only words I could in that moment to make her understand the severity of what Rafael would do to her if she behaved so foolishly again. "I don't command him."

Rafael's eyes snapped back to mine, the coldness in them melting to heat as he studied me. He peeled his hand off Odina's throat slowly, turning his body away from her and making his way to me as she collapsed to the floor in a heap and sucked back deep lungfuls of air. "You asshole," she wheezed finally.

"I believe the term you're looking for is *El Diablo*. Asshole isn't quite strong enough," I said, leaning into Rafe's side as he wrapped an arm around me.

Odina fled the room without another word, clutching her throat as she sought refuge with the family I knew would take her side. It wouldn't matter to them if Odina deserved the violence, because no man should put his hands on a woman.

Perhaps the next time I'd do it myself to save him the trouble.

I leveled Rafe with a meaningful look, emerging from the office to go face the shitstorm that I knew would wait for me in the dining room.

My mother glared at me the moment I stepped into the room, her hands touching Odina's red throat where she would bruise. "Pack your bags. We're leaving. Now," she ordered, standing from her seat and shuffling Odina toward the front door.

I didn't move, staring at my mother with all the resignation I felt. Rafael stepped up behind me, a silent sentry as my father pulled my grandmother from the chair. "I'm not going anywhere," I said, leaning back into Rafe's body for support.

While I didn't regret what he'd done to Odina, I would need the support in the aftermath of what would follow.

"Yes, you are. You are my daughter, and I will not leave you with someone who would do that to your sister."

"You mean what she wished a man would do to me when she drugged me and left me to be raped by her friend?" I asked, watching as Hugo shot to his feet with the tension in the room. He looked at me, nodding once as he silently agreed to take my back with whatever might come from the confession. "I hardly feel any sympathy for her. So forgive me if my husband takes objection to her telling me she hopes I die."

My father's chest sagged as he turned a questioning stare to Odina. She didn't respond to my accusation, clutching her throat with a glare on her face. I had no doubt it hurt to speak, but that wasn't what kept her quiet in the moments following my outing her. She'd wait until she had our parents alone to spin the story she wanted to tell however it best suited her.

That served me just fine, because if they believed the lies she spewed then they were already lost to me.

I stepped away from Rafe's grip finally, moving to stand on my own so they could see that I stayed of my own choice and not because he had his hands on me. "I'm calling the police," my father said finally, shaking his head as if he was disappointed in me.

Not the daughter who would watch me bleed if given the chance.

"You're free to try," Rafael said, leaning against the wall with an arrogant smirk on his face. The charming man from earlier in the evening was gone, replaced by *El Diablo* in all his glory. "I promise nothing will come of it."

"You can't assault a woman without consequences," my mother said.

"How nice it must be to live to be your age and still have

no understanding of how the world works, Mom," I huffed a disbelieving laugh. "If you truly think the police are the highest authority in this city, then you haven't been paying attention."

"What happened to you?" she asked, her voice catching with the emotion that clogged her throat. She dropped her eyes to the tattoo and brand on my arm, her eyes widening. "What did he do to you that you would tolerate being with a man like that?"

"I stopped being perfect and started being me," I snapped, turning my glare down to where she clutched my sister in her arms. "I realized that my life was shit when I was living it for everyone but myself."

"Come here, *mi reina*," Rafe said softly, his gaze warm as he held out a hand.

"I suggest next time you leave Odina at home," I said, moving to my husband and leaning into his side. "She has no place in our lives."

19

RAFAEL

Isa's mother glared up at me, blaming me for the way her daughter had turned on her. The loss of the well-behaved girl who had always done everything she was asked became poignant and undeniable in those moments when she stared at her mother defiantly.

The choice was clear. If they made her choose, Isa would pick me.

It was the final nail in the coffin of the meaningful choices she'd made after leaving Ibiza. She hadn't chosen me in that first moment when Chloe revealed the truth to her, but she'd chosen me in every one since then.

It would always be the two of us, no matter what life threw our way. I knew it in the depths of the soul I thought I'd lost years before her. The photos of her as a child only proved that, serving as confirmation that our lives had been intertwined when she was only just a child. This was something that I felt in my core.

Maybe I'd subconsciously recognized her on the street that day. Maybe our lives had been determined by some higher purpose before we could understand the pieces that were in play. All that mattered to me was the end result.

Isa was mine in a way I'd thought I could never achieve.

Her mother glanced down to her face, seeing the steely resolve there and releasing a sigh. "Call me when you're ready to talk," she said, turning on her heel and guiding Odina from the house. I half-wondered if Waban would make good on his vow to call the police, but it didn't matter much to me.

They'd never bother to investigate. Just like they hadn't really when my father had thrown Isa in the river. Our lives were so entrenched in violence between our families, I had to consider the prospect of what would come if Odina couldn't toe the line I'd drawn in the sand.

Would Isa forgive me for killing her?

With her family out of sight, she turned and buried her face in my chest. Sniffling against my shirt, she pressed herself tighter as the strength she'd shown in front of her family faded. Until the pain that she hid so fluently revealed itself, and only those she could trust to support her, no matter what she did, remained.

Hugo and Gabriel nodded, moving out of the room and giving us privacy as I stared down at the top of her head. "We didn't even make it to dinner," she said, her voice muffled against my chest.

"I know," I said, smoothing the hair over the top of her head. She would need to consider the fact that her family may never accept the woman she'd become. That she was too far removed from the one they'd known and loved for them to realize she was the same person.

She was just more.

I'd do everything in my power to protect her from the pain of their intolerance in the long run. Even if that meant hurting her more now to save her from feeling that disappointment over and over.

I guided her outside, the pool water glimmering in the lights from beneath the surface as we stepped onto the terrace. She eyed the water cautiously, keeping her distance from it as if she still couldn't quite bring herself to accept that she'd been forced to overcome that fear once already.

"I don't understand how she can look at me like she doesn't even know who I am, but leave here with Odina of all people. *Nothing* I've done will ever compare to what would have happened to me if you hadn't been a fucking creep and protected me. Not even murdering Maxim can compare. What am I supposed to make of that?" We moved to one of the lounge cushions.

"You may have to accept the fact that your mother in particular will always take Odina's side," I said, staring into the water before I turned my gaze back to her. Her sad eyes met mine, her lips twisting with anguish as she tried to reconcile that with everything she'd spent her life believing.

"I can't blame her for that. I know how powerful guilt can be when Odina wields it like a weapon. She'll never forgive herself for the choice she made, even though if she hadn't made it we would both likely be dead." Isa sighed, stripping her eyes away from me and hanging her head in her hands. I turned her on the lounge, pulling so that she looked back at me. The words I spoke to her next would hurt but she needed to hear them.

She'd fight them, but eventually she'd see the truth in it.

"Your mother doesn't feel guilty for the choice she made," I said, reaching up to stroke her cheekbones under her eyes and wipe away the stray tears that left her cheeks wet. "She blames you."

Isa's breath left her lungs in a sudden sigh. She blinked

up at me, tensing her mouth as she raised her hands to grab my wrists and tug them away from her face. "You don't know what you're talking about." Standing from the lounge, she made her way back toward the house.

"So why is it that Odina can do as she pleases with very little consequence, and yet you face the interrogation of a formal inquisition the first time you step out of line in thirteen years?" I asked, unfolding my legs to stand to my full height as she froze in place. I pulled off my shirt, revealing the brands on my chest as I stepped up behind Isa's still body. The tension there threatened to take my breath away, every muscle in her body locked as she thought about my words.

When she finally spun to find me standing directly behind her, a shocked gasp parted her lips. Raising her hand from where it rested by her side, I touched her soft fingers to the brands that marked me for every failure. As much as Isa didn't want to admit it, we were more similar than immediately seemed reasonable.

Her mother had never abused her. Never said an unkind or unwarranted word, but she'd let Isa's guilt fester unchecked for years. She'd used it to her advantage and required her to keep an eye out for the sister who didn't deserve her time or energy. She'd stripped away her childhood under the guise of loyalty and good behavior. Isa'd always been destined to fail.

"My father wasn't always abusive," I admitted, guiding her finger to the first of my brands. The one he'd given me the day he murdered my mother was the one that always stood out the most.

It was the first time he'd physically harmed me beyond a smack upside the head, whereas before that he'd relied simply on harsh words and threats to other people. His disappointment with me had been vocalized, and I'd known every single time I failed him. Before the day he killed my mother, I'd been desperate for his approval and sought to do everything I could to please him.

To show him that I was capable of being everything he needed in his heir.

The only difference between Isa's mother and my father was that Leonora genuinely loved Isa.

"My mother isn't abusive," Isa said, her voice gentler than I was sure she wanted it to be considering the conversation. Even through the sadness in her multicolored eyes, a storm raged behind the compassion for me sharing the story of my life with her.

"Am I?" I asked, nodding my hand down to the brand on her arm, my name on her neck, and the tattoo she hadn't wanted. "I've kidnapped you, touched you, drugged you, whipped you, and branded you. Most would say that I am the definition of abusive."

"Do you have a point?" she asked, narrowing her eyes on my face.

"My point is, that despite all of those things, you still have more freedom in my gilded cage than you ever did in hers. In the life she chose for you, you couldn't even be yourself. How is that not abuse?"

"She didn't put me in that cage, Rafe," Isa sighed, dropping her head to touch her forehead to my chest. "I did. I took everything dark and shoved it down where it couldn't touch me again. I felt what it was to bear the consequences of my actions when it was a *mistake*. Why would I want to know what it was to feel guilt for something I'd done intentionally?"

I glared down at her as she retracted her hand from my chest, distancing herself from me in body as she pulled back the gentleness she'd shown in the face of an uncomfortable conversation she didn't want. As much as Isa might have argued that I was the difficult one who complicated our relationship, the truth was that it was both of us.

She was stubborn. I was demanding. That was life.

"Did she ever stop you from putting yourself in that cage?" I asked, tilting my head at her as my voice dropped low. The devil rose to the surface with Isa's continued denial of the fact that her mother would never have allowed her to be free. Not without judgment, and definitely not without condemning her. "Or did she happily allow her daughter to be miserable?"

"That's not fair. Not pulling me out of the cage isn't the same thing as her being the one to put me in there in the first place," Isa said, spinning to turn her back on me as she took the last few steps toward the house. I followed her, stalking her inside as she tugged open the French doors. She passed some of my men lingering in the main living space, heading up the stairs for our bedroom. I didn't like seeing her in it, not the way I loved her being in our bedroom at home.

Being away from *El Infierno* felt wrong in all the ways that mattered.

"Maybe not, but they can't expect you to be the same girl who left Chicago. Life changed you," I said.

"You mean you changed me," she snapped, turning to face me with a severe glare on her face. Her cheeks were stained with the tears of her anger, her forehead pinched as if she couldn't quite wrap her head around our conversation. "You made me into a murderer, and you think it's weird that they wouldn't be able to accept that? Of course they can't. People don't love monsters, Rafael. Only other monsters can do that."

"You love me," I said, stepping closer into her space. Staring down into her beautiful face that was so consumed by anger, I waited for her to return the words that would confirm that *mi reina* was still the woman who'd been reborn in Spain. That she wouldn't backtrack because of her family's expectations and interference.

"How fortunate for you that you turned me into a monster then," she hissed, denying me what I needed to hear and turning her back on me and making her way for the phone ringing on the nightstand.

"If they can't love you for who you are, then they don't fucking deserve you," I argued before she could answer the call. The only other people she'd given the number to were her family when she'd called to invite them to dinner, so I could just imagine how well that conversation would go so quickly.

Some people really didn't understand the notion that distance made the heart grow fonder sometimes when it came to family. Maybe that was hypocritical since I would kidnap Isa again before I allowed her to have any form of distance from me.

"Chloe?" Isa asked, squeezing her eyes closed as she pulled the phone away from her ear. The screeching, angry voice of her best friend came through the cell, muffled but obnoxious despite my distance. Placing my hands on my hips, I stared at the floor in front of me and sighed, overcome with the feeling that bringing her to Chicago had been a grave mistake.

It was too much, too soon, to ask Isa to defy the people who had been there her entire life. No matter what she felt for me, competing with them wasn't something I would ever tolerate.

I was her entire world, and that was the way it needed to stay.

"I know. I'm sorry," Isa said, murmuring softly despite her friend's frantic energy. There was something so undeniably soothing about Isa's voice when she tried to comfort someone, and the sound of it reminded me of how gentle she'd been with Luna.

How gentle she'd be with our own child.

Isa was many things, but a monster she was not. Somehow, I would find a way to make her see herself as she truly was, and not overcome with the regret of her actions.

"No! I promise you I'm fine. He didn't hurt me. Look, Chloe, there are things you don't know," Isa said, pleading with her friend.

"Because you didn't tell me!" Chloe shrieked so loudly the sound reached me from feet away. "You didn't even tell me you were home. I had to hear it from your mother when she asked me to talk some sense into you."

"Of course she said that," Isa scoffed, turning to face me with a small smile. "Because thinking for myself automatically means that I've lost my damn mind." The peace offering hit me in the chest, settling there as it was meant to be. She hit the button for the speaker phone so that I could hear Chloe's words more clearly. I repaid the courtesy by shutting my fucking mouth.

I wanted to fault her for doubting my words in the first place, but I knew the denial came from a stage of grief more than anything else. *Mi reina* wasn't ready to see the truth just yet, but she would soon enough either way.

"You're married to a fucking crime boss! Do you know what they say about him?" Chloe asked as Isa moved to the bed and crawled into the center of it. She curled her legs up underneath her, looking far too small in the grand bed as she stared at her phone and considered her options.

"I know who he is, Chloe. I know that's probably hard for you to imagine." She turned a questioning look my way, heaving a sigh as she continued on. "Why don't you come over to talk tomorrow? I'll text you the address."

"Fine," Chloe barked, disconnecting the call. Isa tossed the phone onto the nightstand as I sat down next to her, drawing her into my side as I lay down on the bed.

"Just say the word and we can go home. You don't have to deal with them in any way you don't want. If that means you just call regularly enough for them to know you're alive, then that is what you'll do."

"They're my family, and we need answers."

I pulled her into my chest as she stained my skin with her tears of frustration.

Dead and scattered into ashes on the wind, my father still managed to fuck up everything good in my life.

20

ISA

Hugo flung open the front door when Chloe's frantic knocking echoed through the house. In the interest of preventing World War III, Rafe had seen fit to go check on the progress of sorting through the files at Matteo's. Most of the men had cleared out of the main space, leaving just the Cortes brothers to keep an eye on the situation as it unfolded.

Tucked behind the walls and the gate of Rafael's estate away from home, there was very little risk of a security threat. At least, one that would require me to have a dozen guards on my person at all times. The watchful eyes had quickly become stifling, even with just the three brothers in my space constantly.

I sat in the breakfast nook, waiting for Hugo to lead Chloe inside. The dining room table would have offered more seats for the five of us, but I couldn't stand the thought of sitting there after the clusterfuck that Odina had made out of dinner the night before. It felt like bad juju to repeat it again so quickly, and if I'd expected complications with convincing my family that Rafael and I were happy together?

Well, my mother had nothing on Chloe when she was worked up and ready to defend me.

Silence reigned in the moments after I heard the front door open, hinting at Chloe's shock. It surprised me that my mother wouldn't have mentioned Hugo's presence, and I honestly hadn't stopped to consider how things might have gone down between my two best friends in the end.

After Chloe had called to warn me, what had Hugo done?

Shit.

"You fucking asshole! I *knew* you were covering for him!" Chloe yelled, and I bolted from my seat to hurry into the foyer.

"Chloe," Hugo sighed, rubbing his temples in frustration. "Can you maybe get inside before you start bitching at me?"

"Wrong choice of words," I scolded him. "Complaining. Yelling. Those are both fine, but women are not bitches just because they disagree with something you did and chew you out for it. Safe bet: if you wouldn't refer to Rafe's rages as 'bitching' then don't do it when you're talking about a woman."

Chloe's eyes shifted to me, settling on me where I stood at the entrance to the foyer. In the casual strappy sandals and pretty wrap dress Rafe had set out for me this morning, I lifted my chin in an effort to look more confident in my skin. The scar on my thigh peeked out the bottom of the dress, and having it out in the open for people who knew me to *always* hide it felt strange. Vulnerable in a way I hadn't expected.

I'd gotten used to people's eyes on my skin, on that part of me that was so marked with what had once been my greatest shame. Where I might have once shifted to tug the dress down my leg to hide it, I felt strangely proud of the marks.

Of the fact that I'd survived when Miguel Ibarra tried to kill me in cold blood.

"You look beautiful," Chloe said, her brow furrowing as she stared at me. Confusion was written into the lines of her face, the stress of worrying about me undoubtedly having weighed on her in my absence.

I smiled to reassure her, stepping up to the doorway and taking her arm. I guided her into the house, her steps hesitant and slow in her surprise. "You were expecting to find me beaten and broken," I said. Her eyes dropped to Rafe's name carved into my skin, and she raised her brow at me sardonically but refrained from saying a word.

She nodded, dropping into the seat at the breakfast nook where I deposited her. The chess set was on the other side of the table, because as much as I loved to play chess in Rafe's office when he was there to keep me company, I greatly preferred the natural light of the kitchen. "Everything I heard about him...." she trailed off.

"Is probably true," I admitted, not bothering to blow smoke up her ass and call it the truth. "Rafe is complicated, but you don't have to worry about him hurting me. Not like that." I moved to the kitchen, grabbing two glasses of the fresh lemonade that I couldn't seem to get enough of. I handed one to Chloe, watching as she puckered her lips against the tartness of it.

"Your mom said he strangled Odina," she said, her face twisting with something cruel.

There was that. As much as the darkest part of me had enjoyed watching her struggle, I regretted allowing it the next day. I hadn't liked seeing his hands on her in any way.

"Strangled is a strong word for what he did. Honestly I think he's probably choked me harder when he fucks me."

Chloe sputtered on her second sip of lemonade, her eyes going wide as she stared at me. "And you're okay with that?"

I smiled at her, sipping my own lemonade through the straw as my eyes glimmered with the need to laugh. "I'm not a virgin anymore. We all have our kinks," I teased. I wasn't certain that was necessarily a kink of mine.

I just liked feeling Rafe's hands on me, whether that was on my throat or my breasts or my ass was irrelevant. I'd take whatever he gave like an addict and still beg him for more when he was done. I didn't care to dissect what that said about me.

"There's a big jump from virgin to liking being choked and cut up," she said, swallowing uncomfortably. There was no chance that it was the subject of sex that bothered her, because I knew Chloe had her share of experiences and had tried all manner of different things, though admittedly the knife might have been a stretch for her. She'd never been shy to talk about any of them with me. The main thing that bothered her was who my partner was. "Where is Rafe, anyway?" she asked.

"I thought it best that he was out of the house while we talked," I said, running my finger over the condensation on my glass. "I don't want you to think that I'm saying anything because he's listening."

"And what about the watchful eyes?" she said, lifting her chin to gesture to where the brothers had settled into the living room. Located within eyesight but not so close that they were smothering us, they didn't exactly blend in with the furniture.

"For my protection. Rafael has enemies, as I'm sure you can imagine. Hurting his wife would be a very efficient way to get to him." She nodded her agreement, even as she rolled her eyes at Hugo's arrogant grin when she turned her attention back to me.

"Are you happy?" she asked, glancing down to the rings on my finger. It appeared my mother had informed her of our marriage among other things.

I paused, letting her see as I thought through my answer. I wasn't sure happy would ever really describe my life with Rafe. Happy implied content. It implied being satisfied. "He makes me feel like I'm alive for the first time. My heart never stops racing and my body always thrums with this excitement for what comes next. I like being with him, and I love him. If that's not happiness, then I don't know what is."

"You have Stockholm Syndrome," she said, reaching across the table to take my hand in hers. She squeezed, her eyes warm and understanding as she tried to compel me to believe her.

"Probably," I admitted, huffing a laugh as she reeled back from my easy admission. "I'm not that naïve. I know what I feel for Rafe isn't normal and most people won't think it's healthy. It isn't. But that doesn't make it any less real. Giving it a name doesn't make it a figment of my imagination."

"I never said it was," she said, tapping the table with her free hand. "But my point is that once we get you away from him, we can get you help. Therapy. Understand why you developed these feelings in the first place and work through them."

"Chloe, I have to want that in order for it to work," I said, smiling gently. It was my turn to squeeze her hand as she tried to pull back. "I am not going to leave him. I'm not going to see a therapist and work through my feelings. I've accepted who he is and his place in my life. All that's left is for the people who claim to love me to do the same, because no matter what you think of this? It's my choice. Not yours."

"So I'm supposed to just let you stay married to him?" she asked, pushing her chair back and standing. I followed, smoothly unfolding my legs. I felt more like Rafael in those moments when my body moved passively, not showing the aggravation that I felt building under my skin. "He's a murderer, Isa!" she yelled, her hands waving as if she didn't know what to do with me anymore.

"So am I!" I shouted back, watching as her eyes rounded in shock. Her hands fell to her sides as she stumbled back a step as if I'd struck her. Trusting that Rafael would take care of me and that there would never be any consequences for what I admitted, I continued on. I couldn't tell my family the whole truth of who I'd become. But Chloe wasn't my Catholic mother. She wasn't my Menominee grandmother who believed in never harming another living creature. "I have killed a man. I have pressed a knife between his ribs and into his heart. I have watched the life bleed from his eyes, and I don't regret a fucking second of it because he deserved it."

She shook her head, her feet moving through the house to take her toward the door. "This isn't you. You'd never hurt anyone—"

"Maybe just like everybody else in my life, you never really knew me," I said, my voice dropping to a pained whisper. With the reality staring me in the face, I couldn't deny the truth to Rafe's words the night before. They would never understand, and they'd certainly never accept me like this.

I was a stain on the way they thought people should live. Law-abiding and constructive parts of society. If being with Rafael had taught me anything, it was that the world wasn't so black and white. We painted in shades of gray with accents of blood to offset the monotony, but nothing was ever what it seemed. Real life was complicated, and only those with their heads buried in the sand didn't realize it.

"You're my best friend," she said, her throat clogging with emotion that threatened to make mine spill over. "You think I don't know you, but some guy you've known for a month does? I was there with you for *years!* I saw—"

"Exactly what I wanted you to see," I murmured, watching as her body went still. "You saw me being who everyone wanted me to be and never once stopping to think about what *I* wanted."

"I know that! God, do you remember the number of times I told you that you could do something just for you?" she asked, putting her hand on the doorknob to the front door and looking back at me over her shoulder.

"And now that I have, it's unacceptable because it isn't what you would have chosen for me. You can't want me to make my own choices and then complain when I do. Do you think it's easy to sit here and have you and my family condemn me for my choice? It is *breaking* me that you can't just trust that I didn't make this choice lightly. You have no idea what I've been through or what I've overcome, but I *chose* him anyway. I don't expect you to understand that," I said, heaving a sigh as she turned the knob. They would never and could never comprehend the gravity of that choice. Of the decision to forgive Rafael for everything he'd done. "But I expect you to respect me enough to let me make that choice."

"Call me when you're ready to listen to reason," she said, ignoring what I said and pulling the door open.

"Chloe," I called as she stepped through the open door. "If you make me choose, it will always be him." She nodded with her back to me, not bothering to face me before she stepped out and closed the front door behind her.

Staring after her for a few moments, I jolted when Hugo stepped up behind me and wrapped his arms around me. His chin rested against the top of my head, holding me steady as I watched one of the last pieces of who I was before Rafael walk out of my life.

I had a feeling she wouldn't be back.

21

RAFAEL

The house was silent as I crept inside, the guards turning to watch me as I made me way toward the steps to our bedroom silently. In the wake of our attack, I couldn't escape Isa's plea to not be helpless anymore. As much as it killed me to admit that her knowing how to take care of herself might be useful, I would do whatever it took to protect her.

Even teach her to stab me more effectively than she had with her fork.

The bedroom door loomed in front of me, cracked open just the slightest bit to give her privacy without shutting herself off from the security in the house. I nudged the door open slowly, fully expecting to find my wife curled up in bed and lost to the depths of sleep. The fact that she stood staring out the window, her back to me but her eyes blazing in the reflection from the terrace, told me everything I needed to know about her conversation with Chloe. It hadn't gone well at all. I already knew from Joaquin's report of the day and what he'd overheard.

The ski mask covering my face made me feel like an

invader in my own home, and only the call I'd placed to prepare the men to know what to expect when I came home kept them from treating me as one. They would hear Isa's screams, and that would damned well be the only time in her life they'd ignore them.

If she wanted to be able to defend herself, if she wanted to be anything more than a liability that I had to shield with my body, then she would need to first figure out how to fight through the pure terror that would consume her. In my father's days, the first part of training a soldier was desensitizing them to the screams of innocent people. To the fear of death and pain. Until nothing remained but the slowing, logical count of the brain as it processed the steps and strategy to gaining freedom.

Isa never took her eyes off the flames outside the window, lost to the same paralyzing fear that I saw in her face every time she looked upon the fire. After her confession, it was all I saw, no matter how hard she tried to hide it. I stepped up behind her, moving so slowly that the air didn't ripple as my body cut through it. The heat of Isa's back radiated through the room, reassuring me that she hadn't taken another ice shower and risked freezing to death to escape the memory of a kiss of flames on her skin.

When her breath left her in a heavy sigh, I lunged. Snapping my arms around her to wrap her up in my grip, I put one hand to her mouth and muffled her startled scream that bubbled up in her throat. My other arm wrapped around where hers were crossed over her chest, pinning them to her body as she jolted and thrashed in my grip. The muffled scream vibrated against my hand as I tugged her back into my body, stepping away from the window to move her toward the bed.

She dropped her weight to the floor, tipping me off

balance until I had to compensate by shifting my grip lower on her waist and hauling her up off her feet. With her hands free, she launched a full scaled attack on my forearms, digging her nails in and shoving at my grip around her waist. The fabric of my suit mostly protected me from the wounds she would have inflicted, and regret claimed me.

I wanted her marks to gouge into my skin, evidence of the fighter I'd married and the vicious little demon hiding inside her.

I worked to steady her, guiding her to the bed. She lifted her feet, catching the edge of the mattress and kicking back into me as I stumbled back a few steps. A dark laugh bubbled in my throat, my grin hidden in her hair as it flew around her with her struggles. Sinking her teeth into the palm of my hand, Isa bit until she drew blood. My hand slipped along her mouth with the slickness of it when I tore it free from her tight grip, and her scream echoed through the room as soon as she was able.

"Let go of me!" she screamed, kicking off the edge of the mattress a second time when I approached it again. Lifting her higher, I tossed her onto the bed. She scrambled for the other side after her weight bounced and settled, her hand clawing around the edge as I grabbed her legs and spread her out on her stomach. Nudging her legs apart slightly, I stared down at the fawn skin of her thighs where her dress rode up.

What had started as a lesson quickly evolved into a dangerous game, my obsession with Isa knowing no limits. I'd lay her out and take her, torment her to the breaking point, and only when she acknowledged that she knew who I was and was as aroused as I was would I finally drive inside her tight heat and give us both what we wanted.

Toxic. Consuming. Obsession.

And what was love but a mutual obsession?

She was everything rolled into one, and I'd be damned if I ever stopped feeding the darkness inside us. I covered her weight with mine, pressing her stomach into the bed as my hips settled between her thighs. My cock touched her ass, nestling against the center, pushing her panties deep as I ground myself against her.

She stilled for a moment, the fear of what was to come locking her body solid. "What do you want?" she asked quietly, those fingers of hers gripping the bedding as she tried to find purchase. Her attempts to shove to her knees and dislodge me went nowhere, and *mi reina* was well and truly caught.

She'd be fucked soon enough.

I grabbed her hair in a hand, wrenching her head to the side as I dropped my exposed lips through the hole in the mask to her shoulder and sank my teeth into the claiming mark I kept there. It would never be enough. My brand, my ring, my name. I wanted to imprint myself on her very fucking soul until anyone who looked at her knew who owned her. When I removed my teeth from her bruised flesh, I pressed a sweet, demented kiss to the skin of her jaw, trailing my lips over her throat. Goosebumps raised in the wake of my touch, her body recognizing its owner even when her brain hadn't caught up.

"This is why your sparring with Joaquin would always be useless," I murmured, feeling her body sag with relief at the sound of my voice. "Nothing can teach you to cope with your own fear."

"You fucking asshole," she gasped, her chest heaving with the exertion of trying to fight off a man twice her size. I nipped the side of her throat, tugging her head to the side even harder as one of my hands slid down to touch the side of her thigh.

"Don't stop fighting me now. We both know what I'll take when I win, and we both know how much you'll like it," I growled, smiling against the pink flesh of her neck where I'd bitten her. Removing my weight from her back, I stood at the side of the bed and stared at her as she spun to her back to glare up at me. Taking in the black ski mask on my face, she widened her eyes briefly as my hands dropped to my suit jacket and unbuttoned it before shrugging it off my shoulders.

"What are you doing?" she whispered, furrowing her brow as she watched me strip. My fingers went to the button at the top of my dress shirt as Isa raised up onto her elbows. Her body tensed, reading the language in my body as I prepared myself to relive my favorite game with her.

Another button, another twitch of her body as she moved to sit on the bed in front of me. I tilted my head, a dark smile consuming my face as fear swirled in her gaze. "Were you going somewhere, Princesa?" I murmured, watching as her brows drew together in confusion. I watched the moment understanding dawned in her eyes, her mouth dropping open as if she couldn't believe the words.

"No," she mumbled, licking her dry lips and pulling her legs up onto the bed to clutch to her chest.

I leaned forward, resting a hand on either side of her body and touching my lips to hers briefly in the mockery of a sweet, gentle kiss. There was nothing gentle about the things I wanted to do to *mi reina*, not after being starved of her touch for so long. Not after thinking she was dead and not being able to relieve myself in her body.

In the fact that my wife was still alive.

"You should be," I said, grasping a strand of hair between my fingers and twirling it as she stared up at me with fear filled eyes. Even loving me, even accepting the nightmare inside me as hers, Isa knew I would hurt her.

Part of me craved it; part of me needed the rush that came with watching her get off on the pain only I could give her.

"Rafe," she whispered.

I pulled back, standing and returning my fingers to the remaining buttons of my shirt, watching her stare up at my face in the mask, looking as if she might defy me in this game I wanted to play. I glared at her, promising without words that I would be even rougher with her if she didn't give me what I wanted. "*Run,* Isa," I growled.

22

ISA

His eyes glimmered with the dark promise of all the things he'd wanted to do to me the first time he'd chased me. Even the knowledge that this wasn't real, that it was all a game, couldn't detract from the fear coursing through my body.

My heart thudded in my chest, and my soul felt like it would be ripped free with the realization that this was no more a game than it had been then. Rafael might be my husband, but he was still *El Diablo*. No matter what he'd made me into, he would never stop enjoying the pain of breaking me.

Of taking me to the edge of my limits and then putting the pieces of me back together to form the woman he knew fit at his side. The woman who could look the devil in the eye and not be afraid. I wasn't her yet, and I still very much feared the consequences of disobeying Rafael in his twisted game.

I bolted off the bed, racing for the bedroom door so quickly that my heart felt like it stopped in the moment when I made it through. I slammed into the wall on the opposite side of the hallway, my bare feet unable to get the traction I needed as I skidded to my hands and knees and then sped down the hallway and toward the stairs.

Glancing over my shoulder, I put a hand on the railing to steady myself as my feet thumped down the stairs one by one. I paused when I reached the bottom, sucking back frantic breaths and listening for the sound of my husband following. Of the devil in a ski mask who would hunt me through the night, taking everything that he knew belonged to him without a thought for what that might mean to me.

I moved to the French doors to the terrace, unlocking them with frenzied fingers that couldn't seem to grasp anything. The taste of Rafael's blood still lingered on my lips as I licked them in an effort to concentrate, tugging the door open and then pausing. I turned to stare back at the steps, closing the door and leaving it unlocked before I turned to the kitchen and looked for a hiding spot within the house itself.

I was under no illusion that I would be able to keep Rafael from fucking me, and if I was entirely honest with myself that wasn't even what I wanted despite the fear consuming me. I'd grown addicted to his darkness, to the adrenaline he gave me and never knowing just how far he would take it.

If one day he'd kill me while he fucked his rage out on my body.

But something about his hunt made me want to defy him, to make it as hard as possible for him to finally get what he wanted. I scrambled into the kitchen, sliding myself into the cupboards in the kitchen island. Pots jangled as I settled into a position at the back, holding as still as I possibly could as I listened. He moved like a panther, so quiet that it was impossible to tell where he was.

Until the sound of the shower curtain ripping back in the downstairs bathroom sounded through the room. I jumped despite myself, even knowing that it put distance between us. Covering my mouth with my hand, I tried to still my lungs and quiet my breathing to a normal pace while I waited.

As I'd hoped, the doors to the terrace closed. Still, I stayed put. Waiting to find out if it was a lie for him too. When no other sounds came through the house, I slipped out of the cupboard as quietly as I could and looked around to see if he hid in the shadows. I padded through the kitchen on quiet feet, making my way to the stairs barefoot.

Halfway there.

My spine tingled with the feeling of eyes on me, and I stilled my body as my heart leapt into my throat. Turning to look over my shoulder, I froze the moment my eyes landed on Rafael's shirtless form standing in the doorway to the terrace. Bathed in the shadows from the outdoor lights, he tilted his head to the side and studied the prey he would devour soon enough. His head was tipped down, his eyes gleaming from the holes in the ski mask as his lips twisted into a cruel smirk that took my breath away even through the mouth hole.

Sprinting for the steps, I pushed past the fear as I heard him follow. His bare feet slapped against the floor as he caught up to me quickly, his long legs simply too much for my shorter ones to overcome. I was halfway up the steps when he grabbed me around the thighs. I toppled forward, wincing as I prepared for the landing on the steps, but it never came.

He supported my body, adjusting my balance for me as he pressed into the back of my knees until they folded for him. I dropped, the collision of my knees with the stair vibrating up through my body. He gave me no time to react before he shoved my dress up over my ass, grasping my panties in his hand and yanking them down my thighs. They caught at my knees, restricting my movement as I tried to scramble up the steps. Those powerful hands of his grabbed the top of my dress, tearing it down the back until it fell around my sides in scraps.

"Stop it!" I hissed, turning to face him so my ass rested on the step. My palm connected with his mask-clad cheek, the dull thump less satisfying than the sting of his flesh would have been.

He'd take it too far if something didn't snap him out of the overwhelming darkness that had consumed him.

Where I'd hoped to discourage him, his eyes only darkened further. As if my fighting turned him on more. He grasped my dress in his hands, tearing it down my hands until he gathered the fabric in his hand and twisted it together. "I like it when you fight me," he murmured, leaning into my space until I lay back on the stairs. The steps dug into my spine, painful and intrusive as he gathered up one of my hands and wrenched it over head.

"Rafael!" I gasped, watching as he knotted the fabric around my hand and fed it through the posts and pulled it tight. My back shifted, the step scraping against my bare skin. With only a bra at my chest and my panties bunched around my thighs, Rafael grabbed my other hand and secured it with the same fabric while I tried to kick out at him.

When he seemed satisfied that I was secured according

to his desires, he leaned back. His fingers trailed over my thighs as my lungs heaved, my back arched painfully on the steps. With his other hand, he unclasped the front of my bra, exposing my breasts to his eyes and the cool air conditioning in the house. My nipples pebbled under his scrutiny, his smile turning wicked as he lifted his hands to the mask and folded it up over his mouth.

His lips were parted, plush and seductive as his tongue darted out to wet them. He leaned forward, touching a gentle kiss to my nipple. The feel of his warm breath on my skin made my spine arch more despite how much I shouldn't have wanted it. I should have stabbed him for the twisted game, but the truth of what I'd told Chloe also threatened to consume me.

He made me feel. Good or bad, beautiful and ugly.

He wrapped his lips around my nipple, flicking his tongue over the tight bud and then nipping it gently with his teeth as his eyes held mine. "This is what I wanted to do that night when you left me," he whispered before he opened his mouth wide and sank his teeth into the flesh of my breast, sucking and kneading it harshly as his other hand yanked the panties down over my knees and off my feet. He shifted, the support of his body between my legs threatening to make me topple sideways with the awkward angle diagonally across the steps and no way to balance myself. "Do you see now how much I restrained myself?"

As he drew his mouth away from my breast and shifted down my body, his arms wrapped around the back of my thighs and spread me wide. Stabilizing me as those sinful lips hovered at the apex of my thighs, he leaned forward and dragged his tongue through my lips slowly with his eyes intent on mine.

I stifled the moan that caught in my throat, watching as

he smiled up at me. Even with a mask covering most of his face, with the shrouding of most of his features, he was still breathtaking. "You're so fucking wet for me," he muttered, the sound tickling my flesh as his breath covered my sensitive skin. "I wonder if I'd bent you over the hood of the SUV and fucked you, would you have been this wet?" he asked, burying his face between my legs. His tongue slid inside me, fucking me with shallow thrusts that made me writhe on the steps despite the pain to my back.

I didn't respond, because I suspected the answer would have surprised me. I'd been so consumed by my terror that night, by the reality that a killer stalked me through the streets, I hadn't been able to focus on the effects on my body.

Knowing how quickly my body reacted, how he'd trained it to do his every bidding on command, I couldn't expect anything else. I would have welcomed him inside my body, and then I'd have hated myself for it immediately after.

He drove me higher and higher, his lips wrapping around my clit and tormenting it with the pressure he knew I needed, only to ease off when my thighs started to tighten around his head. I whimpered, desperate for the release following the adrenaline that had consumed me. "When you come, it will be on my cock," he said, rising up from between my legs. He shifted my body around to my hands and knees, maneuvering me like it was nothing to him to change the way a person moved. To control me entirely.

His hand came down in a firm swat to my ass, the flesh of the globe bouncing as if it too wanted to get away from the intensity of his possession. Pulling me back until I almost sat on my feet, he put one foot on the step next to me and drove into my pussy with a hard glide. Striking the end of me on that first thrust, he pulled a cry from my lips.

"*Fuck*," he groaned, pulling all the way free and doing it again. With the fabric twisted around at my wrists to accommodate the change in positions, I had even less mobility. "I should let you go. Knowing what my father did to you." He reached up a hand to untie my wrists as he moved inside me with slow but hard drives.

I paused, listening for more words as doubt settled over me. He'd sworn he would never let me free, told me he loved me. I couldn't imagine the end would come from something so deeply buried in our past, but the doubt crept in even as he fucked me like he hated me. "But?" I prodded.

He wrapped one hand around the front of my throat, squeezing as he drew me up until his chest touched my back. His free hand reached around my hip, slipping between my legs to touch the space where we connected. His fingers surrounded his cock where it slid in and out of me, the heel of his palm brushing against my clit with every stroke. "I will *never* do the right thing where you're concerned. I'll do anything it takes to own you. Including fucking you so often that my cum leaks out of your pussy every step you take."

His hand tightened at my throat, pressing harder until my vision clouded and my world narrowed down to the feel of him inside me. The stairs digging into my knees didn't matter as I reached up my hands to claw at his arms as self-preservation took over. "Rafe," I gasped.

"And if you ever try to revert back to the girl who takes your sister's shit and tries to please your parents, I'll fuck you until you remember who you really are. *Mi Reina*," he growled, releasing his grip on my throat suddenly as his hand dug into my clit and circled in tightly. I came, my chest heaving as I sucked back desperate lungfuls of air and ecstasy rushed in. He bit into my shoulder as he followed, filling me with heat as his mouth sucked at my flesh until I bled.

Our love had been born in blood, and Rafael Ibarra seemed determined to never let me forget it.

23

RAFAEL

Cradling Isa to my chest, I stared over her shoulder at her nude form in the bath tub. The hot water turned her skin a light pink in a way that should have been relaxing, but her body was tense. "Is it the heat?" I asked, murmuring the words as I dipped my face down to brush my nose over her cheek.

"Is it the fucking heat?" she snapped, turning her head to glare at me. "You just mauled me on the staircase after you *hunted* me in a ski mask."

"But did you die?" I asked, quirking a brow at her.

Her mouth parted in shock, her lips tipping up as a snort burst out of her. "What did you just say?" she giggled, covering her face in her hand.

"Am I not allowed to make jokes?" I asked, smiling down at her and the joy on her face. As much as I loved seeing her afraid, feeling the heady mix of her arousal and her fear of me and the way they combined to drive her higher and higher, that smile was everything. "You're spending too much time in the sun. You have a new freckle," I observed, tapping the side of her nose gently.

She flushed, her chin dipping as the smile drifted off her face and her lips twisted with the shyness. Given that I'd seen everything there was to see on her and fucked every orifice, it seemed unreasonable that my wife would still blush in my presence.

Even knowing that, I wouldn't change it for anything. I hoped she spent the rest of our long lives together being intimidated by my presence, because I wouldn't ever stop trying to overwhelm her.

My thumb trailed over the corner of her mouth as I cupped her cheek in my hand, tugging her back until she rested firmly against my chest. She snuggled into my neck, her breath a reassuring caress on my throat. "Tell me about Chloe," I murmured, wincing when the deep sigh left her and she pressed deeper into me.

"You mean your minions didn't already tell you everything?" she asked, a bitter acceptance of the eyes I kept on her at all times. Isa had long since come to terms with the fact that she had no privacy or secrets from me, and that my obsession with her would keep it that way, but that didn't stop her from hating every moment of it.

"Not everything." I didn't bother to deny that Joaquin had given me a brief summary of the conversation. To do so would only be an insult to Isa's intelligence. Keeping secrets to protect her was one thing, but now that she knew the truth about me and the kind of man I was, those were the only secrets I would keep from my wife. There was beauty in those lies that served a purpose, in the half-truths that protected her soul from fracturing. "And I want to hear it from you."

Isa sighed, sitting up straight and turning to face me. "She didn't understand. She didn't even try to," she said, dropping her eyes to the brands on my chest. Her hand raised to touch the fading marks from where she'd stabbed me with a fork on our wedding night. "I can't say I blame her really. That's the hardest part. I know they're only being logical and doing what they think is right for me. They don't mean to hurt me."

"But they are," I said, raising a hand to touch her back. My fingers trailed up and down her spine, making her shiver despite the warmth of the water surrounding us. "Whether that's the intent or not, you can't deny it's how they've made you feel."

"I wanted to come home. I was so desperate to get back to them that I was willing to turn my back on what I felt for you," she admitted, standing from the water and grabbing the towel off the rack next to the tub. I didn't move to stop her even though I would have rather she stayed and let me hold her. Isa didn't like to be naked when she was emotionally vulnerable. She dried off in a hurry, wrapping the towel around her body as I stood. I couldn't contain my smirk as she kept her eyes purposefully off the erection at my waist.

It never seemed to go away when she was near me.

Only when I was covered and pulled the drain on the tub did she move to speak, picking up the comb and starting to frantically work her way through the wet snarls in her hair from our fight. I took it from her, easing the comb through her hair as she leaned her hands on the counter and stared at me in the reflection of the mirror. "I can't stop wondering what it would have been like if you hadn't stopped me. Would I have come home and felt this...out of place in my own home? Would I have regretted leaving?"

"I think we both know the answer to that question, *mi reina*," I murmured, turning my stare to her face as tears threatened her vivid eyes. "The way we feel about each other, that doesn't just go away because you go to the other side of the world. You'd have felt my loss just as keenly as I felt yours."

"You don't think I could have buried myself in the life I'd planned?"

"Do you think you could have?" I asked, my voice dropping lower. Fury threatened a haze at the edge of my vision, that feeling so reminiscent of the moment she'd chosen her family over me.

She stared at me in the mirror, watching the signs of my anger on my face and studying them intently as she considered her answer. I knew Isa well enough that whatever left her mouth wouldn't be a lie. Her ability to reflect on herself and her feelings so thoroughly was something I admired in her, something I hoped she'd pass to our daughters so they'd have more emotional depth than I did.

I was a puddle compared to the ocean that surged inside Isa.

"No," she said finally, and the relief I felt was tangible in the air. I didn't know what I would have done if she'd said she thought she could forget me so easily.

Probably take her back to *El Infierno* and never let her leave.

"I think you were doomed to need me from the first moment I touched you," I said, smirking at the roll of her eyes.

"Were you born so arrogant?" she asked.

"I believe that was likely developed over years of careful practice," I chuckled.

The laugh she gave in response was hollow as her thoughts threatened to consume her. "They don't understand me anymore," she said, smiling sadly as she looked at her reflection. "I don't belong here anymore, do I?"

My heart clenched in my chest, the admission something poignant for the woman who would have done anything to get back to the family who she'd sacrificed so much to please. "No, because you belong with me."

I finished working through the knots in her hair, helped her into a nightie to sleep in and guided her to bed. She was so tired as I tucked her in, the weight of the emotional epiphanies surrounding her family weighing her down. Tucking her into my arms, I held her until her breathing evened out in the peacefulness of sleep.

Rolling away from her, I sat up and looked over to watch her. Her face was so peaceful, unstressed and unperturbed by the events of her life that made her become so trapped in her head. My cell dinged on my nightstand, a text from Joaquin to let me know that all shifts had returned to their posts around the house and everything was secure following my *exercise* with Isa.

The date at the top of my phone gleamed back at me, feeling significant as I tried to think of whatever responsibility I might be missing back at home. It wasn't until Isa rolled onto her back in the dramatic way of hers that I stared at her stomach and awareness dawned. I wondered briefly if she'd done the math and realized it yet, but knew without a doubt she was too stuck in her own stubborn denial and the stress of all the changes in her life to realize the one truth that had always been only a matter of time.

Isa was two weeks late.

24

ISA

Rafe was gone by the time I woke up, the oddly early hour for him to disappear grating at my nerves. After his actions the night before, my heart clenched with the need to be reassured. My body throbbed from the fight, and I stared down at my feet as I pressed them to the wood floor.

With all I'd fought, very little evidence of it remained in the bedroom. Almost as if there had never been a fight at all. The thought didn't fill me with confidence about my ability to fend off someone who actually wanted to hurt me.

I swallowed back the rush of nausea that bubbled in my throat, more determined than ever that I would survive Rafael's specific brand of training. He might be a dick, but even I couldn't deny that he had a point.

In the moments when his arms had wrapped around me and I thought a stranger had invaded the house, *nothing* Joaquin had taught me remained. My panic had consumed me, until the only reason I remembered to drop my weight was because the claws of terror digging into my chest froze me solid.

When the nausea passed, I stood and made my way into the bathroom. I turned on the shower, going through my morning routine while I waited for the water to heat up. The desire to turn the water to cold pulsed at me, making me grip the edges of the counter as I shoved down the urge.

With my head tilted down and staring into the sink, I jolted when the bathroom door opened unannounced. Rafe's face and broad body filled the doorway, sucking the quiet from the room. Despite the smile playing at his lips, everything in my body went still as he prowled into the bathroom and turned off the water for the shower. "You're awake," he murmured, stepping up behind me and wrapping an arm around my waist. His hand rested against my stomach, the heat of his skin through my nightie searing me as his breath caressed my neck.

"Obviously," I said, smiling past the suspicion rising in me. Something was wrong, and I knew it down to my soul. Nothing good ever came from the things that made Rafael Ibarra happy enough to smile as he walked into a room.

"Do you think it will be a boy or a girl?" he asked, his other hand reaching around my body to place a single pregnancy test on the counter. I stared down at the wand in shock, my brain going silent as it tried to catch up.

A second passed.

And then another.

The beating of my heart filled my ears as my mind started working again, processing the words and the date. "I—"

Nothing else followed, silence consuming me as my gasp froze the breath from my lungs. My hand drifted toward my stomach, touching it gently in disbelief, only to be reminded that Rafe's hand was already there. He'd already claimed the space above my womb as his, touching the child he seemed so confident already grew within me.

"I'm not pregnant," I said finally, dismissing him and moving to turn away from the mirror. His hand held me steady, refusing to let me leave the bathroom and the conversation I wasn't ready to have.

"You're two weeks late," he said, his voice soft despite the panic he must have felt in my body. I needed to get away from him, almost as desperately as when I'd thought he was a stranger the night before.

"It's stress. Women are late all the time when you turn their lives upside down," I dismissed, pressing my spine tighter into his chest to put as much distance between the pregnancy test and I as possible.

"If you're so certain, then what is the harm in being sure?" Rafe asked, that invading hand on my stomach rubbing gentle circles. I shook my head from side to side, determined to deny it until the last breath in my body. It was too soon, and I wasn't ready to add *mother* to the list of changes taking over my life.

"I'm not ready," I said, grasping his wrist and tugging his hand off my belly.

I spun, heading for the door only for him to stop me with a harsh grip on my arm. "Take the test, *mi reina*, because we both know you're not leaving this room until you do." He pulled me back into the center of the bathroom, positioning himself between the door and I. "We already know the truth. The plus sign on a pregnancy test will only confirm it." He dropped the instructions on the counter and strode out the bathroom door as suddenly as he'd entered, closing it behind him and giving me a moment of privacy.

I turned to stare down at the white stick on the counter, the offending device that would change everything. I couldn't even consider the fact that things had already changed, that, whether I wanted to be or not, I *knew* the truth of Rafe's words.

I snatched up the stick, hiking my nightgown up my thighs and glaring down at the instructions. I went to the toilet as I tugged off the protective cap. Sitting and unbearably uncomfortable, I followed the instructions with hasty movements, replacing the cap and dropping it onto the counter as if it had shocked me.

Flushing and washing my hands, I refused to look at the test as I counted down from 120 in my head. Rafe knocked on the door when I turned the water off, the sound soft and patient even though I knew he probably felt anything but.

One minute left.

He'd been so determined to knock me up, so insistent that it was what he needed to feel like I was his in every way, he needed to see the evidence of all his plans coming to fruition.

I couldn't even hate him for it, not when I'd known what he wanted and what the consequences of our constant unprotected sex would be. At some point, I'd even stopped fighting him on it, and I'd become just as responsible as he was.

Thirty seconds left.

I paced back and forth in the bathroom, ignoring the door opening behind me as Rafael lost his patience and entered the bathroom. He stared at me as I walked back and forth, his eyes dropping to the test on the counter wordlessly.

"Ten seconds left," I said as I moved toward him, turning on my heel at the last moment and making my way to the other side of the bathroom.

"I hardly think ten seconds will matter that much," he

said, moving to the counter as I sucked back a deep lungful of air. He stared down at it, his body freezing solid while I watched.

"It's negative?" I asked, stepping up beside him with hope surging through me. I just needed more *time*. Time to figure out who I was becoming and if I even *liked* her. Time to decide who I wanted to be outside the confines of my family's expectations and the cage without walls where I'd locked myself.

Two solid, *very* pink lines showed in the window on the stick. My hand went to my stomach, fingers digging into the fabric of my nightgown and swallowing past the lump in my throat.

I was pregnant, and my child would be the son or daughter of *El Diablo*.

"Rafe," I whispered, the burn of tears stinging my throat. The thought that maybe he'd changed his mind, that he'd only thought this was what he wanted threatened to make me collapse in the seconds before he pivoted and snatched me up in his arms.

His mouth hit the top of my head, his breath ruffling my hair as he sighed contentedly. With my arms still wrapped around myself, I made no move to hug him back. His joy filled the bathroom, dancing over my skin as he smiled into the top of my head and laughed happily. "You're pregnant," he murmured.

I stayed silent, not wanting to disrupt his happiness with the storm of emotions raging inside me. I loved Rafe. I even loved *El Diablo*, but to bring a child into his world was at best irresponsible. And at worst? Selfish. What kind of life could a child ever have with two murderers for parents?

"Oh God," I sobbed, crumpling in his arms as he supported my weight. "My family will think *this* is why I married you. They'll think it's because I was stupid and got knocked up. We can't tell them."

"You want to keep our child a secret from its grandparents?" Rafael asked, pulling back to stare down at my face. The clench to his jaw told me just how thoroughly I'd pissed him off with my demand, his eyes blazing with accusation as he didn't even try to consider how it felt to be eighteen and pregnant.

"Not forever," I explained quickly, tugging out of his grip and resuming my pacing in the bathroom. Rafael dropped the pregnancy test on the counter, his arms hanging by his sides with all the tension of a cobra about to strike. I swallowed back my fear, plowing forward even though I *knew* it was stupid. "Just until things settle."

"No," he said, his nostrils flaring in anger. "I will not hide the fact that my wife is pregnant. This should be a time of happiness, *mi reina*—"

"And it would have been, if you'd given me time like I asked!" I shouted, knowing in the deepest part of me that I would have found a way to cope with the reality of my life with the murderer. That I'd have come to terms with raising a child with him and even looked forward to it. But he'd taken that away from me.

Away from us.

I clutched my stomach as he prowled toward me, my fingers digging into the fabric of my nightgown as I sidestepped him and left the bathroom to go to the more spacious bedroom for the fight I knew was coming.

Dropping onto the bed, I hung my head in my hand while the other still held my stomach. As if touching it could make me bond with the child I wasn't ready for. "I'm not ready for this," I mumbled, looking up at Rafael's pained stare. The anger in his body was palpable, and while I wouldn't have said that anything in him was capable of feeling guilt for something he'd forced on me, there was a lingering sadness in his eyes.

Sadness that I didn't want the child he'd so desperately tried to make.

"We're monsters. I *killed* someone, and while his blood covered my hands, I was already pregnant," I said.

"We're nightmares who will protect our children no matter the cost," Rafael said, stepping closer to me. He placed a finger under my chin, tilting my head up to meet his eyes as he cupped my cheek in his hand. Darkness filled his eyes, all that possessive obsession that I'd thought we could overcome.

I'd given him everything. Caved to every demand he'd given, with very little resistance.

All because I loved him.

"I don't understand how it happened so quickly. Some couples try for years and never conceive," I whispered, watching the skin on his cheek twitch as he pursed his lips.

"You were given a fertility shot when you were unconscious," he said, holding my chin as I jolted back from his touch in shock.

My body seized, staring up at him and waiting for the moment when he would take it back. When he'd tell me it was a cruel joke. "What?" I whispered when it didn't come.

He clenched his jaw, not bothering to repeat the words he knew I'd heard loud and clear. He didn't take them back or apologize, only staring at me and watching me process from where I sat on the bed I shared with him.

The bed I'd shared with the man who'd proved time and time again that he would deceive and manipulate to get what he wanted, and never care what *I* wanted. "When I brought you to *El Infierno*, a doctor gave you a fertility shot.

It was the right time of your cycle to take effect before you ovulated."

I didn't even want to think about the amount of planning and forethought that had gone into tracking my cycle. To knowing *when* I would be ovulating.

"You did what?" I whispered again, shaking my head as I stared up at him. He sighed, reaching up a hand to cup my cheek as if it didn't matter. What difference did it make to Rafael when the end product was the same, regardless?

But it fucking mattered to *me*.

I slapped his hand away, watching as fury filled his eyes and he raised that hand again. When it came near me, I swatted him away more harshly, the slap of my hand against his skin echoing in the silence of the bedroom. "It was bad enough that you took away my choice, but this?" I asked, placing two hands on his stomach and shoving him back with all my might. He stumbled, his brow furrowing as I stood and moved away from the bed. I couldn't even look at it, couldn't think about sleeping in the same bed as him.

Maybe not ever again.

"What does it matter?" he asked, shaking his head as he followed me to the little sitting area next to the massive windows. I spun, panting as I glared at him. My lungs heaved with the need to make him feel every bit of the pain he'd given me.

The betrayal.

"I knew you were an asshole. I just didn't realize how much. At least telling me I wouldn't be on birth control was honest, but I guess you just aren't capable of telling the truth, are you?" I asked, hurrying past him to get downstairs. I was under no illusion that any of Rafael's men would intervene if he crossed a line, a fact that continued to drive a wedge between the brothers and me, but I couldn't stand to be in his bedroom any longer.

I couldn't stand to look at him.

He wrapped harsh fingers around my bicep, refusing to let me get to that door at the other side. He used it to hold me steady until he could wrap the other hand around the back of my neck and squeeze. I winced, a ragged groan leaving my lips as I stumbled and he guided me back to face him.

"When do the lies stop?" I whispered, trying to shove back the angry tears that made my eyes burn. The first stung as it dropped and trailed down my cheek, and Rafael's eyes narrowed in on it as his own breath caught.

His anger surged in response, whether it was hatred for himself or for me I didn't know. He used his hands on my body to maneuver me toward the bed, seeking the one place where I deferred to him in all things. Where his dominance was not only accepted but encouraged.

"No," I said, pushing back against his hand at my nape as I tried to get free. "I can't believe you did this. Will I ever be your equal?"

"Have I not given you everything you could possibly want?" he asked, his voice rising as I squirmed in his grip as we got closer to the bed. I stomped my heel on his foot, taking pleasure in his pained grunt. When he pushed me toward the bed and I fell onto the mattress, I spun to my back and panted as he stalked toward me.

"Do not fucking touch me," I warned. "I mean it, Rafael. *Do not touch me.*"

He froze, tilting his head to the side as that cruel smirk claimed his face. "If you would like to be my captive in truth, that can be arranged, *Princesa*," he said, his tone mocking. As if by fighting him on something so insignificant reduced me back to the naive girl who'd fallen in love with her phantom, no longer worthy of being his queen. "Say the fucking words, and I'll send you back to *El Infierno* where you can live out the rest of your days barefoot and pregnant and protected from all the realities of the life you clearly aren't capable of handling."

I swallowed back my fury, my face paling at the threat and the menace on his face that told me he would follow through. He would make me disappear again, and I'd go back to the island where freedom didn't exist and his will was law.

"You wouldn't dare," I challenged, flinching away from his touch on my thigh as he dropped a hand to trace the scar there.

"Try me, Isa. Did you think that I would become your lap dog just because I told you I love you? That you could wrap me around your finger and I'd suddenly be docile?"

"There is a difference between expecting you to be docile and expecting the decency of honesty," I hissed. "I can't be your *mi reina* if you're keeping secrets from me."

He pressed me to my back on the bed, sitting on the edge beside me and touching his hand to the spot where my stomach would swell soon enough. He trailed his hand over the swell of my breasts, my body freezing solid with fear of what would come.

He could take whatever he wanted. He might even be able to make me like it.

But I would hate him.

He leaned over me, touching his lips to mine in a soft mockery of the connection I'd thought we shared. When he retreated from my space, he shifted down to press a soft kiss to my stomach that would have been sweet under any other circumstances.

He had what he'd wanted, and I'd been stupid enough to make it so fucking easy.

"Consider what type of marriage you would like to have, Isa," he said, reaching up a hand to wipe away the tears staining my cheeks. There was no trace of the gentleness he'd shown my stomach as his hard eyes met mine. "You can be my pet and the mother of my children, or you can be *mi reina*. The choice is yours." He stood from the bed, his steps retreating from the room as he gave me the distance I'd so desperately wanted.

I pulled myself further into the bed, curling my knees to my chest and staring at the door as he slammed it closed behind him. A lock I hadn't even known existed clicked on the other side, drawing a strangled sob from me as I pressed my face into my knees and cried.

25

RAFAEL

I glanced down at my hands as I stretched them, the cuts across the tops of my knuckles flexing and cracking with the movement. Prowling toward the bedroom at the top of the stairs the morning after my argument with *mi reina*, I spun quickly when I realized the door was open and Isa was nowhere to be found.

I'd left her alone the entire day before, staying at the warehouse and choosing to beat Timofey to a pulp instead of returning home to the wife who didn't want me and could very easily make the choice for me to send her back to *El Infierno* where she would have peace from me for the time being.

Instead of saying something I may come to regret because of my inability to express my displeasure physically, I gave her the space I knew we both needed to prevent something unforgivable. I didn't regret the shot but fucking my pregnant wife while she cried had little appeal for me.

I wanted her to fight me, to claw her rage into my skin and claim she didn't want me as she came on my cock and proved that no matter what I did, she would still be mine.

I hurried down the steps to go in search of my wayward wife, my heart in my throat when I found the main space just as empty as it had been when I walked through the doors. "Isa!" I called, spinning and looking around the house as my fury and panic rose into my throat. Aaron stepped out from the kitchen, pointing toward the pool where Isa sat on one of the round cushions on the terrace.

Hugo was beside her, his arm wrapped around her as she cuddled into his side. His fingers rested against the tattoo on her forearm, so close to the brand that marked her as mine.

How quickly she'd sought comfort from another man in my absence rattled the nightmare inside me, feeling it claw its way up my throat as if it could devour Isa whole for the betrayal she gave in response to mine.

I tugged open the terrace doors as quietly as I could, stepping outside slowly so I wouldn't disrupt their private moment. Staying close to the house, I watched the side of Isa's face as she tugged her head away from Hugo's chest. The puffy, red eye and deep circle under it gave me pause, the physical signs of her sleepless night making something ache inside me.

I couldn't be the husband she deserved who soothed her stress and told her everything would be okay. Her life with me would be tumultuous, and I'd push her far more than I'd ever offer her comfort. Even if I was capable of being as gentle and caring with her as Hugo was, men like that quickly found themselves dead in my world when they were in positions of power. If I couldn't even control my wife, then I stood little to no chance of controlling my men or my enemies.

She could rebel. She could fight me. But in the end, Isa would obey me as her husband, even if I had to force her.

Our lives depended on it.

Isa's voice barely reached me when she spoke. "I don't know what I'm supposed to do now," she whispered, her bottom lip trembling as she looked at her friend. It said everything about how desperate she was for someone to talk to that she'd gone to him in the first place.

She might have tentatively forgiven Hugo for his betrayal, but their friendship was a far cry from what it had been before coming to Ibiza. She never sought him out, tolerating his presence as some of the only company she had available to her, but there was never a doubt in my mind that she'd embrace Regina as her main companion the moment we returned home.

"You have two choices. You can either ask Rafael to send you home to *El Infierno* out of spite so that he misses the pregnancy he risked your unhappiness to have, or you can stay here and make it work for the sake of the baby," Hugo said softly, rubbing a soothing hand over her upper arm. "I hate that those are the only choices you have, but..." he trailed off, letting the words hang in the air between them.

But...I would allow nothing else.

Isa touched her stomach, rubbing a soothing hand over what would become a baby bump, her maternal instincts taking over until her brain had time to catch up with it. "Is staying here really what's best for the baby though?" she asked, her voice hesitant as if it pained her to speak the words. "Being around Rafe, dealing with knowing that he'll *always* lie to me and keep secrets, that kind of stress can't be good for the baby. Maybe it's better if I go home and accept that it'll never be a real marriage."

"Do you love him?" Hugo asked, glancing toward where I lurked by the house. He knew I was listening, proceeding with the conversation as if he knew that I needed to hear

Isa's uninhibited thoughts when she thought I wasn't listening.

"Yes," she said, not even pausing before she gave her answer. Something in my chest loosened, knowing that with that love, we could find a way to work through all the obstacles between us. The secrets I kept couldn't be what tore us apart, not after everything that had transpired to bring us to this point in our lives. "That's *why* it hurts. If I didn't care about him, I wouldn't be surprised or hurt by the lies. But he made me believe that he wanted me to be more than just the wife waiting in his bed and the incubator for his heirs. He made me believe that he wanted me to be strong enough to stand beside him and go toe to toe with the devil."

Hugo sighed as if it pained him to have to say what would come next. "I think you're forgetting how different your relationship was when he brought you to *El Infierno*. He was furious with you, and you'd already tried to run from him. A child makes it harder for you to leave him."

"So... he just wanted to tie me to him? It was never about wanting the baby itself?" she asked, the whisper of her voice heartbreaking. For a child she claimed she wasn't ready for, the potential of me not wanting it seemed to strike her straight in the heart.

"I think Rafael is complicated and those answers can only come from him. I'm not privy to the inner workings of his fucked up head. I just think you're forgetting that he didn't give *mi reina* a fertility shot. He gave his *princesa* one. You were a different girl then, and so was your relationship," Hugo explained, tugging her into his chest once more and resting his chin against the top of her head. Only the feeling of their sibling-like relationship prevented me from ripping his body apart piece by piece, and even still it was tempting.

Isa wouldn't appreciate it.

"I don't know how to be a mother," Isa admitted, her voice an ache that reflected the fresh wounds of her relationship with her own.

"I think you'll be an incredible mother. Just give your child everything you wish your mom had given you. Be your grandmother, without the expectation of a legacy. Being Rafael's heir will put enough pressure on the kid, if he's a boy, at least. They'll just need you to support them and love them."

"You seem to forget I've babysat plenty. I know there's more to it than that," Isa said, a hoarse chuckle escaping her throat.

"Fair enough, but you'll have an entire village who would do anything to help you. You have Regina and the three of us. You'll be lucky if you get any time with the baby at this rate," he said with a laugh. Isa cast a hesitant glance over to where Joaquin watched the scene unfolding with amusement.

I just imagined her trying to picture Joaquin holding a baby in his arms. I somehow doubted it would happen as often as Hugo seemed to think.

"Love finds a way, Isa," Hugo said, shifting his weight so that Isa sat straight up once more. Her eyes came over to mine, shock expressive in her eyes. I wondered for a moment if she would be furious for the fact that Hugo had known I listened to their conversation, but shrugged it off as I moved away from the house and approached them.

Keeping my face neutral to try to prevent Isa from shutting down, I resisted the urge to make a scene out of Hugo's continued touch on my wife.

Only barely.

Isa turned her gaze away, shutting me out as instantly as if she'd slammed a door in my face. All the emotion she'd worn in her conversation with Hugo disappeared in a flash. Gone was the version of Isa that was open to having a reasonable conversation.

"I thought I'd made it clear she was to stay in the bedroom until I came back?" I asked, resisting the urge to wince at the gruff sound of my voice on the air and clenching my fists at my side as I approached the lounge. Isa's attempt to shut me out wouldn't end well for either of us.

"She spent the entire day in there yesterday waiting for you to show your face," Hugo snapped. His nostrils flared with anger as he dared to defy me and realized I would take his attempt to shepherd us into a truce and throw it in the garbage, if Isa continued with her stubborn shit. "You made your fucking point."

"What point was that exactly?" I asked, tilting my head to the side as I tried to shove down my anger. Spending time away from Isa was supposed to give her time for the sadness to fade and the anger to rise to the surface so we could work out our differences in the usual fashion.

With her bent over the closest surface and my cock deep inside her.

Isa spun toward me, glaring as her lips twisted into a snarl. "That you can and will do as you please. What else am I supposed to think when you lock me in a room and spend the night God knows where with fuck knows who?"

I chuckled, the dark tinge of my humor raising the hairs on even my arms as I stepped closer to the cushion. The fact that Isa could be so despondent, that she could claim to consider allowing me to send her back to the island where I wouldn't be a part of her daily life for the foreseeable future, and still feel possessive over me was a comforting warmth on my skin.

She could claim to hate my need to own her all she wanted, but the same dark desire pulsed through her veins.

I grabbed her chin, turning her face to mine fully and shifting her body further away from Hugo's. "*Mi reina* sounds jealous, and yet she is the one in the arms of another man."

She tore her face free from my grip, giving me the back of her head as if she could ignore her husband. "Go fuck yourself, Rafael. You know damn well it isn't like that," she said, wincing as I wrapped my palm around the front of her throat and pulled her head back with careful, even pressure. Hugo's arm tensed, his stare meeting mine as he restrained himself from interfering.

He was smart enough to know he treaded very thin ice as it was. Even if my wife wasn't so aware.

"Perhaps I should go fuck another woman," I said, bending her head back with pressure on her throat until she had no choice but to cave and peel away from the comfort of Hugo's arms. "Maybe if I showed you exactly what your life could be, you would appreciate that I have given you more."

"I would cut off your dick while you slept before I ever let you touch me again," she growled, earning a chuckle from me as the demon came out to dance with her devil.

"I've a feeling I would wake up the moment your delicate little hand touched my cock, *mi reina*, and then do you know where you would end up?" I asked, pulling her back further until she had to shift her knees out from underneath her body. I laid her out on the cushion, her breasts heaving as she fought against my grip on the sensitive front of her throat. "Impaled on the cock you thought to remove, and trying to convince yourself you didn't fucking want it."

She swallowed, hate in her eyes as I stared down at where she was laid out on the cushion. She looked like a feast, just waiting for me to devour her in the middle of the day. Her legs pressed together in an effort to keep from showing her ass to Hugo where he'd refused to move and watched my interaction with Isa with hatred in his eyes.

"Don't worry, she likes it when it hurts," I said, raising my eyes to meet his steady gaze as Isa gasped, and I felt the breath travel up her throat in the palm of my hand. "You're dismissed."

Hugo nodded, standing from the lounge despite his likely urge to stay and protect his friend. He knew as well as anyone that there was no one on this Earth who could protect Isa from me. Joaquin moved, following his brother as the rest of the guards cleared off the terrace.

"And Hugo?" I asked, gliding a hand up Isa's chin to touch my thumb to her lip. I dragged it to the side, staring at her teeth as I wondered how hard she would bite me if I dragged her to the edge of the bed and forced my cock between her lips. "I don't care what you mean to her, the next time you *touch* my wife, I will remove any part of you that has come in contact with her skin."

"Yes, *El Diablo*," he muttered, walking into the house with his older brother at his heels.

"I hate you," Isa growled, anger twisting the beautiful features of her face into a grimace that set my blood on fire. As much as I loved it when she was pleased with me and obedient, the moments like these where we pushed each other and tested the boundaries of our addiction to one another were some of my favorites.

She fed the nightmare with her fight and her fear, and I gave her the darkness that her soul craved.

"Do you think this tantrum will matter in the end?" I asked her, sliding my thumb between her lips. She bit it as I'd expected, thrilling me with the thought of her teeth gently scraping against my cock while I fucked her throat. "Do you think you'll ever be free of me? I *broke* you and reshaped you."

I grabbed her by the throat, using it to pull her to the edge of the lounge until her head hung off. She strained her neck to keep it from falling back, slapping my hand away when I reached to cup her breast where the angle made it threaten to spill out the neckline of her dress. "I own your soul. You will never be free, *mi reina*."

Unbuttoning and unzipping my pants, I pulled myself free. I rubbed the hard shaft of my cock against Isa's cheek, watching as she flinched away. "Don't touch me with your cock after you spent the night in someone else's bed."

"If I wanted another woman, I wouldn't be standing here with you. If I'd wanted other women, I would have fucked them before you were mine," I said. She glared up at me as I tilted her head back, rubbing my cock over the lips she refused to part. "Do I smell like another woman?"

"No, you just smell like a fucking prick," she said.

"Open your mouth like a good *Princesa,* and maybe I'll let you come when I'm done with you," I ordered, smacking my length against her cheek hard enough that she gasped. Stretching out one hand to flip up her dress, I slid a hand between her tightly pressed together thighs. Her pussy was as wet as I'd known it would be, ready to take me even when her brain tried to fight what her body knew.

It would be inevitable.

"You're going to fuck me either way, aren't you? Even if I tell you no," she said, staring the devil in the face as she waited for the words she needed. As much as Isa might rail against me and try to fight my control, she needed it as much as I did.

She thrived off of having her power stripped away.

Knowing I would only walk her to the edge of her limits, never quite shoving her off that cliff, and be there waiting to put back the pieces when she took that final leap on her own.

"Yes," I said, watching as that need to be possessed shone in her light eyes. She dropped her head back, opening her mouth so that I could slide inside. I thrust forward, not giving her any time to adjust to having her throat stuffed with my cock as I bumped into the back of her throat. She gagged around me, her throat tightening to protest the sudden invasion as my hands wrapped around the sides of her throat.

My thumbs rubbed over the sensitive front, feeling her try to swallow to accept me as I forced my way in and out of her mouth. Her throat swelled with breath when I pulled back, giving her time to breathe before driving into the wet heat of her mouth and bumping against the edge of her. The delicate skin of her throat called to me, the vulnerable part of her body something that the nightmare inside of me wanted to mark.

I wanted to mark every inch of her skin. I pulled out of her mouth suddenly, feeling her frenzied breaths against my balls as I drew back and stared at her flushed cheeks. She moved back onto the bed, resting her head at a more natural angle and staring at me as she waited for my next move. There was an odd sense of detachment in her face, a distance between us that I felt when she turned away from me and a heavy sigh came through her parted lips.

She waited, stripping away the only thing she could in the moments when I demanded her body. She deprived me of her eyes. Her mind. Her *heart*.

And that was something I would never tolerate.

26
ISA

We could call it love or we could call it a toxic obsession that thrummed through our veins. Whatever the words were, whatever label I tried to assign to what we were, nothing would change. Deep and embedded in my soul, I'd lost track of where Rafael started and I began, until he seared himself on my soul in a way that I would need to tear part of myself away to be free of him.

What we had wasn't healthy. It wasn't defined by the conventional rules that marriage needed to adhere to. Maybe it was Stockholm Syndrome, or maybe it was just that Rafael's darkness called to mine. That we were two sides of the same coin, meant to stand back to back and face the world as one.

That had been what I'd thought, at least. What I'd hoped was true in the moments when I'd abandoned the girl I'd pretended to be, for the entirety of my life.

Rafael's lies had unraveled everything I believed about our marriage—that on the other side of his initial deception, we'd found a way to have a true marriage built on honesty.

It was flawed and raw, but I'd at least thought he would do me the favor of not keeping secrets. What did he stand to lose from being honest, when I couldn't ever leave him?

Rafael moved around the lounge, kneeling on the edge of the cushion at my feet. His rough hands touched the sole of my right foot, gripping it firmly and running his thumb over the arch in a steady pressure. The feeling traveled up the muscle of my calves, forcing me to relax muscles I hadn't even known I clenched. He lifted my foot, touching his lips to my shin and dragging them up the bone softly.

I swallowed, stifling back the moan that threatened at my throat.

The Rafe I'd fallen in love with in Ibiza had been gentle as often as he'd been rough, tempering the intensity of his physical ownership of my body with sweet touches and gentle teasing. I'd thought him lost to the devil I'd married —the lover who'd been my introduction to the sins of the flesh a thing of the past that had only ever been a figment of my imagination.

His fingers gripped me around the back of my knee, pressing into the sensitive point there so very gently as those sinful lips trailed over my skin and brought goosebumps to the surface. He made his way up my thigh, pressing easy kisses to my flesh as he worked to pull me back from the place where I tried to shut him out. *"Mi reina,"* he murmured, the warmth of his breath blowing against my panties as he eased my legs apart.

My heart thumped in my chest as he touched his lips to the fabric, giving only the slightest teasing pressure where I needed it. My hips rose to seek more contact, my eyes clenching shut to try to ignore the sensations I knew he would wring from my body.

Rough fingers touched the straps of my underwear,

tugging them down my thighs and off the legs that he raised to hook over his broad shoulders. Spreading them once they were free from their confines, he shifted his weight and settled between my legs.

His mouth sealed over my pussy, a warm balm as he gently explored the outer part of me with his lips and tongue. When his fingers finally moved to spread me and his tongue slid inside me, I turned my stare down to the beautiful devil worshiping my body.

He consumed me slowly, tormenting me with each press of his tongue as he slid a finger inside me and pumped leisurely. As if he had all the time in the world to remind me exactly what our marriage could be if I stopped fighting.

If I let him have the control he so desperately needed.

"Tell me you love me," he murmured against my flesh. The demand traveled through my body, drawing a shiver from me as those wicked lips wrapped around my clit and sucked softly. My thighs clenched around his head, my ankles crossing over his shoulders and pulling him closer in my desperation for everything I needed.

"Rafe," I begged, tears stinging my eyes as I realized that he'd used my body to bring me back. To prove that the man I loved beneath the monster still lived inside him, and that our lives could be both addictive and full of love.

That he could be both terrifying and gentle.

He nipped my clit in warning, a gentle reprimand that he still waited for the words he wanted to hear. I thrust my hands between my legs, gripping the soft strands of his dark hair with harsh fingers and pulling him tighter. Humming against me, he kept me just at the brink of my orgasm. "Tell me," he murmured.

"I love you," I sighed, the knowledge that he already understood that what I felt for him wouldn't just disappear with a lie easing the sting of my submission. I wanted his honesty, and I'd find a way to prove that.

Another day, when his mouth wasn't working me to a frenzy between my legs and the sight of all that muscle and his beautiful face between my legs didn't threaten to drive me to the edge of my limits. For that moment, I'd take what he gave.

He sent me spiraling over the edge, hooking his finger inside me to stroke my g-spot at the same moment that he intensified the press of his tongue against me. He moved his finger inside me rhythmically, his mouth sinful as it worked me through my orgasm that I bit my lip to keep from crying out for all the guards to hear.

His mouth trailed up over the fabric of my dress, his fingers continuing to pump inside me gently as he touched his lips to mine and swallowed my heaving breaths for himself. He slid his fingers out and guided his length to my entrance, pushing inside me slowly with gentle thrusts as my flesh quivered around him.

"*Te amo tal cual eres,*" he murmured, his lips brushing against mine as the words slipped free. "I love you just the way you are." I felt the words against my skin, warming me from the outside as the meaning of them sank into me. I wrapped my arms around him as he gripped the back of my thighs, guiding my legs to surround his hips. Holding him to me, he took me in slow but hard drives of his cock inside me.

His eyes held mine, love swimming in his gaze as he stared down at me with all the intensity of his obsession. I felt every inch of him as he slid through the flesh swollen from my orgasm, his breath mingling with mine as he made love to me for what felt like an eternity.

There was nothing and no one around but the warmth

of him surrounding me, the comfortable feeling of his weight on mine, until he finished inside me, sending me into a second, rolling orgasm that made me long for the sleep I'd missed the night before.

Only then did he take me inside and hold me as I drifted to sleep, knowing that the secret would need to be dealt with still, but needing the peace of a dreamless rest before I could function.

27

RAFAEL

"I don't regret the fertility shot," I said, rubbing a washcloth over the healing wounds on Isa's neck and shoulder in the shower the next morning.

She flinched, leveling me with a glare that was so unlike the languidness of her body following the emotional overload of the few days she'd had, and what I suspected was the very beginning of pregnancy tiredness. "Next time?" she hissed.

"I can't promise there won't be a next time. I can't promise that I won't do anything and everything to keep you mine." I slid my hand down to her stomach, stroking the skin there as water ran over my skin. "I can tell you that I love knowing you're pregnant. That I can't wait for your stomach to swell and for us to get to see the baby for the first time. I don't think that will go away after the first baby."

She swallowed, biting her bottom lip as I softened my face away from the harshness that I felt. The need to punish her for her distance, to show her how it enraged me to know she didn't feel the same joy I did, threatened to consume me in ways that I didn't think I'd ever be able to control.

I needed her to want me. To love me, and be as consumed by our love as I was.

Not wanting my child was a step past my limits.

"I don't *not* want children," she said, her voice quiet as she looked down at my hand on her stomach. "I'd even started to accept that it would happen sooner than I was ready, but what you did—"

"Changed nothing in the end. You'd have been pregnant regardless."

"It wasn't the *what*. It's the *how*. You kept it a secret. I don't agree with the choices you make for me a lot of the time, but I thought I could at least say you were honest. Unapologetic and unremorseful, but honest. Now I have to question everything, because I don't feel like I can trust anything you say or *don't* say. What else are you keeping from me just because it's more convenient for you?" she asked, covering my hand on her stomach with hers.

I dropped the cloth to the shower shelf, tracing my fingers over her forearm and to the skin above her elbow. "Trackers. Here," I said, touching the small lump that Isa never would have noticed on her own. I moved my hand to the space between her shoulder blades, touching the area where the other one was implanted inside her. "And here."

"Trackers? Like, *inside me?*" she whispered, her brow furrowing as she grasped her elbow and felt the lump beneath her skin. "In case I escaped," she breathed, nodding as if she understood even as it pained her.

"And for your protection. In case it ever came to a point where you were in danger, I could find you quickly and efficiently. I wasn't willing to wait for you to be with me in a way that you'd allow it. So we did it while you were unconscious," I explained, watching her face for sign of the anger that had come from the fertility shot.

It never followed, her face remaining relatively peaceful and understanding. The lines we drew in the sand weren't always consistent, and there was no logical explanation to what bothered her more than the other things I'd done.

It was all part of what made her, *her*, but I still didn't care for the detached look on her face as she considered it. I had a feeling it would take time for Isa to get over what she saw as a violation of her trust.

The time before taking her to *El Infierno* didn't count. She'd forgiven those transgressions and accepted that there had been a shift in our relationship after she'd learned the truth of them. Knowing that I would continue to keep secrets to protect her and to guide us where we needed to go, I didn't bother to lie and tell her there were no other secrets.

Isa didn't ask, as if she could sense that what loomed on the horizon was bigger. That she was somehow not ready to deal with the knowledge that would come from it.

"Did you do anything else to me while I was unconscious?" she asked instead, narrowing her eyes on my face and studying me for something. As if she'd be able to feel the lie in my words if I wasn't honest.

I chuckled, picking up the cloth and placing it in her hands and guiding her to the wounds on my chest. Whereas hers were healing quickly, the deeper marks in my skin would take far longer to close until they scarred permanently.

My love for Isa would never die, consuming every part of me until my body burned in the pyre. Her mark on my skin lasting that long only seemed fitting.

"I licked my pussy to make sure you had sweet dreams of me," I said when she pressed the cloth into my wounds. I welcomed the subtle hint of pain and the reminder of what I'd done to her, even knowing that hers were shallower.

I'd just have to do it all over again when they began to fade.

"I already knew that," she said, giving me her eyes briefly before turning her attention back to my self-inflicted wounds.

"I waited until you woke up to fuck you," I offered, my voice laced with the smile that claimed my face.

"How restrained of you," she said, rolling her eyes to dismiss the kindness it had been. I didn't tell her how much I'd contemplated sinking inside her while she dreamed.

Once the soap rinsed off my skin, she leaned forward and touched her lips to her name. The kiss was hesitant, as if she couldn't quite wrap her head around the fact that she liked seeing it there.

As much as she might want to condemn me for what I'd done, she liked seeing it on me. Her fingers drifted up to touch her own healing wounds, my name stark against her fawn skin. "How am I supposed to explain this to my family? I can't keep it hidden forever."

"So don't." I shrugged. "I don't particularly care what you tell them to explain it," I said, bending over her to run my tongue over my name. She shuddered as the pain ran through her, and I hoped that every time I touched it she would remember the way it felt when I'd dragged my tongue through her bloodied flesh as I fucked her.

"There is no way they don't look at this and see it as abuse. It *is* abuse," she said, heaving out a sigh. "How am I supposed to convince them that I'm with you by choice? When I can't even make sense of it myself, given the things you've done."

"Don't convince them. You tried and that didn't work. I

think it's time they see the truth of our marriage for what it is. Maybe, if nothing else, that will make them understand how futile it is to try to appeal to you and make you see that you should leave me. I'd much rather they hate me than hate you, because I don't give the first fuck what they think of me," I explained. "Let them think you're a victim of my obsession. It isn't untrue."

"I don't want them to hate you," she murmured, and something inside me warmed that she cared what her family thought of me. Even after everything I'd put her through and what I would undoubtedly keep putting her through in the interest of keeping her safe and keeping her mine, she still cared.

"They're going to hate me no matter what you do," I said, kissing the nape of her neck behind my name. "Just let them, *mi reina*. You can't control what other people do. Only how much energy you put into fighting it."

She nodded, accepting the truth to my words. We'd both seen just how furious her mother was for the change in Isa's personality and for the involvement that she had with me at all.

Once they knew about the baby and the truth of the kind of man I was, there would be no point in fighting my claim on their daughter.

28

ISA

A miracle had happened. My family sat at the dining room table, polishing off dessert after making it through an entire meal. It was relatively peaceful, a calm before the coming storm as we spoke about little things and nothing of importance regarding my life with Rafe.

My grandmother smiled as she spoke of the kids at the Center, of the difficulties that came with trying to teach a culture that was rooted in nature, in the center of the city. The familiar cadence of her voice as she spoke about her life's passion was a comfort, a subtle reassurance that maybe we could find our way toward some semblance of normal.

My stomach turned as I picked at the cinnamon rolls I'd made for them, the smell overpowering despite the way my family dug into them. They'd long since been a favorite in our home.

I'd have to make sure my mother knew the recipe.

Rafe eyed my plate, satisfaction in his eyes as he settled on my barely touched, picked-at cinnamon rolls. He'd taken far too much enjoyment out of watching me nearly gag while they were baking, his hands continually drifting to wrap around my stomach as if he wanted to tell the baby he was proud of it for making me sick.

Him? Her? I didn't even know what to call the baby growing in my stomach, and 'it' felt so wrong.

"We did have a reason for inviting you here again so soon," Rafe said, grasping my hand in his and tugging it up to kiss the back of it. Even knowing that this had been the purpose of the evening, the *only* reason we'd asked them to come back so soon after the way the last dinner had ended, I wasn't ready.

I bit my bottom lip, wordlessly compelling Rafe to understand that we should wait. That we should let the evening finish without any drama and tell them later, maybe after we had an ultrasound photo to share. Wasn't the first trimester risky?

Hopefully we'd be home by the end of the first trimester and I wouldn't have to see the disappointment in my mother's eyes that her well-behaved daughter was pregnant at eighteen. Husband be damned, *that* was not something that any mother wanted for her daughter.

"Isa is pregnant," he said, not taking pity on me for the dread making my heart stall in my chest. I shouldn't have been surprised. He was never willing to wait for me to catch up to the speed that he plowed forward at.

My mother dropped her gaze down toward my stomach even though the table blocked her view, her eyes accusing as she glared at it. "Well I guess that explains the shotgun wedding," she said, the disappointment in her voice evident.

"We just found out a couple of days ago, actually," I said, forcing a smile to my face. I couldn't even blame her for the assumption that it had been an accident and I'd done something stupid. What eighteen-year-old got pregnant on purpose?

One who was married to a ridiculously impatient Rafael Ibarra, apparently.

"We're both very happy, and I know it would mean the world to Isa if you were supportive of this next phase in her life," Rafe said, staring down my mother with a warning gleaming in his eyes.

"She doesn't look very happy," Odina muttered, her first words since they'd brought her to dinner. I'd notified them she could come, but if she wasn't on her best behavior she wouldn't be permitted on the property in the future.

That had been a fun conversation, but I hadn't expected her to show up. Odina had more important things to do than spend the evening with the sister she wanted dead.

My father nudged her with his elbow, making her quiet immediately as I turned a beaming smile toward her. "My happiness and yours don't look the same. Probably because I can be happy when I'm sober," I said, smiling sweetly and sipping my water. Odina raised her glass of wine, downing the rest of it pointedly.

"Of course we'll be supportive if this is truly what you want, Isa," my father said, smiling toward my grandmother. She nodded her agreement, even though I could see the traces of pain evident on her face. Rafael was nothing like the man she'd wanted for me, a betrayal of our culture on my part that I'd chosen someone so vastly different from her beliefs.

But love was love, even if in my case it shouldn't have been.

"Of course," I said, dropping my hand to my stomach and cradling it. I may not have chosen it, but that didn't mean I wouldn't whole heartedly love my baby when it came. "I wouldn't change it." Rafe's hand squeezed mine, his hand tightening as he studied my profile. I turned to him, watching him search my face for the lie in the words.

I couldn't explain how quickly the feeling of responsibility for the baby had taken over. How attached I'd grown, talking to my stomach in the hours he'd left me locked in our bedroom alone. No matter how it had come to be, or how horrible the timing was, the child was a part of both of us.

I had to hope for the best parts, and not the darker impulses that consumed both of us.

"Well, you'll have to teach her all the ways of our people," my grandmother said, tears stinging her eyes as she took my free hand in hers from across the table.

"You will teach her yourself, *nōhkomach*," I said, biting my bottom lip and suppressing the smile that tugged at my lips. Of course the matriarch of my family would assume her great-grandchild to be a girl, even before the first time we heard the heartbeat.

"I hope so," she said, nodding her head in agreement as she pulled her hand back and used her napkin to dab at her eyes.

My father cleared his throat, pushing out his chair and looking awkward as emotion clogged his throat. "I'm happy if you're happy, but I would like a word with your husband," he said, turning his eyes to Rafael.

Rafe smiled, deceptively calm as he glided to his feet. The reassurance of my father's acknowledgement of him as my husband probably went a long way toward convincing him that he could walk into the conversation without being prepared for war. "Of course," Rafe said, kissing me on the forehead and walking toward the hallway where his office was located. They disappeared around the corner, cut off from view as I tried not to focus on whatever my father might have to say and what it could mean for the bloom of promise I felt in their acceptance of the baby.

"Have you thought about names?" my mother asked, pursing her lips as she sipped her wine.

I laughed. "We just found out two days ago, so we haven't talked about it yet. If it's a girl, I'd like to name her Daniela after Rafe's mother," I said, smiling lightly. The name felt right, settling over me like the whisper of a caress. A tingle that I felt down to my toes, as if she was watching out for him. I had to hope she approved of me if she was.

"And a boy?" my grandmother asked.

"Something to do with the stars," I said, glancing toward the hallway where Rafe was with my father. "If I can find something we agree on anyway."

"Why the stars?" Odina asked, her stare incredulous as she tried to shake me.

"When we were in Ibiza, Rafe told me the story of how he and his mother used to lie out and try to count the stars. He knew it was pointless and a waste of his time in his father's eyes, but those are some of his most vivid memories with her." I left off the part where he'd counted my freckles, the knowledge of it feeling too personal.

I'd have throttled Odina when she tried to make a joke of it or mocked how sickeningly sweet it was.

"Who would have thought him capable of sharing such a sweet memory," my mother said, chewing the corner of her mouth.

"He's a man like any other, Mom. He's complicated and there are lots of different versions of him that you'll only ever get to know if you give him time and accept him." I swallowed back the surge of love that consumed me in the wake of my words, even as the marks on my neck that were visible for the first time twinged with phantom pain. My grandmother's eyes landed on them for what felt like the hundredth time that night, but she didn't say anything about them.

Just as she'd kept quiet about the tattoo and the brand, she chose not to judge me for what I let Rafe do to my body. Her questions would come, but her relationship with me was trusting enough that she would give me the benefit of the doubt and ask when the watchful eyes of my mom and sister weren't on us and studying our every move.

"I'm going to go check on them," I said, standing and making my way toward the hallway. I knew as soon as I rounded the corner that Rafe had left the office door open, probably to reassure the rest of my family that he wasn't stealing my father's soul while he had him to himself.

"She's my baby girl," my father said, his voice catching on the emotion of the words. "I just want to protect her. You're about to become a father, so I truly hope you can understand that."

"Of course I do. I would never hurt Isa. I know some of what you've heard of me and our relationship has given you pause, but I love your daughter," Rafe admitted, and there was a pause as he let those words sink in.

"Just please don't hurt her. I've seen the tattoo and the burn, your name on her neck. The signs are all there and plain to see. I am begging you not to hurt my girl any more than you already have." My heart ached with the strangled sob in my father's throat, with the emotion I felt knowing that I would do the same for my daughter.

I'd go one step farther and kill anyone who threatened her, but how could my father expect to kill Rafael Ibarra?

"The marks you've seen on your daughter are a part of our relationship. I assure you, I wear her marks on my skin. One for every time I've marked her," Rafe returned. I swallowed back my tears, moving back to the main space and rejoining the three women of my family. Leaving the men to have their discussion in privacy once I was satisfied that Rafe was handling my father with about as much tact as I could expect of him.

He handled my father with care, and my heart swelled to hear it despite the ominous words he'd spoken about not caring if they liked him.

Maybe, just maybe, there was a chance we could find a way for them to be a part of our lives.

29

RAFAEL

I handed Isa's father the crystal tumbler filled with scotch, his grimace falling on the marks on my chest with my shirt hanging open. My name on Isa's skin was smaller, much more localized despite the length of my name.

Hers took up the majority of my chest, the wounds angry and red as they healed. He tossed back the scotch quickly as I took a sip of my own and set it on the desk. Leaning my ass onto the surface, I watched as he stood from his seat.

"I don't think I want to know anything about your relationship with my daughter," he said, swallowing back the nausea I was sure he felt at seeing her name carved into my chest.

"Probably not," I admitted with a smirk. I'd damn well kill anyone who went near my daughter eventually one day, so I liked to think I had an inkling of understanding about burying his head in the sand to deny the things he couldn't stop. "I won't tolerate people coming between us, but if you want to have a place in our life, I won't stop you. So long as you accept her place in mine and what she means to me."

He nodded, moving toward the door. "And you swear to me that you won't hurt her?"

"I swear to you that I won't hurt her in a way that the entire purpose is to cause her pain. There will be things in our relationship that she doesn't agree with and choices I take away from her, but I do it with her best interest in mind and to enable her to better survive in my world." I took another sip of my scotch as he left the office without another word, wondering how I'd ended up catering to Isa's father. I much preferred when we were home on *El Infierno* and I didn't feel obligated to explain myself to anyone.

The answers we needed couldn't come soon enough.

I finished my drink, setting the glass on the desk one final time and sighing before I worked myself up to facing the negativity of her mother and sister. Something would need to be done to bring her mom to heel for Isa's sake.

I just didn't know what, given that Isa would castrate me if I dealt with her in the way I typically handled the people that annoyed me.

A soft feminine knock came on the door, making me snap my head to face it as Odina stepped into the space and leaned her weight into the door she closed behind her. Her eyes tracked up from my feet, trailing over my black slacks and to the defined muscles of my abs. Given our previous encounter had ended with my hand around her throat, my only hesitation in killing her being her parents in the other room, she was either incredibly stupid or unreasonably fearless.

Probably both.

Her gaze caught on her sister's name etched into my skin, a scowl twisting her lips that were identical to my wife's. "That's a shame," she muttered, raising her eyes to meet mine as she took a few steps closer. She stayed a few feet away, replacing her scowl with a cruel smirk that I recognized all too well from what I saw in the mirror before I hurt someone I hated.

"What do you want, Odina?" I asked, my face shutting down to complete and utter boredom. How someone could look nearly identical to *mi reina* and still be nothing to me blew me away. Not even the trace of an emotion tugged at my chest, seeing the hatred on her face and knowing the place of pain that it came from.

"If you wanted to hurt her, you should have just cut her throat. Well, a little deeper anyway," she said, stepping forward until she was only a foot away. She reached around me, pouring scotch into the tumbler I'd emptied and helping herself to the liquid. I'd already thought it odd that her parents allowed her to drink in their presence considering that the twins were only eighteen and illegal in the United States, but I supposed they'd long since given up on keeping Odina sober.

Alcohol was the least of her addictions, and from what I'd seen in my time watching Isa, Odina was far more tolerable to be around when she was plied with booze.

"I don't have any interest in hurting my wife," I growled, reaching for the bottom of my shirt and tugging the two halves together. I buttoned it slowly, not making any sudden movements out of a desire to keep Odina from pushing the limits with me once again.

I wouldn't hesitate to strangle her again, but without Isa to stop me I couldn't promise that I *would* stop. There was no denying that Isa's life would be far simpler without her sister in it. She would have been better off if Odina had died that day in the river, and I didn't care what it said about me that I was willing to admit it.

"Hugo promised me you would hurt her," she said, stepping closer and touching the second button on my shirt as I fastened it. I pushed her hand away, quirking a brow at her to try to tell her just how foolish it would be to touch what wasn't hers. "I didn't say anything that night or when Wayne mysteriously turned up dead. I kept your dirty little secret because I wanted her to suffer. Tell me, how is she fucking suffering?" she asked, glancing around the lavish office and glaring at the books as if they represented the worst crimes of humanity.

Because they'd been given to Isa.

"You can't make her hurt just because you do," I said, dismissing her and moving to step past her for the doors.

She caught my arm in her grip, her nails digging into the skin. "You know *nothing* about me and my pain. She deserves to rot for what she took from me."

"And what was that exactly? Your humanity?" I asked, tearing my arm out of her grip. "You are nothing but a spiteful cunt. You can't handle that your sister has everything you could ever want, because you know you don't matter to anyone."

"Please. You think the husband with the nice house and the pretty clothes matters to me? I've seen the pitch black *nothing* that comes when you die. I have felt the burning in my lungs while I watched my mother choose her. All that matters to me is making that go away and forgetting that every day I am one step away from going back into the black pit of death," she said, her voice dropping to a gentle murmur.

I felt a moment of compassion, imagining what that black must have been like, but it didn't explain the witch she'd become when she could have made the choice to live her life differently. The compassion wasn't for the woman standing in front of me, but for the sister that had shouldered her hatred all her life and tried to make amends for something she hadn't done intentionally in the first place. "What exactly does that have to do with Isa?"

"Seeing her hurt makes me feel better," she said, her lips curving into a smile as she darted forward and touched her lips to my chest, directly above Isa's name. I grabbed her head in my hands, shoving her off of me until she stumbled backward with a chuckle. "Oops," she said, her voice mocking as she cast her eyes toward the doorway.

Where Isa stood, watching with her arms hanging limply at her side. Those hands curled into fists, her jaw clenching as she twisted her mouth into a grimace.

She couldn't possibly think—

Her eyes dropped to my still partially unbuttoned shirt, glaring at the smeared lipstick Odina had left on my chest. I grabbed a tissue off the desk, using it to clean the red stain from my skin as I leveled Odina with a hard glare. "*That* was very fucking stupid."

"I agree," Odina said. "Risking your happy marriage when your wife is pregnant is the epitome of a low point. I can't imagine what Isa must feel knowing that her husband would fuck her sister."

"Get out," Isa said, her voice quiet and deadly. If Odina had been the slightest bit smarter, she would have run from the room at the empty stare Isa turned her way.

Instead, she dug her heels in stubbornly and tried to stick to the story she'd concocted in a pathetic attempt to hurt Isa. "What? You thought you were special?" she asked, huffing a laugh. "I'm you, Isa. Just more fun. A man like *Rafael* knows that I will give him things you would never even think exist." My name was a dramatic purr on her lips, and I clenched my teeth together to allow Isa to determine how the rest of the evening went.

If she gave me the word, I would slit her sister's throat for touching what belonged to *mi reina*.

"I said get the fuck out," Isa growled, the first hint of malice leaking out of her vivid eyes. They seemed to glow with the rage burning inside them, and she took a single step toward her sister. My body hummed in response, feeling the pure rage in the motion as she tilted her head and Odina took a step back. "Do not make me say it again."

Odina paused, watching her sister for a moment before she laughed uncomfortably and threw up her hands. "Fine. Stay with the asshole that would fuck anything that bent over for him." She retreated from the office, leaving me staring at the back of Isa's head as her back heaved with the deep breaths she drew into her lungs.

"Would you like to explain to me what you're doing in a room alone with my sister, with your shirt open?" she asked, a cool detachment in her voice as she spun to stare at me with those rage-filled eyes looking too big on her pale, empty face.

"Your father was worried about my name on your neck. I showed him your name on my chest," I said, watching her as she stepped toward me like a caged animal.

"You expect me to believe that? When I walked in and found her lips on you?"

"Yes, I expect you to trust that I would never fuck your goddamn sister, *mi reina*. What use would I have of her when I have you?" I asked, reaching out a hand to touch her cheek. She slapped it away, her glare intensifying as her cheek twitched.

"You wouldn't be the first boyfriend to screw my sister," she said, moving further into the room and staring up at the ceiling.

"I'm not your fucking boyfriend," I reminded her, my

anger rising in response to her lack of trust and the dismissal of me as her husband.

"You're right. You're my husband, and that makes this even worse," she said. A trace of the emotion lying beneath her anger slipped free, making her shake her head as she hung her head and her old insecurities surfaced. She glared at the exposed skin of my chest, her eyes lifting to my face as she searched for other places where her sister's lips might have touched me.

I'd never have allowed even the first touch if I'd been prepared for her to do something so ridiculously stupid.

"*Mi reina*," I said, dropping my voice low to the command that she responded to so thoroughly. Her skin pebbled with goosebumps, but she shook her head to reject it.

"I can't do this right now," she said, shaking her head again and slipping out the door to the office. Short of physically restraining her, she gave me no opportunity to stop her. I could have forced it, but if it came to that I wanted to do it after her family was the fuck out of my house.

Yelling came from the main room as I trailed behind her a moment later, picking up my pace and hurrying to find the source. "He tried to force himself on me!" Odina yelled, pointing her finger in my direction as I stepped into the room.

I huffed a laugh, crossing my arms over my chest. "Why would I want you when I have the better version of you in my bed every night?" Isa spun to gasp at me, her glare settling on my face.

I supposed talking about her in my bed with her family in the room was slightly inappropriate. I'd give her that.

"He forced himself on you?" Isa asked, cocking her hip to the side as her head tilted.

"Yes. Is that so hard to believe? Look at what he's done to you! I can't imagine you were willing for that!" Odina said, touching a hand to her own neck as she swallowed like she couldn't stomach the thought of my blade carving through her flesh.

She'd be dead by the time I finished with her.

Isa hung her head forward, her chest spasming as laughter bubbled up her throat. "God, you almost had me." Odina furrowed her brow at her sister as the rest of their family watched in confusion. "If you hadn't made up the ridiculous lie about him attempting to rape you, I would have believed your bullshit. So fucking stupid to believe anything where you're involved."

"What are you talking about?" her grandmother asked, settling Odina with a glare and turning patient eyes to Isa.

"When I walked into the office, Odina had her lips on him. Does that sound like a rape attempt to you?" Isa's grandmother's jaw clenched, her glare hardening on her other granddaughter in fury.

Isa turned her eyes to where her mother held Odina close despite the condemning evidence that Odina was lying, and I knew before her mother spoke who she would believe. "You would lie for him. You've made it very clear that he's more important to you than your sister," her mother said, her gaze softening as she turned her attention down to Odina.

Isa's breath left her in a rush, the shock of that betrayal hitting her straight in the chest. She'd always perceived herself to be her mother's favorite, the well-behaved child who she could control and who did as she was told, even if she didn't realize that was exactly why she preferred her. "One of these days, you'll remember why she's not worth your defense," Isa said, turning her back on her mother. She hugged her grandmother and her father where he watched the drama unfold. I didn't doubt that the two of them believed Isa's story of what she'd seen; they weren't blinded to Odina's toxicity in the same way Leonora was. "Don't come back until you see her for what she is. I have no place for either you or Odina in my child's life."

Isa went for the stairs, retreating up them and leaving her mother gaping after her. "I believe that means the two of you can kindly get the fuck out," I growled, my lips twisting into a snarl as I locked eyes with Odina. "There's a special place in Hell for men who rape women, but there's a spot right next to them for the women who accuse innocent men of the same crime. Believe me when I say, I know a thing or two about the Hell that's waiting for you if you don't stay the fuck away from my wife."

Leonora guided her out the door, her father nodding to me hesitantly as if to say he would try to talk some sense into his wife.

I just worried it would be too little, too late for *mi reina*.

30

ISA

The front door closed.

Even though he moved silently, I felt the moment Rafe stepped into the bedroom. "You thought I touched her," he said, his voice gentle as he came up behind me. I spun, refusing to let his hands touch me in the wake of knowing my sister's mouth had been on his skin.

"You need to shower," I said, storming away and into the bathroom. I turned the shower to hot, determined to watch him boil alive to wipe the stain of her touch from his skin. He walked into the bathroom, smirking arrogantly when I raised my hands and tore his shirt open with a brutality that felt foreign to me. Buttons popped free from the fabric, scattering through the bathroom as they pinged off the other surfaces.

I shoved the fabric down his arms, wincing when his hands came to rest against my cheeks. "Isa," he said, tilting my head up until I looked him in the eyes.

"Please," I whispered, dropping my hands to his belt when he didn't move to take off the shirt. He sighed, stripping it off finally as I shoved his pants down his legs. He stepped out of them and his boxers, kicking the shoes off his feet and moving into the shower without me needing to ask. I followed, uncaring about the water splashing against the front of my dress as I picked up his loofa and squirted shower gel onto it. Rubbing it over his chest frantically, I removed all traces of Odina's touch from his skin.

He took it from me, stilling my hand when he lost his patience with my scrubbing against the raw flesh of his wounds. My hand trembled in his, my eyes turning up to face him. "It's okay," he murmured, leaning forward to touch his lips to mine.

Shuddering against him, I touched a hand to his chest tentatively. Waiting for the slimy feeling of what Odina had done to cover my skin. For the questions to come about whether Rafe had encouraged it.

But they didn't. I seemingly couldn't trust him not to keep secrets from me. But after my rage had faded from the shock of seeing Odina's lips on his skin, I knew without a shred of doubt that I could trust him not to touch another woman. Even when the wounds she'd caused in our lives before Rafe threatened to make me lose grasp of everything between us, somehow Rafe's dedication came through.

He slid a hand beneath the curtain of my hair as the water drenched it, turning me until my back pressed against the wall. The sharp curves of his muscles pressed into my breasts, my name on his skin so close to my face as he leveled me with a stare so potent with need that the breath caught in my lungs.

He took my hand in his, guiding it to touch the wounds that I'd turned an angry red with my frantic scrubbing. Blood dotted the places where I'd rubbed away the healing flesh, turning the drops of water pink as they dripped down his chest.

The intention behind the contact was clear. He'd done everything in his power to tell me he was mine as much as I was his. The thought of my sister's touch on my name on his skin made bile threaten my throat, an inability to process the severe, inescapable possession that flooded through me.

I knew without a doubt that I would kill her the next time she tried to touch him. What bothered me was that I wasn't sure the realization worried me. It should have made me question everything I'd become.

"Eres la única estrella en mi cielo," he murmured, dragging my finger to trace the name on his flesh.

A chuckle fought its way up my throat. After all this time, he still spoke Spanish like I could understand a word of it. I'd need to remedy that soon enough. "I don't know what that means."

"You're the only star in my sky, *mi reina*. How could I want another woman when all I see is you?" he asked. I touched my forehead to his chest, inhaling the clean scent of him deeply into my lungs and holding him there until I relaxed. "If it helps, I would have killed her should the roles be reversed. You're still less murderous than me."

"I don't think that's as big a compliment as you think it is," I whispered, tipping my head back. With his hand tangled in my hair, he leaned forward and touched his lips to mine. He kept his eyes on mine for the soft press of his mouth, a whisper of the things that would come shortly enough.

He pulled away, dragging the sleeves of my dress down my arms one by one as he waited for me to stop him. The darkness in him swirled beneath the surface, tucked away safely for the moment as if he could sense that the nightmare wasn't what I needed then.

I needed Rafe, the lover who had shown me the wonders

of life in Ibiza. Rafael could wait until the morning, consuming me with his darkness when I wasn't soft and pliant in his arms but a queen ready to fight.

I was so tired of fighting, of being at war with my sister and my family while the battle between us continued on.

My dress fell to my feet in a wet mess, and I kicked it away. Reaching up trembling hands to unclasp my bra, I shoved it down my arms and tossed it to the side of the huge rainshower as Rafe guided my panties down my thighs. They joined the rest of my clothes, the movements between us slow and unhurried as he moved us toward the corner of the shower. His lips pressed to mine again, a skillful seduction of his mouth as he guided me to open for him. The taste of him overwhelmed me, the smokiness of his scotch a bite against my senses.

He invaded me, claiming my mouth for himself. I'd never have enough of his delicate possession, just as I'd never have enough of his darkness. My world would stop turning without him in it.

I moaned into his mouth as I wrapped my hands around his shoulders and pulled him tighter to me. He rewarded me by deepening our kiss, pressing me tighter into the wall as his strangled groan rattled against my mouth.

His hand left the back of my neck, gliding over my collarbone and cupping my breast in his massive palm. He kneaded the flesh gently, prying his mouth from mine and tormenting the front of my throat with the soft caress of his lips that drove me to the brink of madness.

When his mouth finally touched my nipple, it was a teasing, barely-there contact that sent a ripple of heat to my center. I moaned and arched my back, watching in fascination as his wicked lips wrapped around it and sucked. He stared up at me as he sank a hand between my thighs, slipping his fingers through my wet heat and pressing two inside me to pump slowly as he tormented my breast.

"Rafe," I moaned, my hips moving instinctively. Begging for more, helplessly caught in his trap all over again. He pulled his fingers free, wrapping his hand around the back of my thigh as he lifted my leg to touch my foot to the adjacent shower wall. I dug my toes in, gripping it as hard as I could to keep the position as Rafe lowered to his knees in front of me.

His breathtaking stare held mine as he pressed a kiss to the top of my center, a teasing caress before his warm breath blew over the part of me that was so starved for his attention. His fingers dug into the skin of my thigh as he helped to support my leg, leaned in, and licked my clit slowly.

He took his time, touching every part of me with his mouth before he gave me what I wanted. Worshiping my flesh despite the pain of the stone tiles on his knees.

El Diablo was on his knees before his queen.

He finally used his free hand to pump two fingers into me, driving me higher and making me writhe in his grip. My foot slipped along the wall, his eyes scolding as he wrenched my leg higher to hold me in position. Only then did his mouth cover my clit, his tongue working it over with firm and slow touches that drew gasps from me. "Come for me, *mi reina*," he murmured against me, a groan rumbling through him when I slid a hand to the back of his head and pressed him tighter to me. The inky strands of his hair caught in my fingers, and I tugged furiously as my hips moved to help find my release.

It crashed over me like a storm, swallowing me in a tidal wave of pleasure that left me shuddering against the shower wall. My foot slipped, only Rafe's steady strength keeping it aloft as I went limp in his hold.

I hadn't recovered, hadn't managed to pry my eyes open before I felt him sinking inside me. His body pressed against mine, his free hand wrapping around my other leg to grip my ass as he lifted me in his arms.

His length slid through my tender tissue, still convulsing with the force of my orgasm, as my eyes opened to watch his darken with pleasure. He groaned, using the sheer strength of his body to hold me still against the wall while his hips thrust in and out of me slowly.

There was no rough possession or anger to the movements, only the obsessive love that ran between us like a current. That moment with his eyes on mine and us entwined in the shower was everything I knew we could be.

Everything we would have shared had I never run from him, turning the threat of dark obsession into overwhelming rage. He loved me. He hated that I hadn't chosen him. And the stain of that choice had determined our relationship from that point forward.

But it didn't have to be our forever.

I cupped his hand in my cheek, swallowing the moan that threatened as he bumped against the end of me with every slow but hard drive. "You'll always be my night sky," I murmured, leaning forward to kiss his parted lips. He went still, pausing inside me as he studied the emotion written into my face. "I should have chosen you."

He growled, pulling me away from the wall so suddenly that I yelped and wrapped my other leg around his waist. His movement inside me resumed, driving more furiously as he stepped out of the shower. We were still dripping wet when he guided us onto the bed, shoving as deep as he could inside me and pulling back to take me more firmly.

Without the awkward standing position, he hit the end of me with every thrust. His arms caged me in, holding me still as his wet skin slid along mine and he watched me. "You're mine," he said, his voice a rumble as his lips hovered only a breath away from mine.

"Yes," I agreed readily. "I'm yours, Rafe."

"Te amo, mi reina," he said, punctuating the words with hard drives inside me as my flesh tightened. They were the words I needed to hear, the confirmation that all of his methods were for a reason, even if it often felt lost to the brutality of his actions. The inexplicable bond between us demanded them, because Rafael didn't know what to do with love.

Except to own me.

"And I love you," I murmured back, burying my face in his neck as he drove us higher toward the release that hovered just beyond the horizon. Rafe groaned into me, flooding me with the brand of his heat inside me that sent me spiraling into my second orgasm.

My life before had been simple. It had also been empty.

Real life, *real love*, was bloody and unforgiving, but it was worth every bit of the pain just to feel it.

31

ISA

"Señora Ibarra, your mother is here," Aaron said, stepping into the kitchen where I sat at the breakfast nook with my chess set in front of me and played by myself. Running through the strategies I'd spent weeks studying.

The specific methodology to chess, and the ability to respond and analyze all the pieces on the board, was something that I had to imagine came easy to a man like Rafael who was used to manipulating people to serve his purposes.

"My mother?" I asked, furrowing my brow as I stood from the chair. I peeked around him toward the entryway, not hearing any noise from inside the house.

"She's at the gate," Aaron agreed. "Señor Ibarra indicated it was up to you if I let her on the property."

I glanced out the window, knowing there hadn't been enough time for her to come to the realization that Odina was a leach and would continue to take the patience and kindness she offered her and abuse it. That she would continue to abuse everyone in her path.

Especially if Rafe was right, and my mother's tolerance

didn't stem from her own guilt but from humoring her because she too blamed me. I swallowed back my nerves, nodding to Aaron as I moved to the kitchen to pour the lemonade that I now knew was a pregnancy craving.

Sour things kept the increasing nausea at bay, and sometimes it felt like I could drink a jar of pickle juice and feel like I was walking on a cloud.

A few moments passed, with me using a spoon to add extra sugar to my mother's lemonade so that her stomach wouldn't turn from the tart flavor. When the front door finally opened, I returned the pitcher to the fridge and turned to stare at my mother as Aaron led her into the room. "Would you prefer I send for the brothers, or are you comfortable with me staying?" he asked, his face soft despite the usually harsh lines I saw on the man's face.

I paused, considering the words as I turned to stare at my mother.

"Surely I can be alone with my own daughter?" she asked, crossing her arms over her chest and leveling Aaron with a glare.

"After the issues of your last several visits, I would prefer you not be alone with Señora Ibarra. Perhaps one day you'll be worthy of trusting, but that is not today," he said, raising an eyebrow as if he dared her to argue with his point.

"Thank you, Aaron. Could you call for Joaquin? I think his calming presence will be beneficial today," I said, giving him a soft smile to ease the blow of the dismissal. I'd have sent for Hugo, but the fact that my mother knew him meant he would only be a distraction. Joaquin was mostly a stranger to her, but he challenged me to be my best self.

He pushed me to stand up for myself and take no shit, and if I'd learned anything in dealing with my mother since coming home, it was that I needed that push.

No longer could I be the whipping girl for the crime I had committed as a child.

Aaron pulled his phone from his pocket, stepping into the entryway but keeping us within his line of sight as he spoke into it. "Would you like some lemonade?" I asked, pushing the glass to the other side of the island.

She stepped forward, shaking her head as she perched on top of one of the stools. "I had hoped to have a word alone with you." She shot a look to where Aaron had hung up his phone, his hands crossed behind his back in a military stance as he watched wordlessly. "I think what I have to say will come as quite a shock, and since it is about my life and personal business, it is none of your husband's business."

"That may be the case, but I keep no secrets from Rafael. Regardless of Joaquin's presence, I would have told him what we discussed when he returns home tonight." I nodded my head to Joaquin as he swapped places with Aaron, turning to settle in at the breakfast nook. He took the seat I had occupied previously, studying the board and looking for weaknesses in my play.

I'd forced him to play with me far too often since coming to Chicago.

"I won't relay anything that he doesn't need to know," he said, moving one of my pawns and giving me a smirk that told me he knew how much it irritated me when he touched my pieces. "I'll leave that up to Isa to decide. I am just here to make sure this conversation is a productive one. Otherwise it doesn't need to happen at all, Leonora."

"Fine," my mother sighed, settling into her seat more thoroughly as I took a sip of my lemonade. "This may come as a surprise to you considering the way I tried to raise you to be better than me, but I was not a virgin when I met your father."

I stilled, wondering what could possibly come of discussing my mother's sex life. While I'd never given it any thought, I had assumed her no sex before marriage stance had applied to her as well.

The hypocrite.

"Okay?" I asked, a small smile curving my lips despite the grimy feeling sliding through my body. "There's no harm in that, Mom."

"I was involved with a man before I met your father. He was—" She paused, a bitter grin taking her face as her eyes went wistful. "He was incredible. Wealthy and charming in a way that I never thought to experience for myself given my upbringing here."

I'd never met my mother's family. Never had the opportunity or explanation, purely because she said that they weren't a part of our lives and never would be, and that was the end of it. "He sounds like he treated you well."

"He did, and I needed that after I'd disobeyed my mother to go on my whirlwind trip in Europe. It wasn't safe for a girl like me, but I wanted to know the country where she'd been born. I thought she would understand when I came home, but while I was in Spain I met him. I decided to stay with him, thinking myself in love like a fool," she scoffed.

I froze, possibilities running through my mind as I gaped at her. She'd never spoken of a trip to Europe before, never even hinted at what might have been the biggest adventure of her life. "You spent time in Spain?" I asked, the breath whooshing out of me suddenly. The memory of the fear in her eyes, the cautionary tale that must have run through her mind when she said goodbye to me before I left for Ibiza was all consuming. Too fresh in my mind as I stared at the mother who felt like a different person.

"Nearly a year," she said, smiling sadly. "He put me in an apartment and we dated. He told me his family life was complicated, and I knew there was a woman he was supposed to marry for business purposes. I believed he loved me, and that he would never go through with the wedding to a woman he barely knew, but they were married six months into our relationship," she said, shaking her head as if she was disgusted with the memory of it.

"But you were there for a year?" I asked, staring at her and waiting for her to continue. For her to tell me that she hadn't been the other woman in a marriage.

"It wasn't a marriage built on love. There were no feelings between them, so I agreed to remain his mistress. After a few months passed, he came to see me less, until the visits stopped altogether or remained platonic in nature. Like visiting a friend, when months before he hadn't been able to keep his hands off me," she said, pausing to reach across the counter to take my hand in hers. All the judgment I'd felt for my relationship with Rafe made me refuse to squeeze her hand back.

At least I hadn't been involved with a married man.

"He ended it?" I asked, swallowing around the nausea in my throat as I pulled my hand back. I tried not to judge, tried to keep the shock off my face knowing that everything I'd believed about my mother and her stringent beliefs had been a deception. Or, at the very least, hadn't always been what she thought.

"He ended it. He said he fell in love with his wife as he got to know her and that he'd come clean about our relationship. She would forgive him for what he did, so long as he never saw me again. Martina was pregnant—"

"Where in Spain was this?" I asked, my heart stalling in my chest as the familiar name erupted through the room. Joaquin's head shot up at the table, his eyes intense on mine as I turned my shocked eyes to his to be sure it hadn't been a figment of my imagination. Martina was a common enough name, but the odds seemed impossible. "Where, Mom?"

"Barcelona," she replied, staring back and forth between Joaquin and I.

"What was his name?" Joaquin asked, standing from his seat and closing the distance between us. His hands hit the island counter, leaning into her space and waiting for her to give him the answer we both knew was coming with rising dread.

"Andrés," she whispered. "Ibarra is a very common name. It seemed impossible that they would be related, but they are. Aren't they?" she asked, placing her head in her hands.

"Andrés is Rafael's uncle," I said, leaning my ass into the stove behind me.

"This isn't where I thought this conversation was going. I didn't come here to warn you off his family. I just wanted you to understand that even good men falter. They aren't always loyal and you can't trust that your husband will be faithful to you. Andrés was a good man who made a mistake, but it didn't change what it did to his wife when she found out the truth. I don't want that for you," she said, rubbing a hand over her face.

I couldn't even think of the implications of what the new information meant for my family going forward or about how intertwined our pasts truly were. "Did you ever meet Miguel Ibarra? This is very, *very* fucking important. I couldn't care less about your affair with Andrés right now, but this matters," I said, leaning forward and taking her hand in mine.

She nodded hesitantly, her eyes glancing toward where Joaquin watched with wide eyes. "Andrés and I ended on good terms even though I was hurt, but his brother thought I knew too much. He wanted Andrés to keep me in the family and offered to take over my care." She paused, swallowing down whatever surge of emotion came from remembering a conversation where she was talked about like a pet. "I wasn't interested. I just wanted to come home, so Andrés snuck me out of the country and that was that. I never saw either of them again."

"But I did," I said. Joaquin pulled the cell from his pocket, unlocking the screen and calling Rafe as he paced back and forth in the room. There was no answer, unsurprisingly. The twisted fucker was probably covered in blood, busy interrogating Timofey once again. What he hoped to learn from a man that had to be barely alive at this point, I didn't care to know.

He just needed to answer his damn phone.

"Who is Miguel to Rafael?" my mother asked, blinking back her shock. "Is he his father?"

"He was. He died a few years ago," I said, watching as Joaquin typed furiously on his phone—presumably a frantic text to Rafael to call him immediately. "But not before he threw Odina and me into the Chicago River."

My mother's eyes widened, her shock palpable in the air as Joaquin's ringtone erupted in the room. He answered, stalking to the doorway that went to the foyer and speaking rapidly in Spanish without pause. "Miguel Ibarra threw you in the river?" my mother asked, swallowing as she touched a hand to her chest. "But why?"

"That's what we've been trying to figure out," I

murmured, sliding the lemonade closer to her to encourage her to take a sip. I moved around the island, taking the stool next to hers and sliding onto it slowly. "Is there anything else you know? Anything that might explain why he came back after all those years?"

"I was *nobody* to Miguel. I only ever met him a few times. He terrified me, Isa. If that man is Rafael's father, then you're in danger. Andrés told me stories about the things his brother was capable of so that I knew to keep my distance. You wouldn't believe—"

"Mom," I sighed, taking her hands in mine and guiding her to face me. "I know exactly what kind of man Miguel was, and I know the kind of man my husband is. Rafael may be a far cry from perfect, but he is not Miguel."

"The apple doesn't fall far from the tree," she groaned, rolling her eyes as if I was being naive.

"If that were true, Odina and I would be like you. We'd be more happy to have quiet lives and go to college and do what is expected of us. We wouldn't be consumed by this darkness inside of us and desperate for adventure," I explained.

"You think I wasn't? You think I went to Spain on my own and fell in love with a man like Andrés Ibarra because I craved safety and comfort?" She scoffed, turning her face away from mine and finally taking a sip of her lemonade. "I was just like you two, and look where that got me! With a broken heart, shipped out in the night so a madman couldn't claim ownership of me, only for him to come back and try to drown my daughters years later."

I recognized the signs of guilt weighing in, the way her shoulders sagged under the realization that her choices all those years ago had been what led to Odina and I ending up in that river.

With it came the realization that clenched my heart in my chest, making my eyes sting with the tears of what I hadn't wanted to see. This guilt was different than what I'd thought she felt before.

This guilt was hers to carry, and not just the shadow of the blame she'd shifted onto my shoulders.

All my life, I'd thought she catered to Odina because she felt guilty for the way her choice had affected her. Instead, she'd given my sister everything she needed because she blamed me for the decision I'd made that day.

Rafael had been right. He'd seen the truth in my mother's actions when I'd been too close to them. "Miguel Ibarra did whatever he wanted and didn't care who it affected," I said. "If you didn't feel guilty about your affair with Andrés before today, then you shouldn't now. Nothing has changed."

Regardless of whether we'd known it, her affair had to have been the driving force that led to the events that shaped the rest of our lives, but that had been true the day before too. "I was so mad at you," she murmured, squeezing my hand in hers. "For going with him that day. How many times had I told you not to talk to strangers? I was so grateful you were alive, but still so mad at you."

"I know," I said back, nodding my head as Joaquin stepped back into the room. "But I forgive you for it. I just hope you can find a way to forgive me for that mistake. I've stopped expecting it of Odina, but it took me a long time to realize I still needed to hope for it from you."

She leaned forward, wrapping her arms around me and tugging me off the stool until she crushed my head to her shoulder and kissed my forehead. "Of course I forgive you, Isa. I should have forgiven you a long time ago," she said, sniffling back tears as Joaquin watched the interaction with a soft smile on his face.

I bit my lip to stifle the emotion threatening to make my lip tremble. We had a first hint about why Miguel had bothered with me in the first place, and I finally felt closure over my choice that day.

It never would have mattered what choice I made, because all roads would have led me right to that moment in the kitchen.

Rafael and I had always been inevitable.

32

RAFAEL

Sliding my phone into my back pocket, I turned to level Ryker with a look that communicated just how little fucks I had left to give. Joaquin's urgent voice rang in my ears, the discovery of a connection that shouldn't have existed making me wonder what else I'd missed that had been right in front of my face.

I'd never told Andrés Isa's last name, and especially not her mother's maiden name. Isa looked nothing like her mother, taking after her father's side of the family with the fawn skin and almond-shaped eyes. Her every feature was different from her mother's, striking in a way I couldn't ever imagine Leonora achieving.

She looked like she'd been born in Spain.

I picked up the sledgehammer from Ryker's stash of tools, swinging it with all my might and a loud roar. It landed on Timofey's kneecap, shattering it instantly as he screamed. "Fuck!"

I rattled off the date of Isa's drowning, grabbing him by the hair and snapping his head back until his lazy half-swollen eyes met mine. "What was my father doing in

Chicago?" I repeated the question I'd asked far too often in the time since the attack.

"Visting Bellandi and probably fucking everything that walked." He spat at my face, barely missing before it dribbled back onto his chin. "The anniversary of your bitch of a mother's death was always the worst."

Ryker moved at my side, but held back when I raised a hand to stop him. The answers I needed were a step away. Defending my mother's memory could come when I made sure Timofey died painfully, when he had nothing left to tell me.

"What does that have to do with Isa's mother?" I asked, watching as understanding lit in his eyes. The fucker knew, had known about that connection the entire time, and why he was protecting a dead man went beyond me.

"He liked to check up on Leonora from time to time," he wheezed, a smile pulling at the cracked skin of his lips. "Just to make sure she hadn't been naughty and talked about family business. You know how it goes. But there was no way she ever said a word. From what I saw the one time I went with him, the house was all but dilapidated. The information she had would've been worth money in the right hands."

"It seems excessive to still be checking on her twenty years after her affair with Andrés," I said, quirking an eyebrow.

"So he had a little crush. It wasn't often that women dared to say no to Miguel Ibarra, and the protection your uncle put on her only made her more interesting. I don't think he went to see her every year by any means, or even every visit to Chicago. He just kept an eye on her, because if she ever stepped out of line Andrés protection would be meaningless."

"Why did he throw her daughters in the river?" Ryker asked, his eyes darting back and forth as we worked to catch up on the information he'd missed in my conversation with Joaquin.

Timofey laughed, turning his face to mine. "This doesn't have the answer you're looking for. There's no deep plot twist to explain the madness that consumed Miguel's mind and rotted his logic."

"Fucking tell me," I snapped, crushing the bones of his hand with a swing of the sledgehammer. He groaned, the sound of his voice drowning out the cracking as he tried to wiggle his fingers in the aftermath.

"Did he ever tell you that he heard your mother nagging him even after he fucking killed her? God, he wished he could kill the bitch all over again for the way she tortured him. It was always the worst in the summer, which was why he never stayed on your fucking island for the anniversary of her death, and sent you to stay with Andrés when you were too young to be on your own. He was so much fucking fun to be around in the summer months. Half-crazed and ready to throw down with any man who so much as looked at him. Willing to fuck anything that caught his eye," he said, closing his eyes slowly as if he was picturing a rather fond memory. "Dima said he and Miguel were walking along the river. Looking for something to *fuck* while Miguel did his compulsory check in on Leonora."

"Dima was there with him," I said, the breath escaping my lungs in surprise. "He was practically a child then." The very same Kuznetsov who had purchased Isa had been there the day she drowned.

That hardly seemed like a coincidence.

"He was probably ten. Our father gave us whores to play with as soon as we could fight, much like yours," he said, giving me a pointed look. While my father's women hadn't been the same as the Kuznetsovs', who were forced to work for the family, it was no secret that my initiation to sex had come far earlier than it should have.

"That doesn't explain why he tried to kill Isa," I said, a warning sounding in my voice. To be so close to the answers I needed, then to have the man who had them dance around the subject needlessly—I wanted to slit his fucking throat.

"She never stood a chance," he said, a demented laugh bubbling free. "He took one look at those fucking eyes of hers and *knew* that she was a witch. On the anniversary of the day he burned your witch of a mother at the stake? That could hardly be a coincidence to Miguel. He figured if he gave your mom a present, maybe she'd let him off the hook and stop fucking haunting his crazy ass."

"What?" I asked, going still at the demented answer. After hunting for it for what felt like forever, *that* was it? Another symptom of my father's madness, another victim to his witch hunt.

"I'm sure it didn't hurt that Leonora would lose her daughter, well, daughters, since the other one was stupid enough to follow Isa. Your mother always wanted a daughter," he said, tipping his head to the side with that deranged smile on his face. He knew damn well that his time was coming to an end, that I'd kill him when I was satisfied I had all the answers.

The pain in his beaten and broken body had to be enough motivation to finally give me what I wanted. I glanced over the parts of his body, the missing nails and skin peeling off his arms, the leg and arm bent at awkward angles even though he was secured to the chair.

"A witch for a witch," I said, humming my dissatisfaction. "But Isa lived."

"And your father's obsession ensued," he said, twisting his lips into a frown. "What do you think your sweet little wife will think of you when she finds out you watched your father and Dima sign her life away and did nothing to stop it? Will she be so forgiving of that?"

"What did Dima want with her?" I asked, ignoring his attempt to prod at the regret I felt over the inability to save the children my father had hurt.

I'd done what I could, when I could. It hadn't been in time for the others, but it *had* saved Isa.

I was selfish enough that she was the most important to me, but not enough that I didn't feel the weight of the other's lives.

"Dima and your wife have far more in common than you think, *El Diablo*," he said, tipping his head back to relax the muscles in his neck. I hefted the sledgehammer in my hands, ready to begin the process of deciphering that cryptic message.

The one that he wasn't ready to share.

33

ISA

Rafe stepped out of the French doors as I hurried from my seat to meet him. Spots of blood covered his white dress shirt, the signs of the torture more evident than ever on his clothes. Rafael was always so immaculate, so undisturbed when he came home, even after being gone for an entire day of violence.

"Rafe?" I asked, watching as I stepped up to him. His eyes snapped to mine, something missing in that stare as he walked toward me. "Did you get answers?" I asked, letting him pull me into his arms.

"Yes," he murmured against the top of my head, breathing deep as he nuzzled into my hair. Shrugging off his shirt and pants quickly, he ran a hand through his hair and didn't seem to care that his men might see him in his boxer briefs. "Your mother was telling the truth. She had an affair with my uncle."

"How? How is it possible that all of this is connected and we never knew?" I asked, watching as he moved toward me. He wrapped his arms around me, lifting me off the floor and carting me toward the lounge. Laying me out beneath him, he brushed his nose up the side of mine sweetly. "Your uncle...and my mom."

He shuddered, shoving the thought away with a shake of his head. "My father kept tabs on her to make sure she didn't talk. He saw you when he was checking on her."

"So he threw me in the river because of his issues with her?" I asked, trying to wrap my head around it. I'd started to accept the truth to Rafe's statement that my mother had spent her life blaming me for going off with the stranger who threw Odina and I into the water. I'd watched shock fill her face as she realized that it might not have been my fault at all.

But a result of the affair she had thought long since buried in her past.

"No," Rafe said sadly as if he could follow the path my thoughts wandered. "He saw your eyes, and decided to give my mother the daughter she'd always wanted."

"A daughter through death?" I asked, considering the thought processes of a man so deranged by his fantastical beliefs that he actually believed it worked that way. "Like a gift?"

"Yes. Like a gift for her. I think that's why he muttered something about her not deserving two daughters to Odina. She was just there and she had to be a witch too because she had the same eyes. You were the target, whether it was because he saw you first or just because you were the one who was willing to go with him, I guess we'll never know."

"When I didn't die, he hurt other kids with eyes like ours. He hurt other people because of me," I whispered, my heart aching for the ones who hadn't been so lucky to survive his ruthlessness. "Why not just come finish the job?"

Rafe sighed, hanging his head as he paused. "I'm not entirely certain," he admitted, but something in his voice felt like a lie. Something felt like guilt, but I wasn't sure I was ready for the truth if it was worse than what he'd already told me. "You said you heard a woman screaming when you were in the water, that you heard an inferno burning."

"It was just the water rushing and my mother. That's all that's possible," I said, dismissing the way the reminder made me feel. I'd questioned my memory far too many times over the years to even consider it anymore.

"We'll never know what really happened in that river. I don't believe in God or anything of the sort, but I remember how fierce my mother was when it came to protecting me. I remember her standing against my father and trying to fight back. If anyone could protect you in that river, it's her," he said, touching his lips to mine. "She knew I needed you more than she ever would, so she kept you safe. And then she led me to you," he said, murmuring the words against my mouth. The sentiment was oddly sweet, coming from the man I knew didn't believe in anything beautiful after life.

Only suffering and pain.

"My grandmother would say that her ghost was discontent," I said, smiling lightly at his words. "That she stayed here to keep an eye on you."

"Your grandmother sounds like a very wise woman," Rafe said with a grin, touching his lips to mine again. I didn't know what I believed regarding his mother and the path that had led to him finding me, of all the people in the world who didn't share this odd connection.

All I knew was that he was mine, and that was what mattered in the end.

But his father was Miguel Ibarra, and I'd seen the marks on Rafael's flesh as proof of what happened should he disappoint his father. The burns on his chest were horrible.

They were the physical reminder of everything that was evil about Miguel. But they were nothing compared to what the other kids, taken after the day in the river, must have suffered at the hands of people like Pavel Kuznetsov.

The stars twinkled overhead as I lay back on the lounger. In some ways, Rafe was no better than his father. He'd branded me. He'd abducted me.

He'd taken things I didn't want to give and pushed my body in ways I hadn't imagined possible.

But he'd also freed me from the cage of my mind, showing me that there could be freedom in physical submission, but there would never be freedom with my darkness locked away. He'd taught me to embrace who I was, instead of living a life for someone else.

The other kids would never find freedom, and I would carry the weight of that with me every day. We still didn't know for certain that I'd been the first, but I *knew*. Deep in my heart, I knew the fact that I'd lived had been what set Miguel over the edge into this frantic pursuit.

Rafael sat on the edge of the lounge cushion, leaning back onto his hand and staring down at me. There was silence between us for a moment as I kept staring at the stars, thinking of what must have happened to the little boy who'd counted them with his mother. What he must have survived between that version of Rafe and the young man who could watch children sold into slavery without trying to stop it.

"My father never kept any of the children for himself," he said, lying down beside me and staring up at the sky as he heaved a sigh. The weight of the confession that would come settled over my skin. It wasn't often that he spoke of his upbringing or what life had been like on *El Infierno* with his father. "That wasn't his particular taste. He preferred his victims to be women, especially women who had children that they would do anything to protect. His favorite pastime was making a mother think she could find a way back to her child if she just did as he asked, and usually, if they did, he would let them go when he was done," he murmured, his voice oddly distant as if he could remember the pain.

I could only imagine the screams of a woman howling to be set free, trying desperately to get back to her child, and the knowledge of what came when she finally went quiet. My heart felt heavy, sinking into the sound of Rafe's distant voice and trying to set aside the emotion it brought.

"And if they didn't?" I asked, even if I didn't want to know the answer. I knew whatever he'd come to tell me would have a purpose, because he would never volunteer information about his childhood without reason.

"It depended on any number of things. If the child was particularly 'pretty' he might sell them after he killed the mother. But sometimes the children stayed on *El Infierno*. Knowing my father, he thought that raising the children in his lifestyle, to work for him, was the ultimate way to get even with the women who refused to give him what he wanted. The kids weren't treated poorly, but my father was fond of threatening me with them," he said.

"What do you mean threatening you with them?" I asked, turning to look at him finally. He kept his eyes on the sky, ignoring my presence beside him.

"They trained with me, along with the other children who were raised to be soldiers. They became my friends in some ways even though my father forced me to keep my distance. I was the heir to his empire, and I couldn't have friends. But I got to know them well enough that watching them be hurt for my disobedience kept me from speaking out. I couldn't take a stand against my father, not until I knew I could win."

I turned my body, touching a hand to his shirt-clad chest. He still didn't give me his eyes, but his hand covered mine. "He used them against you?"

"I think that's what their purpose was the entire time. He kept them because they were easy to manipulate. They grew up with adoptive families on the island, but they were always his leverage. Until I killed my father, they were secondary to the *real* families," he paused, finally turning to level me with his eyes. "Hugo was only a toddler when they were brought to the island along with their mother."

My lungs emptied of air, the sudden realization of why in my, albeit limited, time on *El Infierno*, Hugo had never bothered to introduce me to his parents. Someone had raised him, but it didn't seem as though they were parents in the way he needed when it came down to it. "Your father killed their mother?" I asked, swallowing past the sudden burning in my throat. That one man could cause so much carnage, destroy so many lives, he'd deserved to die a thousand deaths.

Burning was too merciful for him.

"My father's men had snatched them off the streets of Ibiza while they were at the market. I don't know that Hugo and Gabriel have any clear memories of their birth parents, but Joaquin was old enough to know what was going on. He fought the entire time his mother screamed and he vowed vengeance even though he was just a boy. Joaquin was the one who made me realize that my father had given me the army I needed to take control. I just had to wait for them to be old enough to fight. So I made friendships off the island. I acted as my father's liaison and turned his allies who didn't agree with his actions against him. I bided my time, and when I was strong enough I put an end to it all." Rafe's words washed over me, his eyes intense and blazing with the guilt I knew he must feel for the ones he hadn't saved.

His life had never been black and white, and he wasn't a good man.

But he'd done what he could to end the suffering of innocents on *El Infierno*.

"Joaquin himself tied my father to the post he died on. And when he went up in flames, he stared at the faces of all the children he'd stripped from their mothers. I hope the ones who weren't there with us keep Miguel from peace in whatever comes after life," he sighed, leaning forward to touch his lips to my forehead.

I hoped Miguel Ibarra never found peace in the afterlife, and that whoever or whatever haunted him while he'd been alive had shown him what true pain was after his death.

I'd never be able to forget that I'd been the first, and that the weight of all that followed rested on my shoulders purely because of my survival.

34

ISA

I picked at the remnants of our late dinner, exhaustion creeping in from the emotional high earlier in the day. My mother's confession weighed heavily on my shoulders, and so did the hesitant step we'd taken toward finding a new normal. I hoped with the entire truth out in the open, perhaps we could find a way to form a new relationship that was built on truly understanding one another for the first time.

I didn't have to force myself into the mold she created for me, and she no longer had to pretend to be something she wasn't. We could just *be*.

The survivor's guilt would be what haunted me. The knowledge that I'd somehow played a role in the destruction of other people's lives, all because I'd still breathed when my mother pulled me out of the river.

Rafe finished his food, moving to rinse his plate and deposit it in the dishwasher. He turned, leaning his ass on the counter and gripping the edge in the way that drove me crazy. The muscles of his forearms stood out in stark relief as he flexed to hold the counter, and my stare caught on them.

The bastard smirked as if he knew exactly what those forearms did to me. He opened his mouth to speak, as if he might taunt me with the promise of what would come later in the night. He cut off abruptly when Joaquin sauntered into the room, his expression tight as he turned to me. "Odina is at the gate and demanding entrance. Should I phone your mother to come get her wayward *child*?" he asked, emphasizing the last word to show his distaste for my sister.

In the days since we'd returned to Chicago, I'd realized just how far apart Odina and I were. For being born only minutes apart, the chasm between us felt enormous once I finally saw her for what she'd allowed herself to become in an effort to deal with her trauma.

Spoiled. Entitled.

The word choice was intentional, reducing Odina to the choices she'd made and the fact that she seemed unable to act responsibly. I sighed, glancing at the time on the stove.

I'd spent so long waiting for Rafe to return home from his torture session that it was already past ten at night. I already missed having Regina to tend to the meals, and then immediately felt guilty for such a thing.

It wasn't like I lived a particularly busy life while we were in Chicago. I could cook meals.

"Just let her in and call my parents to come get her. We can't exactly leave her at the gate throwing a tantrum," I sighed, rubbing my temples between my fingers. I could already imagine the nightmare she'd given the guards, her shrieking and entitled behavior something I'd dealt with far too often.

Joaquin nodded his agreement after a shared look with

Rafe, confirming that the choice was one he agreed with. "I think it's best you make yourself scarce," I said, wincing at the glare Rafe leveled me with. "Don't look at me that way. You rejected her, and she'll see that as being solely my fault. Having you in her face is only going to antagonize her further. I'd like to survive the time it takes for my mom or dad to come get her in relative peace."

"Since when do I care what hurts Odina?" he asked, tilting his head thoughtfully. As if he truly needed to consider it to decide if there'd ever been a time when he might have. I suspected the answer was no, but perhaps there had been a moment before discovering how terrible she was to me that he valued her life in relation to mine.

It was likely short lived.

"You don't," I murmured, standing from my seat and moving into his arms. I wrapped mine around his back, holding him to me firmly as he looked down at me with an unimpressed expression. "But you care about what hurts me. I just want to get through whatever she wants until my parents come to get her. That's all."

"Fine," he said, leaning down to kiss me. "Joaquin stays with you. I don't trust that little snake in the slightest, and if someone doesn't come get her soon, I'll kick her to the curb. I don't want her upsetting you, and you need to sleep."

"I'm pregnant, not a child," I reprimanded with a scowl. "I'll go to bed when I'm good and ready."

Rafe smirked, shaking his head before kissing my forehead and rubbing my stomach briefly before prying himself away from me. He went down the hallway toward his office, leaving me standing and watching the subtle sway of his hips as he moved.

If *this* was any indication of what pregnancy hormones could be, I'd be a Rafe addict by the time the baby was born.

Joaquin moved toward the front door, his shoulders sagging and head dropping forward as he muttered to himself and disappeared into the foyer. The sound of Odina's brutal knocking echoed through the house, making me wince with every loud blow. Even aside from the obvious fact that we knew she was here, because of the armed guards surrounding the property, what did impatient people have against doorbells?

I watched through the open doorway to the foyer as Joaquin heaved the heavy front door open. Odina shoved through the space he created dramatically, her shrill voice echoing through the house as she sang. "Isa! Oh, Isaaaa." I winced, knowing the only time Odina sang was when she'd been drinking.

She stumbled into the main area, her face flushed from the alcohol she'd consumed. "For fuck's sake, Odina. Did you *drive* here?" I asked, watching as she moved for the living room and stumbled over her own feet when she tried to pivot and drop onto the couch.

She nearly missed, her eyes widening sluggishly as she barely caught herself on the very edge and pulled herself back onto the cushions.

"Yes, *Mom*," she groaned, dropping her head back as she sank into the couch. "How'd you get to be such a buzzkill?"

"Someone had to be," I said, moving to the fridge in the kitchen and grabbing a bottle of water. Joaquin walked past the room, moving through the parts of the house that enabled him as if he needed to check all corners. His anxiety nearly set me on edge, but he'd been paranoid about security checks after the bombing.

Who could blame him after that really?

Holding the bottle to Odina's lips and tipping her head back enough not to spill, I poured water into her mouth slowly. "Your father is on his way," Joaquin said, taking up his place over in the breakfast nook of the main space to keep an eye on us from a distance.

"Mom hasn't been the same since she came here," Odina said, her voice surprisingly clear despite her obvious drunkenness. "What did you say to her? Poor little Isa is *always* the victim."

"It's sweet that you think I've ever had any control over what Mom did, but I promise you I do not. She came here to tell me a story. One that isn't my place to tell you, so you'll have to ask her if you want answers," I said, wondering if my father knew about the man who'd come before him. My parents had married later in life, and it wasn't unreasonable, even if surprising, to think they'd both had love lives before each other.

"You trust him," Odina said, narrowing her gaze as she stared back at me with cloudy eyes. "You've never trusted them before."

"Rafe is different," I explained, standing from the couch and moving to the kitchen. I grabbed a dishcloth from the drawer, running it under cool water and taking my seat next to her once more. I dabbed the cloth over her forehead, watching as she settled into the touch. No matter how much Odina hated me, she'd always wanted to be cared for when she hit the point where alcohol numbed the pain and made her vulnerable.

Those were the nights when I got a brief glimpse of what I thought our bond could have been if it hadn't been for that day in the river, and when I clung to a glimmer of hope that maybe one day things could be different for us.

I'd given up on that hope, but I had continued to show her kindness in the moments when she'd accept it and when she needed it. Where I'd once thought it a strength, now I saw her for the weakness she was. My love for a sister who didn't deserve my affection weakened me, but it would take a very sharp knife to sever the bond between us completely.

"He's a man," she scoffed.

"He loves me. In a way that I hope you find one day. Maybe then you can understand that I'll never forgive what you tried to do. We both know there was no chance of us ever being true sisters again after what you did with Wayne. But trying to seduce my husband was the icing on the cake." I hated to admit the words, even knowing that they were well and truly said in earnest. I couldn't help but hope that one day Odina grew to love a man, and someone she should have been able to trust came and threatened that for her own pettiness.

I felt terrible even thinking about it, but the thought was there nonetheless. The bonds of sisterhood didn't mean I had to *like* being so tied to her. As terrible as her actions with Wayne had been in high school, my territorial feelings where Rafe was concerned meant she'd straight up pissed me off.

"He killed Wayne for what we did," she said, and there wasn't a trace of doubt in her voice. Even if it had never been addressed, she knew the man who had interfered on that night came back to make good on the threat that was fuzzy in my memory. "Why didn't he kill me?"

"Because you're my sister, and he knows I would have a hard time forgiving that. He let you live as a kindness, so I suggest you keep your distance from now on," I said, pressing the cloth into her face. I glanced out the windows, my eyes narrowing on where Odina had parked our father's truck next to the house. "We live separate lives now —"

My words cut off as Joaquin shouted. "Get down!" A

flash of light blinded me, making everything disappear in a shock as I tucked my face into my chest to protect my burning retinas.

Boom.

Glass shattered at my side, raining down on us as I put my arms up to cover my face and tucked my head in instinctively. The shockwave knocked us off the couch, forcing us to the floor, and I rolled to my stomach protectively. My ears rang, the repercussion of the blast making that too-familiar sound consume all of my thoughts. In the eerie, ringing, near-silence that followed, I moved into a crouch slowly, peering out the window.

The place where my father's truck had sat before was now a raging inferno, my gaze catching on the flames and terror filling me as I cradled my stomach tightly in fear.

The baby I hadn't been sure I wanted suddenly felt like something I couldn't live without—something I needed to protect at all costs.

A second blast rocked the night, the air rippling with the force of it even though it seemed further away. Not trusting if that was because of true distance or simply a consequence of the ringing in my head, I crouched even lower and moved to check on Odina.

Joaquin closed the distance between us, wrapping an arm around my back as he crouched with me to try to remain out of sight. His gun was already drawn and clutched tightly in his hand, ready for whatever might come our way in the wake of the explosions. "Get to the panic room," he grunted, gesturing me toward the hallway where the men's quarters were located. His voice was muffled from the pressure in my ears, as if I was in the water of the river and not feet from the flames.

"Not without Rafe!" I argued, yelling despite the intent

to stay quiet. My throat burned with the way the words felt torn out of me.

Odina held her ears in her hands, the side of her face covered in cuts from the glass. My face stung with the same, tiny abrasions that felt so miniscule compared to the pain claiming my entire body. Still, there was an oddly familiar sensation of deja vu as I pushed through that pain.

I'd survived a car bomb once before, and I'd be damned if this one got the best of me. "Hurry up," Joaquin ordered.

"We have to move," I said to Odina, nudging her with my foot as gently as I could. With the pain overwhelming my body, I didn't know that I could move to help her to her feet. Only the adrenaline and the will to protect the baby kept my limbs functioning despite my terror.

The heat of flames on my face was more than a memory —a reality that seemed inevitable for me to escape. As if the fire of the fate I'd escaped followed me through my life with Rafael, waiting to consume me within the flames.

"I can't," she sobbed.

"Get up!" I yelled, holding out a hand for her. If she didn't take the offering, I'd have no choice but to leave her. To let my sister suffer a fate meant for me once again, purely because if I had to choose between her and the baby, there would be no choice at all.

She took it hesitantly, leaning her weight into mine as soon as she stood on wobbly legs. I shouldered it, nearly collapsing under her as I made my way toward the back hallway where Rafe's office was. Joaquin kept his hands free, that gun clutched in his hands far more valuable than helping my sister walk. His face conveyed everything he felt about watching my twin use me to support herself, disgust written into the twist of his mouth.

Smoke curled out under the office doorway, my heart

catching in my throat at the sight of it. Odina paused her steps, freezing in place as she stared at it and looked back toward the front of the house. "I'm not going in there," she wheezed, holding up a hand to cover her mouth and breathe through the smoke.

"Then go," I said, shrugging off her arm as I clenched my eyes shut against the burn in them. She gave me one last lingering look, briefly turning it to Joaquin who made no move to leave my side. She shook her head before she turned on her heel and retreated toward the front of the house. It was up to her to save herself. The only thing that mattered was getting Rafe and making our way to the bunker.

I took one last smoke-filled breath of air before I put one foot in front of the other. Joaquin led the way, attempting to stand between me and whatever might be on the other side of that door. Even going for Rafe's office at all came as a surprise, when I'd have half expected him to cart me to the panic room no matter what I thought of that plan, but he couldn't fight me and protect me at the same time.

A window at the end of the hallway in front of me crashed open, glass spraying through the space as a bottle cracked against the wall. Flames erupted, consuming the hall in fire that made me stagger back a step as the heat of it touched my skin.

"Rafe!" I screamed with a cough, the sound ringing in my ears.

Only the fire answered me.

35

RAFAEL

The house vibrated with the force of what had to be an explosion at the front, sending me vaulting to my feet immediately to make my way to Isa. The window at my side shattered as a Molotov cocktail crashed through, lighting the books I'd so carefully selected for Isa aflame on impact.

She would not be happy about that.

Pulling my gun from my pocket and the spare one from the space where it was taped to the bottom of my desk, I hurried for the door, keeping one gun aimed at the window for any sign of an enemy, before it too could be consumed by flames. The second crash came closer, speeding inches past my face to strike the wall with the door and render it impassable.

I moved to the shattered windows, aiming my gun outside while knocking jagged pieces off the sill with my other gun without care for what they might do to my hands. The need to get to my pregnant wife overrode all else, leaving me with the distinct feeling that I would do *anything* to see her safely tucked into the bunker.

A face popped up from outside, warranting a hasty shot to his face without thought before he could do the same. There was no regret as I pressed my hands to the windowsill and stepped up onto it. Jumping down to the ground outside, I spun and crouched low quickly to keep an eye out for any others.

No one appeared, the area oddly quiet despite the roaring of flames both inside the house and out.

Standing straight, I quietly made my way along the side of the house and kept tight to the structure itself. With the wall at one side, I only needed to watch three others for combatants who might pose a threat.

The French doors to the pool area were closed but unlocked when I reached them, the entry to the house guarded by my own men who kept watchful eyes on all the distant shadows. Aaron turned to me as I approached, his gun raised and ready to fire before he heaved a sigh of relief at the sight of me. I walked past him with a nod, emerging into the main space where I'd left Isa.

The memory of standing in that doorway and watching her pull herself out of the cupboards filled me with bitterness. By the time the flames had finished their job, very little would remain of the house we'd called home in Chicago for a brief time.

Searching the room, Isa was nowhere to be seen, the window next to the sofa all but gone. What I thought must have once been her father's truck sat just outside that window, a blazing ball of fire consuming it entirely.

Gabriel stepped out of the foyer, and my lungs heaved with relief for a very brief moment when I thought I saw Isa tucked safely under his arm. The harshness of his grip on the nape of her neck and the savage scowl on his face gave me the first hint that the woman thrashing against his grip was not my wife.

"Where's Isa?" I demanded, looking around the main living space and into the foyer behind him.

"She says they went to look for you," Gabriel grunted, pinching Odina's neck tighter. "She thought she'd bail on them and find a place to hide. There are men out front. They bombed the gates too and more keep coming. I lost contact with the perimeter guards."

"Pavel?" I asked quickly to confirm, watching when he nodded his head hesitantly. "He wants his son back."

"Bellandi sent men to guard Timofey at the warehouse, and back up should be here shortly."

"Rafe!" Isa screamed, making sure my feet carried me toward the hall that led to my office. The thought of her trapped in the same fire I'd escaped, having wandered into it to find me, threatened to make my body explode along with the cars.

Gabriel followed, trailing behind me as he spoke. "There's no better way to achieve getting his son back than to take something you value." He raised an eyebrow when I looked at him over my shoulder, digging his teeth into his bottom lip as he glanced down at Odina. "I have a plan, but *reina* will hate it."

"So long as it means she walks away alive, I don't particularly care if she likes it," I grunted. He dropped back, taking it as the permission it was. I already knew from the look on his face exactly what Gabriel had planned.

And there was nothing I would not sacrifice for my wife and child.

36

ISA

Joaquin wrapped his arms around my stomach from behind, lifting me off my feet as I yelled in panic. "Shhh, *mi reina*. You have to be quiet," Joaquin said, his voice muffled by the continued haze. I turned my head to get a good look at him, wincing when he lifted me higher and carrying me back to the mouth of the hallway and away from where Rafe had last gone. Tears barely touched my cheeks before the heat of the air dried my skin.

We moved toward the main space, Joaquin working to hold me as still as possible as I struggled against his grip. I couldn't leave Rafe and hide in the bunker, not until I knew he was alive. The thought of a life without him just felt...empty.

"Let me go!" I begged, yelling over the noise from the fire and the muffling to my ears. My hands shoved at Joaquin's grip, pushing him away to the best of my ability. It was pointless, his grasp like iron in his determination. "Rafael!" I screamed.

Like an omen and a summons, his thunderous face

suddenly filled my vision as he stepped in front of me. His hands cupped my face, the cold bite of the metal of the guns he held touching my skin a stark contrast to the heat of his skin against mine. Relief shoved away all the panic, my breath leaving me as a strangled sob escaped my throat.

Rafe took me out of Joaquin's grip as I threw my arms around his neck and lunged for him, relief tangible in my veins. The sight of him alive and well, mostly unharmed, felt like a miracle I hadn't earned.

He moved as soon as I was in his grip, murmuring softly in my ear as he clutched me tightly. I didn't even care about the weapons touching my body, only grateful to have him with me. He walked toward the hallway that led to the guard's rooms.

"Are you hurt?" Rafael asked, and I knew he meant the deeper kind of hurt that he wouldn't be able to see. The scrapes on my face from the glass would heal, but the potential damage to the baby was something we'd never be able to see.

Not until it was too late.

Hugo emerged from the men's quarters, blood staining his shirt as he heaved his lungs. He threw open the first door in the hallway, the room I knew the brothers shared, and where the entrance to the secret bunker hid.

Most of the guards didn't even know it existed, a secret only afforded to Rafael's most trusted men—in particular the ones who would be assigned with getting me to it in the case of an emergency.

Hugo pulled back the rug on the floor, exposing the latch that led to the underground bunker that couldn't quite be called a basement. It was too enclosed, too bombproof to be anything so casual.

Hugo lifted the lid off the control panel tucked into the

floor, entering the code with hurried fingers and then lifting the metal hatch covered in wood flooring when the lock was released. He disappeared down the ladder first. "All clear!" he called.

"Go on, *mi reina*," Rafe ordered after he kissed the top of my head. I turned back to look at him, pleading with my eyes for the moment I knew was coming.

He wouldn't hide away in the bunker with me.

"If I go, are you coming with me?" I asked.

"I'll be right behind you," he agreed, cupping my cheek briefly and nodding for me to follow Hugo. I climbed down the ladder as quickly as I could with the way my body ached, wincing with every move of my sore muscles. Hugo's hands landed on my waist, pulling me into him and away from the ladder as Rafael and Joaquin followed.

The door to the bunker was closed, locked up tight until Hugo entered his passcode to open that too. The thumbprint scanner lit as it took the imprint of his thumb, the seal on the heavy metal door releasing. Hugo stepped inside, leaving me to hover at the door as I felt Rafe's eyes on me. I turned back to face him, my heart in my throat as he hesitated.

"I'm sorry, *mi reina*," he murmured, his brow pinched as if he actually meant the words for once. Something pierced my neck, my hand moving to touch the spot as heat spread from the too-familiar spot. Hugo wrapped his arms around me from behind and supported my weight as I stumbled. "Forgive me."

In the moments before everything went black, Joaquin's fuzzy shape pushed the door closed and he and Rafael's faces disappeared on the other side. "When you wake up, it will all be over," Hugo murmured gently as he lifted me into his arms. My head lolled as he carried me through the long, tubular bunker.

I'd come so far, but when it came down to it in the moments when it mattered, I was still something to be tucked away and protected.

A Princess instead of a Queen.

37

RAFAEL

Joaquin and I left Isa in the bunker, my lungs heaving with the effort to breathe past the smoke. I knew that when Isa woke, there would be hell to pay. While I might not regret doing whatever it took to keep her safe from the danger above ground and from the risks that came if Hugo had to physically restrain her, I definitely regretted the way it had to happen.

And the fact that she would know this plan had long since been in place in the event of an emergency.

"Gabriel has a plan. Go see if he needs help," I instructed Joaquin.

That was exactly why I needed him outside the bunker, even if it went against both our instincts.

I grabbed an assault rifle from the brothers' room and stashed my handguns into the back of my waistband. Nodding to Joaquin, I watched as he pushed open the bedroom door and made his way back toward the main space of the house. I followed shortly after, veering toward the front after pointing up the stairs to signal that was the last place I'd seen Gabriel. I didn't speak, keeping my breaths as shallow and minimal as I could to prevent too much smoke in my lungs.

Making my way out the front door, I moved through the rain of gunfire and took cover behind one of the SUVs closest to the house, looking for higher ground as bullets flew past my head when I ducked down.

Peeking over the hood, I stared in shock at the familiar shell of the old Ford at the gate. It was a crumpled mess beneath the flames. Nothing remained of what it had once been, not even the charred body that I could barely make out within it.

My phone pinged with a text, and I ducked back down to quickly glance at the words that filled my screen. Relief filled me with the confirmation of everything I already knew to be true. Isa and the baby were safely tucked into the bed in the bunker, sleeping away the worst of a tragedy that would undoubtedly haunt her for the rest of her life.

It was devious in the way I'd come to expect of the quietest Cortes brother. It was always the quietest ones you had to worry about.

Bullets rained down on the SUV I hid behind as I lifted my phone to my ear to call Joaquin to see if he'd found Gabriel. His plan was the best chance we had at walking away with the least casualties possible. "Did you find him?" I asked as soon as he answered.

"You're sure about this?" he asked, and the hesitance in his voice might have made me hesitate. He knew as well as I did that some acts in life were unforgivable.

This wasn't one of them, not for me anyway.

"Do it," I ordered, ending the call and shoving my phone into my pocket. I darted for the next SUV in the driveway, hiding behind it and getting a little further from the house. Raising my gun to notch against my shoulder, I ignored the twinge of pain from the bullet wound from not long past when it settled into place.

The front door burst open as Joaquin emerged from the house. Odina sucked back lungfuls of air as smoke billowed out behind them, adding validity to the deception. Instead of her usual jeans, she wore one of Isa's favorite dresses. I was immediately struck with the hatred of seeing it on her skin, an irrational loathing of watching her impersonate the sister who she'd done nothing but harm.

Even if this time around it was to Isa's benefit.

I hadn't taken the time to inform myself about how they would follow through with the lie, far too driven by the need to make Pavel's men believe they'd already accomplished what they set out to do. Even with Isa tucked safely away in the bunker, that wouldn't keep her safe forever.

I needed to get her the fuck out of Chicago and home to *El Infierno*. To do that the fastest way possible, I needed Pavel's men dead or gone. My preference was dead, but if they took one of my very inconvenient problems off my hands, it would be no loss to me.

In time, Isa would understand it wasn't a loss for her either.

Odina didn't struggle, keeping oddly still in Joaquin's grip as he moved her toward one of the vehicles like he might take cover.

They never made it that far.

Joaquin's chest jerked suddenly as the bullet struck him dead center, his face going slack as his hand fell away from Odina's waist. Fucking Dima Kuznetsov stepped out from behind one of his vehicles, hurrying to close the distance between them as his men focused their fire on the SUV where I hid. I peeked out around the far end as much as I dared so I could watch the scene unfold without taking a bullet to the brain.

Under the rain of bullets, there was no way for me to step out and move toward the woman they all thought was my wife. They'd forgotten the one simple truth in the game we called life though.

A King always protected his Queen.

Joaquin dropped to the ground, spinning as he fell until he landed face down and went perfectly still. Odina's mouth opened as if she might scream, but there was no sound as her legs crumpled beneath her. Dima closed the distance between them, wrapping an arm around her waist and lifting her dead weight from the ground. She still didn't struggle, even when he wrapped a hand around the front of her throat and placed the barrel of his gun to her temple.

His dark eyes gleamed as they met mine around the corner of the vehicle. "Where is my brother, Ibarra?!" he yelled, pressing the gun tighter to Odina's head.

"Let her go, and I'll take you to him!" I shouted back, locking eyes with Dima as he guided the woman he thought was my wife backwards. Odina didn't move or say anything to try to tell him that she wasn't who Dima believed her to be.

She couldn't. Not with the drugs Gabriel had given her and the conscious sedation gripping her body. She likely felt every moment of fear, of knowing that her body had been stolen from her and used for a nefarious purpose.

Exactly as she'd done to her sister a year and a half prior.

Eventually, Dima would learn the truth. But Isa would be out of Chicago by then.

"You can have her back when you give me my fucking brother!" He continued dragging her dead weight, yelling curses at her as he thought she refused to cooperate. My men returned fire after he tossed her into one of the vehicles closest to the gate, climbing in and escaping with the prize he'd thought he caught and the few men he valued the most.

But his brother would soon be dead, and he'd stolen the wrong sister.

I didn't give the first shit if Odina died, and in time Isa would come to understand I'd done only what I had to do.

With the deception achieved and Isa safely tucked away, my men and I returned fire with new vigor at the remaining men Dima left behind. The sound of gunshots filled the night with constant noise, the bangs reverberating through the air driving me to a place of peace that only came when I sent my enemies exactly where they belonged.

I drew in a deep breath, sinking into that place where fear didn't exist. Only death and destruction mattered when the world narrowed down to war. Shifting gears from the husband who wanted to do everything to make sure his wife was safe, I embraced the devil who killed everything that stood in his way. The fact that it took effort spoke to just how much Isa had already changed me when we hadn't been paying attention.

Love was weakness, but it was one I would happily embrace to have her in my life.

My lungs filled with air, and I moved on my exhale. Standing fully and moving in the direction of the men who closed ranks in an attempt to finish off my men, I didn't wait for the insurgence of my men coming from around the rest of the property.

I moved with quick, methodical steps. Veering sideways, never following a steady trajectory.

Head shot.

And the man closest to be dropped as blood sprayed out of his forehead. The air shifted to my right, the coming sense of malevolent energy warning me of the impending danger.

Throat shot.

He froze in place, his gun dropping as his hand raised to touch the wound in his throat as blood pumped out of the carotid.

Chest shot.

I sank into the melody of gunfire and the almost rhythmic rolling of two fingers on the trigger, finding beauty in the music of it as death filled the air around me. Gabriel emerged from the side yard with the rest of the men after telling them that protecting the house no longer mattered.

No one would gain access to the underground bunker, and most didn't even know it existed. I moved further down the driveway, picking off the stragglers who were wounded and putting them out of their misery with a shot to the head.

Blood and brain matter covered the once pristine pavers lining the drive, leaving a trail of my rivals as I slowly made my way to check on Joaquin and to the gate and still burning car to seek the answers Isa would need from the body inside. My men moved past me, closing in on Dima's men who thought to try to escape the fate waiting for all of them. They should know better.

Death came for all who fucked with *El Diablo*.

Rafael & Isa's story concludes in Until Death Do Us Part. Coming soon!

>>Pre-Order Now.

. . .

*F*all in love with a Bellandi? You can find Matteo, Ryker, and Enzo's stories in Adelaide's Bellandi Crime Syndicate series.

>>Start with Bloodied Hands.

*W*ant more Rafael & Isa right now?
>>Download an exclusive deleted scene from Until Retribution Burns.

ALSO BY ADELAIDE FORREST

Bellandi World Syndicate Universe

Bellandi Crime Syndicate Series

Bloodied Hands

Forgivable Sins

Grieved Loss

Shielded Wrongs

Beauty in Lies Series

Until Tomorrow Comes

Until Forever Ends

Until Retribution Burns

Until Death Do Us Part - Coming soon

Other Dark Romance

An Initiation of Thorns - Cowritten with Tove Madigan

Pawn of Lies - Coming May 14th

Romantic Suspense Novellas

The Men of Mount Awe Series

Deliver Me from Evil

Kings of Conquest - Cowritten with Lyric Cox

Claiming His Princess

Stealing His Princess